RAISING *the* DAD

Also by Tom Matthews

Like We Care

RAISING
the DAD

Tom Matthews

Thomas Dunne Books
St. Martin's Press 🙚 New York

This is a work of fiction. All of the characters, organizations, and events portrayed in this novel are either products of the author's imagination or are used fictitiously.

THOMAS DUNNE BOOKS.
An imprint of St. Martin's Press.

RAISING THE DAD. Copyright © 2018 by Tom Matthews. All rights reserved. Printed in the United States of America. For information, address St. Martin's Press, 175 Fifth Avenue, New York, N.Y. 10010.

www.thomasdunnebooks.com
www.stmartins.com

Library of Congress Cataloging-in-Publication Data

Names: Matthews, Tom, 1960– author.
Title: Raising the dad : a novel / Tom Matthews.
Description: First edition. | New York : Thomas Dunne Books/St. Martin's Press, 2018.
Identifiers: LCCN 2017045657 | ISBN 9781250094766 (hardcover) | ISBN 9781250094773 (ebook)
Subjects: LCSH: Dysfunctional families—Fiction. | Family secrets—Fiction. | Fathers—Fiction. | Domestic fiction. | GSAFD: Black humor (Literature)
Classification: LCC PS3613.A8276 R35 2018 | DDC 813/.6—dc23
LC record available at https://lccn.loc.gov/2017045657

Our books may be purchased in bulk for promotional, educational, or business use. Please contact your local bookseller or the Macmillan Corporate and Premium Sales Department at 1-800-221-7945, extension 5442, or by email at MacmillanSpecialMarkets@macmillan.com.

First Edition: April 2018

10 9 8 7 6 5 4 3 2 1

In memory of
Gip and Jeanne Matthews

One

They came blinking into their new fluorescent-lit freedom with hollow, dusty stares. Having served their time with the county for drug offenses or battery convictions or any one of a million knucklehead schemes supposed to deliver them to lives much plusher than this, they were set loose to try again. About a third of them had family waiting. A third of *those* got warm embraces, while the rest met shrugs and listless escorts back to the parking lot.

Almost all stopped first at the county-run snack bar for cigarettes. While waiting for his brother for almost two hours, John Husted calculated that with the county markup on cigarettes being at least fifty cents above retail, each ex-con immediately reimbursed the system a tiny portion of the cost of jailing them.

Those who knew John Husted best sometimes told him that he overthought things.

The de-incarcerated came one by one, ambling down the bleak linoleum hallway to rejoin society. Each clung to a sad paper bag that held their belongings.

"I hope he brought me something," John's mother, Rose, said expectedly as she strained to see around all the bodies in front of her.

"He hasn't been on vacation, Mom," he sighed. "Remember? Mike's been in jail."

His mother's memory began failing alarmingly after John's brother got sent up eleven months earlier. Along with all the other frustrations this presented John, the worst was having to remind her over and over again that her eldest son was a convicted criminal, this time put away for possession and a gun charge.

Her dementia still played games with her; catch her on a good day and she'd remember the sad news about Mike. But when rattled or tired, the most basic memories drifted away from her and came back in confused tatters. If they came back at all.

Every time John explained Mike's situation to his mother, the look on her face gently went from despair to blissful acceptance. As if to think, "I am sorry to learn this about my son, but in no time at all I get to forget it all over again."

They scanned the parade of the freshly sprung, and there he was: big brother Mike, looking shabby but still clinging to a bit of his rock-and-roll swagger. The tattoos still snaked up his forearms, and the ratty rock star hair still framed a well-sculpted face made flinty by hard living. Now forty-five, Mike's hair thinned up top.

Mike signaled to his brother from across the room with a cool cock of his chin, but then his expression darkened as he saw their mite-sized mother standing at John's side. She darted across the room and hugged him before he could deflect her, her cheek pressed to his scarecrow-like sternum.

"I wish you had been on vacation," she said quietly.

Baffled by this welcome, Mike pried himself from her grip. John turned to steer the family out the door.

"Hang on," Mike said as he got in line to buy cigarettes.

They took a booth at Denny's. Mike left jail flat broke and his mother paid for his cigarettes with the last few dollars in her purse. This was going to be on John.

Mike shoveled half the breakfast menu into his mouth while his mother ignored her chicken salad and spoke excitedly. "It was between Mrs. Kerry and Delores Steddick, but the judges felt that the azaleas along the edging made the difference, with the colors. And those were *my* idea," Rose boasted. "Mae told me that I *had* to be in the picture with her in the bulletin, but my hair—"

"Ma, you told me this story," Mike interrupted. "Like in every letter you sent me. You and Mrs. Kerry, kickin' the other flower lady's ass. I got it."

He sawed into another waffle, oblivious to the fact that his curtness caused his mother to withdraw and grow smaller. Mike was using the exasperated tone with Rose that John fought to control the past several months, not always with success.

"Sorry," she said.

Because Mike brought their family reunion to an awkward silence, John felt it was his job to find them a new topic.

"Tell us about jail."

Mike stared a hole through his younger brother and ground his teeth as Rose revved back up. As John knew she would.

"Your father would be so ashamed. He was a respectable man. And look at your brother. John has a good job, a lovely family. Never once a bit of trouble from him. What is *wrong* with you?"

John wasn't surprised to hear his mother play the Larry card. His father died thirty years ago, his ghost only resurrected after all those years to tell Mike how far he had fallen from his father's expectations. Teenaged Mike and the old man fought bitterly right up until the day in 1985 when a sudden stroke killed Dr. Lawrence Husted. The loss crushed Rose and she never recovered a complete reattachment to her life and the sons she was left alone to raise. When John began to notice her memory slipping a couple years earlier, it was impossible to tell if this was a new crisis or just the manifestation of what had become a crippling frailty since her husband's sudden death.

Other than to nag Mike from the grave, Larry Husted didn't come around much anymore.

"It wasn't my fault," Mike said. "I was just holding the gun for a guy."

"And the dope?" John asked snottily.

There was a time when Mike would kick John's ass for this, but John thought he could take him now. Mike was two years older than John and he had abused his body horribly since he was a teenager. Maybe Mike knew this as he scowled into his sticky bun.

"Well, I want you to go see Mr. Lennox," his mother pushed on. "He told me he might be able to find you some work, out of respect for your father."

"I *know,* Ma. You told me in the car, like *fifteen* minutes ago. *Geez.*"

"Sorry."

The waitress, pretty and probably not even twenty-five, refilled Mike's coffee. He winked and she smiled, not finding him as skeevy as John would've wished. Mike the alley cat, back on the prowl.

"Well, I have to go see a man about a horse," Rose said brightly, throwing off the family prickliness as she rose from the booth. She always used this expression whenever she had to go to the bathroom, claiming her generation found it amusing while trying to be discreet.

"What the fuck's the matter with her?" Mike asked John once their mother was out of range. "Can she remember *anything?*"

"She's okay when she's relaxed, when she's poking around the house or arranging lunches with her friends," John said. "But stress sets her off. She didn't want to come today."

"So why is she *here?*" Mike asked with a pissed-off edge. "I told *you* to pick me up. I don't need her seeing me this way."

"So don't *be* this way," John said. Mike accepted John's attempt at shaming him with a sneer.

"She's not even seventy," Mike said.

"She's *almost seventy-five*. I've had her in with her doctor. He thinks it's Alzheimer's."

"Fuck . . ." Mike said.

"She's taking pills that might slow it down, but there's no stopping it," John said. "But it's good, you getting out now. You can move back into the house, not pay any rent while you're getting yourself together, and you can keep an eye on her. You need to learn to talk to her better."

Mike scoffed. "Hey, that'll fly for a while, me taking care of her. But I've got plans," Mike drawled. "Steve Hoover's got a job for him and me that's gonna keep me on the road pretty much full-time."

Mike had that self-centeredness of an addict that caused him to drop names as if John had been paying close attention to his schemes and committed the various players to memory. John had no idea who Steve Hoover was, but he assumed he was Jerry Boyd, and that Vasquez guy, and the cousin of that meth freak Mike had lived with for a few months who was going to make them all rich moving black-market baby formula. Steve Hoover was probably just the next scabby-souled bum who was going to lead Mike back to county lockup, if not worse.

"She *needs* you right now," John said. "I have been handling this on my own for almost a year, and I've got my own life to deal with."

"Well," Mike sniffed, "I'll do what I can. But, you know, I got my shit, too."

He refocused on his breakfast while John stared out into the parking lot. Mike flirted with the waitress some more. When the bill came, he grunted a kind of thanks at his kid brother.

With the tab paid, they stood to leave. They stared fretfully toward the ladies' room.

Mike snagged the waitress. "'Scuse me, Debbie. I'm a little worried about my mother. Think you could stick your head in the john and make sure she's okay?"

The waitress smiled, touched by his concern. Mike managed to help his mother *and* turn his concern into part of his seduction. It's a gift.

They followed the waitress to the bathroom door, then waited awkwardly. They heard their mother's voice echoing angrily from inside.

"Can't a woman go to the bathroom without being spied on?" she barked at the waitress as they emerged, then she turned her wrath on her sons. "What's the matter with you two? Are you in such a hurry to send me home and get back to your lives?"

John quickly grabbed their things. Rose yanked her coat away from him and began struggling to put it on, flustered with the eyes of the customers upon her. Mike and John caught the wordless signal from the waitress: their mother had been lost and confused in the bathroom. Being found out made her pride bristle.

"Thanks," John whispered to the waitress as Rose fumed and ice water doused Mike's seedy growls of romance.

"Yeah," Mike mumbled to the waitress, suddenly laid bare as a guy old enough to have a mother old enough to suffer things like this. "Thanks."

Rose continued to strain to get her arms snaked through her coat sleeves until John finally took it away with a gentle firmness and she allowed him to help. They exchanged the silent sigh the two of them had been sharing more and more.

He put his hand on her back and guided her toward the exit. Mike held the door.

Two

John and his daughter sat opposite each other, worlds apart. They were both on their laptops, seated together at the kitchen table so that John could idly cast an eye over every so often to hold Katie's internet explorations in check. She was supposed to be doing homework, but he knew she had half a dozen texts going while allegedly studying for a social studies test. Her fifteen-year-old fingers danced out fevered teenage chit-chat, her words that crude online shorthand: OMG GTFO WE F/F.

Imagine what The Diary of Anne Frank *would read like if she had had a Twitter account,* John often mused to himself.

He was supposed to be finishing up the federal grant proposal he had been writing for almost three months. His job was finding supplemental funding for Next Step, the nonprofit where John worked as the development director. Next Step provided transitional living for kids who had "aged out" of foster care, and John found the government agencies and foundations that wrote checks for such projects. He was expert at decoding the massive knot of institutional bullshit they spun to make sure no one got their help without suffering first.

Lately, though, he spent these homework sessions getting lost in watching his daughter. It was easy; he could just glance past his screen, knowing she was too transfixed by her conversations to know she was being observed.

Studying her intense gaze as it softly shifted from unguarded smiles to deep concern, he could see the whole range of adolescence play across her face. He should have coaxed her back to her studying but it was too pleasing, just being able to sit there and watch her be.

He and Robin worried about her grades, and about new friends shaping her in troubling ways. An understated goth look had begun to creep into her appearance. It was nothing dire, just a new affinity for dark clothes and an unflattering thickening of black mascara around her soft blue eyes. Despite some new surliness, Katie was still a sweet but overweight teenager, just the sort to embrace a fashion trend that John thought was rooted in a kind of preemptive ugliness. Who could hurt a kid for her body size or her face or her lack of awesomeness when she willfully made herself ugly to all but those who defiantly wore the costume alongside her?

John saw the older goths when he dropped Katie off at school, and their sneering commitment to the pose—the piercings, the tattoos, the whole Bela Lugosi-meets-the-Third Reich facade—struck him as nothing but the insolent armor of sad, wounded kids. It stung his heart to think that his sweet-souled daughter might be lost to such a joyless clique.

He typed something, and then heard the gentle *bing* of a new text arriving on her screen.

"Dad, stop," she laughed before catching herself. "I know it's you."

"No, it's Johnny, your Samoan pen pal. You really should talk to him, I hear his family is loaded."

She shook her head. He typed some more and transmitted it across the table.

She sighed, playing along: "Johnny wants to know how school was today," she said.

"Hmm, I was wondering that myself," John said. "I often find myself thinking like a Samoan."

She typed a terse response. John's laptop beeped. " *'Fine'?*" John read from his screen. "Your day was *fine?* Johnny was hoping for more detail. Johnny wants to know if you've still got a crush on that Brendan kid. With the red Mohawk and the infected nose ring."

She shut her laptop. "I think I'll go study in my room."

"Then you won't need these," he said, relieving her of her computer and phone and handing her her social studies book. "Take a cookie, you look hungry."

She gave her father that irked but tolerant teenage sigh, the one that John chose to believe said, "You *do* understand that mannerisms imposed upon me by my age and peer group prevent me from revealing that I am actually rather fond of you, don't you?"

John was still working at the kitchen table when Robin got home. She taught ninth grade geometry at Emerson, the high school Katie attended and where John and Robin had gone.

She was thirty-eight now. Her looks had taken on a pleasing overlay of age and experience, and John still thought that any fifteen-year-old male would be lucky to have such a woman etching a trapezoid on the whiteboard before him. He knew he should tell her that more often, but figured she would shoot him down as insincere for having deemed her less than centerfold material.

"Hey," Robin sighed with a familiar flatness.

"Hey," he replied.

In every terrific romantic movie, in every great love story ever written, lovers whose hearts were fused as one never once greeted each other with a tired, emotionally detached, *"Hey."*

These were John and Robin's "Hey" days.

"Haven't got dinner going yet," he said. "I'm in the home stretch on this thing, I kinda lost track of the time."

"That's okay," she said as she took a jar of spaghetti sauce from the cupboard and began filling a pot with water.

They married seventeen years ago. John thought they had a marriage that worked. They had a nice house in a better part of town, they kept their bills paid, and they had a smart, mostly responsible daughter whose grades so far hovered around the B range. They weren't the most passionate couple on the block, but all the grabby-hands marriages John saw up close— the attentive husbands, the giggling wives, the cloying hints of post-cookout whoopee when all John *really* wanted to know was how they wanted their steaks done—had all ended in divorce.

Robin and John kept an even keel; they still laughed enough, and shared interests enough, and made love enough to make the marriage endure.

Robin wasn't convinced. She felt they had lost something, and she talked about them trying to find it again. *A lot.* One of the last times they went round and round about it, she said that the two of them were like co-managers of a successful business: they understood what their roles were, they came together efficiently when a crisis hit, and they kept their doors open when so many businesses around them failed.

It wasn't until bedtime that night, when John crawled into bed and recoiled at the frost radiating from his wife, that he realized she wasn't making a flattering comparison. When she compared them to business partners, he actually thought they made a breakthrough. He may have smiled and said, *"Right!"*

Her arms clenched tightly across her chest in bed that night, she continued her analogy with the observation that at the end of the workday, these two "managers" John admired seemed to go their separate ways, to increasingly separate lives.

But it's hard *to keep a business going,* John would think to himself. *I'm proud that our doors are still open. That's all I'm saying.*

While Robin waited for the water to boil she poured some wine and set a glass beside his computer. "Did you call your mother back?"

"Mmmm, no."

"John . . ." she scolded.

Months ago he changed his mother's incoming calls to a custom ringtone, so he knew when it was her. At first it was the "Chicken Dance," John insisting that he needed something frivolous in his head before he took on her increasingly emotionally draining calls. But Rose phoned so often that Robin and Katie threatened to kill him as that insipid polka burrowed itself into their brains, so he changed it to "Over the Rainbow."

Between the ringtone and caller ID, John didn't always pick up when he knew it was his mother. If she left a message he'd listen to it instantly, and he'd call her right back if it was even remotely urgent, but so many of her calls were just because she was lonely or she had to tell John something that she told him five times before.

He was falling behind in his work, indulging his mother every time she beckoned. It made him feel shitty, but he felt that he needed to allocate his time better.

His mother called twice the night before, each message simply, "Call me." But he hadn't yet.

"I'm stepping back," he said with unconvincing resolve in response to Robin's disapproving tone. "Mike needs to deal with this stuff. If it was important, she would've said. Or he'd have called by now for me to take over with her."

"How do you think he's doing with her?" Robin asked, sipping her wine from the other side of the room.

"Fine. I guess. But it's only been a couple weeks. Hopefully this Steve Hoover thing doesn't come through."

"Who's Steve Hoover?"

"The next piece of shit who's going to knock my brother's life sideways."

"The Vasquez guy."

"*Sí.*"

Robin went to change her clothes, leveling an arching eyebrow of disapproval at her husband as she left the kitchen. "And you're leaving her to fend for herself with dirtbags like that hanging around."

He sighed and tapped the screen of his phone.

"Hi, Ma."

"Where have you been? I called you all last night," Rose asked.

"Sorry. I just got caught up in this project that I'm working on, and by the time I heard your message it was too late to call. How are you? Is Mike taking good care of you?"

"Oh, sure. We're already like a couple of old roommates."

John's ear was honed to hear hints of unease. Something was bothering her. "You sure? Is something wrong?"

"Oh, it's just . . . He had some friends over last night, they were up later than me. They're so loud."

"You want me to talk to him? It's *your* house."

"No, don't make trouble. It'll be fine. Listen, I called because Walt Bolger wants you to call him."

"Walt Bolger? *Doctor* Bolger?" John asked. "Why?"

Walt Bolger and John's father were partners as young doctors at Holt Memorial Hospital. On the day in 1985 when John's father had his stroke, it was Dr. Bolger who found him on the floor in the office adjacent to his and fought to save him. Nearly a year later, it was Dr. Bolger who sat Mike and John down and told them that their father finally had to be let go, that while his body lingered on there was no chance of him ever regaining consciousness.

Dr. Bolger had to tell the boys this, because over those ten months their mother pretty much broke down, unable to handle the brutal turn their family had taken.

Other than bumping into him around town a handful of times since John moved back to his hometown in the mid-nineties, he consigned Walt Bolger to that raw-nerved part of his memory that tapped into that precise moment in time when he knew his family would never be the same.

"You must've misunderstood him," John said gently to his mother. "He was probably calling to talk to you. Could he have been confused?"

Dementia, John was learning, was grabbing hold throughout his parents' generation. The brain misfires, and all of a sudden Walt Bolger's calling his dead friend Larry to set up a tee time.

"Why would he be looking for me?" John asked.

"He says he has something to talk to you about. He wants to meet you for lunch. He was your father's best friend, so you call him tonight."

"Did he give you any idea—"

John heard the stereo blast to life at his mother's house. Furious metal. *Mike* music.

"*What?*" she shouted into the phone.

"Ma, tell Mike to turn that stuff—"

"Okay, bye."

She hung up. John stared at the phone, and then called up a phone book. He was apparently having lunch with the guy who pulled the plug on his old man.

Three

They met at Rocky's, a diner across the street from the hospital that had been around since the fifties. John's father had been a regular there as a young resident and later as a flourishing internist, when he had both the time and money to have taken lunch somewhere more refined. There were still waitresses working there who had waited on him.

When John and Mike were young, Larry Husted would bring his sons to Rocky's when he was on call and needed to stay close to the hospital. "On call" became words John resented, because it meant his father—and the family—was forever tethered to his job. Long after his stature at the hospital would have allowed him to scale back, Larry still took rounds in the emergency room he helped build and made himself available for consultation at all hours.

As an adult, John wondered if his father always declared

himself available whether the hospital actually needed him or not. He knew his father loved his job, but as Larry's marriage stretched on and his sons grew more troublesome, maybe work provided him an escape.

Families weren't always easy, John knew.

Almost nothing ever changed at Rocky's. A shadow of a decal for Squirt, the lemony soda that still made John's mouth pucker just thinking about it, scarred the front door. The gumball machine just inside still raised money for the Lion's Club. After all this time, John wondered what kind of empire they must've amassed, a penny at a time. It took quarters now.

The counter where John and Mike spent hours when their father ran across the street to consult on some quick emergency remained. Their mother had been involved with community work on the weekends, so when the hospital intruded on Larry's day off, the diner's owner had been happy to watch the boys. The waitresses doted on them—every kid in school knew Mike and John got free sundaes at Rocky's any time they wanted. Mike was still young then, years away from the misbehavior that would tear him and his father apart.

"Johnny Husted!" A zaftig, sixtyish waitress had sneaked up on him. "Where you been keeping yourself?"

"Hey, Sheila. Ah, you know. Sticking close to home, trying to get some work done."

"And your mother?"

"You'll see her next week. We have a lunch date."

"Good for you!" she smiled as she led him to a table. "I hear Mike is back home."

John flinched. Her discretion was admirable, but he was sure small-town gossip had all the dirt on big brother Mike.

"He is."

"Tell him to get his fanny in here," she said. "I still remember when there was nothing a free sundae couldn't fix for that boy."

John smiled as she handed him a menu. "I'm waiting for someone. Walt Bolger, actually."

"How is he?" she asked with a heartsick concern.

"I don't know," John said warily. "I actually haven't seen him practically since I was a kid. Is something wrong?"

"Cancer. Or that's what everyone says. The old poop is as close-mouthed as he's ever been," she said with a fond gruffness that went back decades. "We'd hear this and that from his wife, but she died years ago."

She took back the second menu. "Well, I can go ahead and get *his* order in. Walt Bolger hasn't changed his lunch order in forty years."

She winked in that motherly way that has been bred out of our younger waitresses, and John was left with his reveries. Out the front window, beyond the strip mall that had grown in well past his father's day, he could see "new" Holt Memorial, which remained a monument to his father's vision and determination. It still towered over the town but no longer appeared like the sleek, modern facility that opened to much local fanfare in 1983.

It would always shine by comparison, though, so long as the *old* hospital remained grafted to its replacement. Coming out of the seventies, Holt City—an hour southwest of

RAISING THE DAD   21

Milwaukee—was a dying town, and the doctors and the hospital's board argued that only a world-class hospital could keep Holt City from falling to dust like so many small Midwestern cities. With the vast tract of land already paid for, they built the new hospital directly adjoining the existing building. They intended to tear down the old hospital just as soon as they found the money for the demolition.

On the day they broke through the wall between the old hospital and new, there was a ceremony where dignitaries and prime movers got to take a symbolic swing at the edifice with a sledgehammer. John's father, never a big man, staggered beneath the hammer's weight, but as he drove it home his pride was clear.

Chunks of that concrete, encased in Lucite, were still on Larry's desk the day the stroke brought him down two years later.

But it was all the new facility could do to keep up with the cutting-edge medical technology required to keep it competitive. The old hospital hung on to rot, affixed to the working building like a tumor.

Memories of Dr. Bolger returned to John when the old doctor finally arrived and sat down across from him. Dr. Bolger had been an imperious name associated with Larry's career and a dour specter pecking at a cocktail at the dinner parties John's parents hosted when he was a kid. John stole looks at the old man while he picked at his lunch. He did look frail, perhaps from disease, but definitely older than John figured he was.

Dr. Bolger had been younger than his father, but John guessed he was into his seventies. Seeing him so weathered, knowing that he and John's father were a team back when they were young and vital, made John wonder what Larry would look like had he earned such a long life.

"How's your mother?" The old man asked after muted small talk.

"Oh, you know," John said. "Not great. I've had her in with Dr. Kelly over the past year. He's pretty sure it's Alzheimer's."

"I've spoken to him," Dr. Bolger said. "He's very good, and he won't sugarcoat anything for you. This is an awful disease and there's not much he can do for her. You just need to keep her world very quiet and be patient with her as her thinking gets more tangled."

He looked John in the eye. "Dr. Kelly tells me you're doing a great job with her. I'm not surprised."

John smiled gratefully.

But then an awkward silence fell over their lunch that stretched into an air of avoidance. Having dispensed with all the fond and sad talk about the past, it appeared that the old man was avoiding the real reason for this meeting.

After Sheila cleared their plates and topped off their coffee, Dr. Bolger cleared his throat.

"John, I've been wanting to talk to you about your father. About how he . . . died," he said. "There are things you need to know."

Going into their lunch, John wondered if this was why his father's old friend reached out to him after so long. His father died when he was thirteen and that whole period was so emotionally wrenching that there were great holes in his understanding of what happened. With his time on earth dwindling, John figured the old man wanted to tell him what he could about his father and the way he died, just to make sure he knew.

"You know, your father was a great doctor," Dr. Bolger continued. "We both were, and we knew it. Everything was changing in medicine, and we saw all the advancements that were on the way. We'd lose a patient and it would *haunt* us to know that if they had just hung on, if they had just gotten sick a few years later, we maybe could've saved them."

John was confused by where this was leading, but he felt the old doctor drawing close to the matter at hand. He looked past John through the front window, toward the hospital.

"Let's take a walk," he said.

Four

They stood at the crosswalk, Dr. Bolger saying that he never got tired of the view of the hospital from the other side of the street. John realized that he would never care about anything as much as Walt and Larry cared about that building.

They entered through the main lobby to a complicated mix of smells: flowers from the gift shop, bland, utilitarian food from the cafeteria, and the medicines that dangled hope before all who entered. Until he had begun escorting his mother to her appointments, John hadn't been in the building since Katie was born.

The old doctor strolled in regally and marched straight toward the private administration offices.

"Excuse me. Can I help you?" a receptionist asked.

"Yes, dear. I'm Walter Bolger. *Doctor* Walter Bolger." He

gestured to a wall opposite her, where portraits of the hospital's founders were on sober display.

The receptionist saw his portrait and squirmed as he smiled unctuously. John got the feeling this wasn't the first time the old man pulled this.

"I'm so sorry, sir. I'm new here."

"Quite all right; we were all new here once. When I was new here, *here* was a cornfield!" He spread his arms wide for effect.

He walked John to the wall of founders and stood him before the image of his father. John remembered being in the hospital lobby for the unveiling of the portrait, within a year of his father's death. Mike was a no-show that day; by that point, he would've been somewhere getting high, or working out with his band.

Larry Husted was no older than forty-five when the photograph was taken in the early eighties. The ghastly remnants of seventies fashion had lost most its grip, but his sideburns were still a bit too long, his glasses still had that racy sort of aviator style that were all the rage back then. Larry had on a vibrant blue suit jacket that his peers might have considered just a bit radical, given his age and status.

The same photo of his father sat eternally beneath a hazing of dust in the family home where his mother lived. The man in the photo was *dynamic*. Whenever John noticed the picture, he sometimes convinced himself that his old man was sporting a loose perm.

John nodded toward the portrait. "Did he do something? With his hair?"

"What?" Dr. Bolger asked with surprise.

"Nothing."

They stood in silence, until it became uncomfortable. The old man finally broke the reverie by leading John farther into the building.

They passed what had been Dr. Bolger's office for decades. Obligatory pictures of his late wife and assorted family members personalized a space that was otherwise efficiently all business.

John stared into the room next door, his father's old office. This was where the stroke got him. That was the floor where he fell. One morning a lifetime ago, Larry Husted walked through the doorframe where his son now stood, and he never walked out again.

At the moment the father passed through this space one final time, the son was across town, at school, not seeing anything coming.

Dr. Bolger stood with his hand on John's shoulder, understanding where his thoughts were. They moved on.

Rounding a corner, they nearly collided with a man in his mid-forties wearing a jacket and tie and an unmistakable air of anxiety.

"Ah, Dean. Good!" Dr. Bolger smiled. "This is John Husted, Lawrence Husted's son. John, this is Dean Durning, our hospital administrator."

Durning shook John's hand as the old man seemed to be forcing them together.

"Hey, John. Good to meet you. I was five years ahead of you, all through school. My sister Peggy was in your class. Peggy Durning?"

"Right, sure," John said. He had no idea who Peggy Durning was, but her brother was trying way too hard.

"I was just giving John a tour of the place," Dr. Bolger said.

"A tour! Great!" He grabbed John's hand again. "Your father is a legend around here. A *legend*. If there's ever anything any of us can do for you . . ."

"Thanks," John said, unsettled by the guy's fidgeting. Durning popped back into his office as Dr. Bolger and John continued on.

"Dean is a good man, he's really taking good care of this place," the old man told John. "You'll like him."

They walked on, seemingly without purpose, until Dr. Bolger stopped at a door marked HOSPITAL STAFF ONLY. The old man punched in a code and as he opened the locked door, John saw stairs leading down and heard the throbbing pound of heavy machinery. "Come on," the old doctor said, ignoring John's skeptical look.

John followed him down the stairs and along rows of generators and boilers echoing through the vast basement. Dr. Bolger shouted to him above the noise.

"This is the guts of this place! This whole building, it's like a living organism, and here is where its life comes from!"

John imagined Walt Bolger and his father as young men

decades ago, poking around here throughout construction like a couple of kids. He pictured lunch-bucket guys in hard hats shooing the two of them off, only to have them slip back down the next day to check on progress. Rather than take John back to the terrible day his best friend died, maybe the old man simply wanted to show John the secret corners of what he and his father had built together.

They pressed on, Dr. Bolger navigating a maze of corridors and vast industrial spaces without slowing. At what had to have been the farthest reach of the basement, in the corner of a cluttered storage room filled with ancient hospital beds and bulky, decommissioned machinery, the old man stood before an exit door.

"How'd you like to have a look inside the old hospital?" he asked with a strangely constricted smile. "Your father put in a lot of hours there, a lot more than he got to see in the new building. When he was just about your age, that old place was his everything."

John hesitated. Old Holt Memorial held strong memories for him. It was the monolithic taskmaster that kept John's father away from him throughout his childhood, but it was also a tangible place where by all accounts Larry Husted helped an awful lot of people get better.

But above all else, it was a spooky old building that few people got to poke around in. A building where people had *died,* where ghosts might still stir the cobwebs.

John liked recognizing the little boy inside him who answered back:

"Sure!"

Five

Dr. Bolger led John through the heavy service door leading out of the hospital and up a rusted set of stairs that brought them back to ground level. John had lost his bearings during the winding tour; they were now standing at a distant corner of the hospital where it joined with the empty building.

John followed the old doctor behind the abandoned hospital, struck by the utter desolation. The corners and crevasses of the long-abandoned building accumulated decades of wind-blown debris: leaves, fast-food wrappers, grocery bags. John smiled to see a Bob Dole '96 flyer tangled in the mess; Dole would've definitely had his old man's vote.

A rusted industrial dumpster blocked another door, this one leading into the old building. Dr. Bolger squeezed behind the dumpster with surprising ease and brought a key to a heavy padlock. His hand was shaking.

The door swung open, and a chalky mustiness rolled over them. The old man reached inside and grabbed a flashlight. "Watch your step," Dr. Bolger cautioned. "It'll take a while for your eyes to adjust."

The light became patchy as they moved deeper into the dead hospital. The walls were a dour institutional green. The floor tiles, cracked and fading, were ancient. The sun came through in dust-speckled beams pricking through boarded-up windows. The stale, unbreathed air hung heavy. John stopped and took in the ghostly surroundings.

"Dr. Bolger?" John whispered, realizing he was alone. He immediately felt a little boy's chill as his adventure turned scary. "Hello?"

Through the pale light he noticed that a path on the floor cut through decades of dirt and debris. In every other direction, not a single footprint, and yet down one hall, a clear trail had been nearly worn clean. The old man seemed to know John would follow.

He found him sitting on a bench outside a long row of closed doors. John assumed the old man was winded, his shoulders heaving as he looked to the floor. But as he turned John saw he was crying.

"He *asked* me to do this," the old doctor pleaded. "When it began, I was just doing what he wanted. Please believe me."

Something grave was suddenly in play.

"Do what?" John asked, his heart beginning to race. "What are you talking about?"

"We knew—that very first day—that the stroke was too severe, the damage was too extensive. But his body wouldn't let go.

"He was *fighting*. And he went on and on, for almost a year," the old man pleaded.

"You and Mike were young, we were all determined to shelter you from more harm, but your mother . . . The pressure, the not knowing, it was killing her. We needed to bring it to an end, John. We needed to say it was over. For her."

He turned and stared at John.

"But Larry just kept on fighting." A pause. "He never stopped."

John looked to a door across the hall. The trail leading from the new hospital ended there.

Room 116.

Something heavy and immutable broke loose in John's mind. He looked to his father's friend for passage back from a dream that could not be happening.

The old man softly gripped John's forearm. "He's never coming back, John, you need to understand that. *He's never coming back.*

"But he's still here," the old man said simply.

John looked again to the door, then turned slowly back to Dr. Bolger.

"What are you . . . ?" John pleaded, the words queasy in his ears.

The old man buried his face in his hands. "I swear, I just didn't know what to do."

John's feet slowly took him down a dusty trail to the closed door. His hand reached for the knob.

Six

The room was carefully preserved, in jarring contrast to the deterioration of the abandoned building. A single lamp burned softly, casting the bed in the corner in a cloak of shadows.

Photographs of the Husted family were throughout the room: Rose as a young doctor's wife, a preadolescent Mike and John smiling with abandon at Disneyworld. Larry Husted and Walt Bolger in seventies era golf clothes, tipping beers on the veranda of a golf course clubhouse. But mixed in with the distant past were a handful of more recent images, candid photos of Rose and John caught smiling at unremarkable gatherings held years after they lost Larry. A class picture of Katie, taken when she was in sixth grade, was on a shelf viewable from the bed.

The door closed behind John as he eased in. The nurturing

tableau before him and the inconceivability of what waited for him in the shadows threatened to send his mind careening into shutdown. Some instinctive self-preservation mechanism kicked in as he knew to take his time acclimating himself. To hold onto for just a few moments more the reality he had believed for thirty years.

He glimpsed a sturdy bookcase filled with medical texts, along with the Ian Fleming and John le Carré novels his father had loved. A Donald Duck figurine stood at the end of a shelf. A framed photo clipped from the *Holt City Times* was propped up among the books. It was Mike at twenty-one, onstage and preening in his full heavy metal finest. Gravel Rash was beginning to draw big crowds down in Chicago, with rumors around town about a pending record contract. The article in the local paper back then had called Mike the next Axl Rose.

Gazing farther along the shelf, John stopped short when he saw it: chips of concrete, set in Lucite. He solemnly took the smooth cube into his hand. That day at the new hospital, with the sledgehammer and the applause and his father hailed as a hero, was a moment around which John fixed all his memories. John long ago assumed the Lucite block had simply been misplaced.

John felt its cool surface as he grimly looked back to the door that would return him to the old man who had the answers.

John's steps were deliberate as he committed to crossing the room. He felt time spinning backward, to a point where two lives diverged, he thought forever. One became a man, formed a life, fell short sometimes but carried on. The other, he had been told, had not.

The faint, sterile tapping of the medical machinery grated against the solemnity of the moment. Vital signs silently triggered spikes on the screen of a digital monitor.

As the form in the bed took shape in the dim light, John met the scent. It was antiseptic, the chilly moist bite of alcohol fused with something warm and human: The muted sour milk smell of a body long dormant. A whiff of breath. The traces of body waste discreetly collected.

Larry Husted had a smell. A living smell.

John arrived at the bedside and looked down.

His father was a gauzy husk of a man, the trauma of his decades-long internment reducing his body to a cruel hollowing out of the human form. He was in a fetal position, facing his son. His eyes were closed; a faint scar ran across his left cheek.

His chest rose and contracted almost imperceptibly.

A tinfoil sting pricked the base of John's skull as he recognized the face despite the effects of age and distress. He gripped the railing at the bedside and felt the reconnection.

His mental processing was blunt and simple:

"Here is Lawrence Charles Husted," John silently explained to himself. "Larry. Dad. Here is my dad.

"I have a dad."

His knees began to weaken as he reached to brush his hand along his father's forearm. The warmth of Larry's body proved to him that his existence was real, and John's steadiness collapsed. Gravity brought him to a chair at the bedside, his fingers never once breaking the connection now that his touch found his father's living skin.

John gently traced the line of a vein in his father's reed-like arm. Their blood flowed here. The son's tears came in jagged surges that wracked his body.

When the door to Larry's room rattled open an hour later, the sound echoing down the abandoned corridor, Walt Bolger stood slowly with his shoulders back, ready to honor his obligation. But the ravaging of John's emotions and the inconceivability of the truth left him too numb to assail the old man with questions or furious disbelief.

Something vastly intricate was at play here. The same man who had engaged in the most macabre deceit imaginable, who had kept John from his father for three decades, had just allowed John to stand again in the presence of that father.

Something mad and tragic had been allowed to live on in this long-dead building, but Walt was now owning up to it when he didn't have to. Time may come for rage, John realized as he met Walt's mournful look, but it would have been profane unleashing it in the reverent quiet outside his father's room.

Instead, John collapsed into the embrace of the old doctor.

"It got away from me," Walt whispered as he wept. "I

never wanted to do this to your family, to *Larry*. He'd be so disappointed in me."

John pulled back from the embrace and grasped the haunted old man at the shoulders:

"What happened?"

Seven

Larry was reading the newspaper that morning in 1985.

"Donald Duck has died," Larry Husted observed to Walt Bolger, who raised a skeptical eyebrow. Walt was going over the chart of a difficult case he'd be seeing later that morning.

"The guy who did the voices in all the cartoons. He died," Larry explained from behind the front page. "Clarence Nash. Leukemia. Eighty."

"Hmm," Walt mumbled.

"He made his first cartoon in 1932, and he retired just two years ago," Larry read. "*We* save lives, and this guy goes into the office and talks like a duck. For fifty years. Think you can get rich doing that?"

Walt said nothing as the medical records before him absorbed him. Ignored, Larry turned the page on the obituary. "I liked Daffy Duck," he shrugged.

Like most mornings, Larry and Walt shared a cup of coffee as they went over the newspaper before their rounds. Just the other day the paper had reported that a third artificial heart had been installed successfully in a man down in Kentucky, and now there was word that the owner of the *second* mechanical heart had just become the first to venture outside the hospital—for a whopping fifteen minutes.

These were days of miracles and marvel, but there was still no saving Donald Duck.

Larry's nurse stuck her head into Walt's office to tell Larry that his workday was due to commence. He rose from his chair in mock anger, doing a credible imitation of a grouchy cartoon duck as he headed back to his office. Walt shook his head at his friend with a familiar, bemused smile.

"I think I'll talk like Donald Duck to my patients this morning," Larry said. "I don't think that would worry them at all."

Walt finished his first file and opened the second when there was a commotion and the rustling of papers from the other side of the wall. Engrossed in the next case history, he didn't give the noise much attention.

"You okay in there, Donald?"

By the time Walt's wife, Marie, brought Rose to intensive care, Walt was gravely concerned by the initial assessment of Larry's condition. He summoned a show of strength as he met Rose with a measured hug—not too long to foreshadow the worst, not too short to underplay the seriousness of the situation. It was not in him to tell Rose what he feared to be true as he led her to her husband's bedside.

Larry looked peaceful, trapped in a nap that had quietly, violently short-circuited him. He hit his desk as he fell, and a gash under his left eye was crudely stitched and stained by drying blood.

"What happened?" she asked, her voice a trembled whisper.

"He had a stroke, honey," Walt said. "We can't tell yet how serious it is, but we're concerned."

He looked past Rose to Bart Ladmore, the neurologist on duty; his face was ashen as he studied Larry's chart. Nurses who worked daily with Larry, who routinely rode out trauma events with professional detachment, hovered anxiously. It would be invisible to a civilian, but their wordless interplay confirmed for Walt that his friend was being swept away while they flailed impotently for lifelines that would all prove to be yards too short.

They all knew. Except Rose.

Walt took her hand. "We're doing all we can. Bart has been on the phone to a neurologist in Chicago, one of the best in the country. He's on his way. But right now, all we can do is monitor his condition and pray he has the strength to fight this."

Rose gently pulled away from Walt and took Larry's hand. She stroked his hair and concerned herself with the cut on his face.

"We'll get this stitched up right," she whispered to her

husband. "I can't be staring at a scar for the rest of our lives."

John remembered coming home that February day in '85 to floorboards that were heaving. Screw Tool, Mike's latest band, had settled into the basement months earlier, and the hours after school were prime for jamming. From whenever Mike bailed on his classes until shortly before dinner, the jackhammer ditties of Mötley Crüe, Judas Priest, and the Scorpions thudded up from the cellar in bone-rattling waves. As he headed home from school, John could hear the bass end as it pummeled the core of the Husted home, a modest but pristine house in a historic part of town.

Neighbors had already called the police a few times about the noise, creating an awkward civic standoff as Larry's status necessitated delicate treatment. Larry had been furious that Rose allowed the band into their home, unswayed by his wife's logic that if Mike was determined to run with a bad crowd, better to have him where they could keep an eye on him.

Larry was not a fool; he knew the band was smuggling liquor in along with their gear, he could smell the pot that hung in the air. While he toiled at work, he imagined Mike and his friends giggling in the basement and exhaling smoke into the window wells, thinking they were getting away with something.

A blowup loomed, and Mike was about to find himself

kicked out of the house along with the band equipment. If Rose protested, that was a strain Larry was prepared to subject his marriage to. The level of contempt between father and son would not continue under his roof.

Arriving home that snowy winter day, thirteen-year-old John shoveled the driveway as his father had instructed over breakfast, then he came in through the back door. His dog, Jerry, who cowered in the coat closet whenever the band played, skittered his way to John's ankles and begged for escape. John held the door open for him.

He grabbed a cup of chocolate pudding from the refrigerator and dug his homework from his backpack as the Crüe's "Looks That Kill" tingled the soles of his feet. John and Mike had a relationship that was typically ambivalent for teenagers born a couple years apart. John resented the perpetual tension that Mike's presence brought to the house. On the other hand, Mike's rock-and-roll status and his rep with the outlaw crowd at school provided John some tangential cool.

And Screw Tool *rocked*. The sonic assault that cleared bird feeders three houses down resonated with John in a way that was not unconducive to homework. He dumped his textbooks on the kitchen table and set to studying, his heels dancing in rhythm to Eric Alvin's kick drums.

Only a desire for more pudding forty-five minutes later broke John's focus long enough to find the note lost under his homework. He read it twice, then headed down the basement with a rising sense of fear.

From the bottom of the stairs, the sound of the five-piece band was clean and furious. John shouted fruitlessly into the gale force onslaught of Van Halen's "Hot for Teacher" to get them to quit playing.

Only when he flicked the basement light on and off, traditionally the sign that their mother was on her way down to change over the laundry or alert Mike to a phone call, did the music crash to a ragged stop.

Mike quickly stashed an open beer while lead guitarist Jay Taggert stubbed out a joint and waved away the smoke, only to see that it was just Mike's kid brother.

"Dude, what the fuck?" Mike sneered at John. "Get outta here!"

The band glared at John, then Eric exploded into the stuttering drum pattern that kicks off "Hot for Teacher." John threw himself into the middle of them—all older and easily provoked into kicking his ass—and demanded that they stop.

Mike slammed his mike stand to the floor with a hateful stab and shoved his brother backward. "You want me to kick your ass, faggot?"

John met his threat with uncommon spine as he waved the note in Mike's face. "Something's wrong with Dad! We're supposed to go to the hospital!"

The staticky buzz of the amps filled the silence as Mike read the note and quickly ran the calculus of how he should respond. Even if it mattered only in how it impacted him, he sensed he should care that something was up with his father.

But here in front of his friends—his dead-souled, heavy metal friends—it would be faggot indeed to show that he cared.

"Fuck it," Mike drawled, flicking the note back at John. "If it was serious, she wouldn't leave a fucking note."

John felt the anxiety rising; he worried that he would cry. "I can't get there by myself! You have to drive me!" Mike, license-less at fifteen, had been known to help himself to the family car when his parents wouldn't know.

Mike studied his little brother, some distant twinge of affection piercing his hard-ass pose.

"Shit," Mike sighed as he turned to his band. "I'll be right back. Keep practicing."

Eight

Over the ten months following Larry's stroke, Screw Tool became Raz'r Gash then BitchBlade (for a week and a half), before falling into what would become Gravel Rash. Mike and Jay Taggert remained the only constants as new players came and went, either kicked out by Mike for lack of commitment, or hobbled by parents unwilling to let their sons practice and party at the Husted house at all hours.

It was a small town; everyone knew that Rose Husted had been keeping a sad, seemingly endless vigil at her husband's bedside. Left alone, their oldest son Mike was running wild.

As the months stretched on, talk around town was that Larry could not survive, but Rose was resolute. Even if Larry finally died never regaining consciousness, she knew that some believed that coma victims were capable of hearing those around them despite their impairment. She knew this, because Larry had told her, reading as he often did from a medical journal he had brought with him on a flight to Phoenix a few years earlier. *He* believed it was possible.

If there were even a chance that her husband was hearing life going on around him, Rose would not allow the darkness he was trapped in to go silent.

A second bed was rolled into Larry's room, testament to the power he wielded at the hospital, and Rose moved in.

Her sons fared the best they could. Friends and neighbors made sure John, who turned fourteen during the crisis, got to school and ate regularly. Otherwise, he was on his own to keep his grades up and ride his bike on wintry streets to see his father and—more and more—to care for his mother.

Her friends all worried about her, and one by one they took John aside and spoke to him soberly. If he could, they said, he should try to get her to go home and sleep in her own bed. No one wanted to see any more harm done to her. Despite his youth, John was charged with luring her home.

"Mom, let me stay over with Dad again," he would plead. "The Andersons want to have you over for dinner, then you can go home and get some sleep. Dad'll be okay till tomorrow."

"You never talk to him," she protested wearily.

"I will," John insisted, producing his backpack. "I have a speech due in speech class, so I'll practice it on him. I promise."

"What's it about?"

"The three branches of government."

She scoffed and settled in. "He'll never sit still for that."

"Then I'll turn on the basketball game. We'll watch the game together, he'll like that. Me, too."

"Well . . ."

"Mom," John reasoned, "if you were sick and couldn't move, would you want Dad talking to you *all the time*?"

She scrunched her face.

"So give him a chance to miss having you around. You'll walk in tomorrow, and he'll be really happy you're back."

She smiled wearily. She walked to her husband's bedside, and pulled the covers up to his chest.

"You boys don't stay up too late," Rose whispered to her husband. "Lights off as soon as the game is over."

She kissed Larry on the forehead.

"I'll call Jeff," John said as his mother grabbed her purse and turned to him. "His mom can swing by and get me to school."

"Make sure you shower."

"They let me use the doctor's locker room whenever I want. The security guards let me into the cafeteria if I get hungry. Don't worry about me, just get some sleep."

He hugged her and she kissed him on the cheek.

"I love you," she said.

"Me, too."

After she was gone, John sank into the chair at his father's bedside and turned on the TV. He didn't like basketball, but it wouldn't distract him while he did homework. If something crucial happened during the game, he'd make sure his father got a clear description of what he was missing. Just to be on the safe side.

Mike, meanwhile, made the most of the ten months that his father lingered. Already a dismal student, he barely went to class once his mother lost track of him. He still put in his time at Pizza Hut to help keep up with band expenses, but otherwise he was living a rock-and-roll bachelor's life for days at a time. From February to May, when he couldn't convince the others to skip school and rehearse with him, he would give his voice a rigorous work out, singing along at stage volume to records. And a couple days a month, he would drive down to Chicago, developing relationships with the club owners who would be essential to Gravel Rash's rise.

Every few weeks, Mike went to the hospital for sullen, obligatory visits. Taggert noted that there might be a heavy metal ballad in his situation, one of those treacly mood pieces that record labels were looking for with the recent success of the Crüe's "Home Sweet Home." So sometimes, Mike made up sad lyrics in his head while he stared down at his father.

Hard rockers couldn't be caught giving a shit about their mothers, but even Mike had to recognize Rose's pain. His mom had tried to be cool about the band. She let them practice in the house and insisted that some of what erupted from her basement was "catchy," making Mike shake his head with a reluctant smile for her sweet, well-meaning bullshit.

At his father's bedside, he would drape an arm around his mother and sincerely encourage the unlikely fantasies she was clinging to about her husband's recovery. When she would unexpectedly show up at home, he would quickly kick the band out and keep the house quiet so that she could sleep.

He cringed to see the pained look on her face when she saw what he and his friends were doing to her home, but any resolve to keep the party confined to the basement wilted with the arrival of the next case of beer.

Nine

Finally, in early December, Walt told Rose that there was no hope in keeping Larry alive. Despite relentless efforts, he and his colleagues—Larry's friends—had determined that he had passed into a vegetative state. His brain had been deprived of too much oxygen, and the damage was irreversible.

His body was healthy and strong. Under the expert care of his colleagues, he could continue to breathe on his own for who knew how long while they kept a feeding tube in place. But is that what Larry would want?

For the sake of his best friend's family, Walt was determined to convince her that it wasn't.

Over those long months that Rose had clung to her husband's side, she had completely lost control of her life. Bills weren't paid, the bank was calling about missing mortgage payments, and her oldest son was running wild. An ambulance was called to her house earlier in the week, and medical records that Walt Bolger was able to make disappear showed that Mike had nearly OD'd.

Walt knew that Rose had become too emotionally frail to assert herself as the sole parent of two teenage boys, but he also knew that Larry would expect her to try.

"Rose, it's time we let God take Larry from us," he began, holding her hand as they stood next to Larry's bed. "He's been fighting so hard, trying to come back, and if we let him, he'll keep right on fighting."

She smiled sadly.

"But there is nothing more we can do to help him," Walt continued. "His brain can't ever work again the way we need it to."

He saw her resist as she looked down at her husband. He put his arm around her shoulder and held her firmly.

"If you tell me we need to let him stay on, that's good enough for me. He will continue to live here until he's ready to go, and we'll keep him as comfortable as possible.

"But I need you to listen to me."

He stood before her and took both her hands. He positioned himself so that her focus was on him, not on her husband. "Rose, your boys *need* you. All this time, you have stayed at Larry's side. And I know, with all my heart, that there will come a day when Larry will hold you close and tell you how much your devotion has meant to him.

"But I also know that, right now, Larry needs you to be the parent he can't be anymore," he said softly. "Mike is in trouble. He could have died the other day, when he should have been in school. He needs his mother to help him get through this. It's not going to be easy."

Her heart sank at the truth of this.

"And John," Walt continued softly, "is a sensitive boy. He's still trying to understand all this. He needs you there, to make sure he's okay."

He put his hands on her shoulders and spoke plainly.

"It's time to go home, Rose. It's time to see to your boys. *That's* how you can help Larry now."

Rose understood the truth of what he was saying; she had known for months it was coming. But that didn't blunt the sudden rush of tears that came upon her as she fell into Walt's arms.

"I'm so scared," she cried as she accepted what lay ahead for her. "I can't do this alone."

"You won't be alone, honey. You have so many friends who love you. We'll get you through this."

They held each other and wept. As she grew to accept what she needed to do, she could no longer look at Larry. There were arrangements to see to, decisions to make. It was all on her.

"I don't know what to do," she whispered. "I don't know where to start."

"Sssh," he said softly. "Marie is right outside. She's going to take you back to our house. I'll stay here with Larry. I won't leave his side until it's over. When I get home, we'll figure out how we'll get through the next few days."

Walt broke the embrace and held her at the shoulders.

"You take as much time as you need," he said, then stepped away. As he reached for the door, it broke his heart to see her standing alone.

"He loved you, Rose," Walt said quietly. "So much."

He left the room; she felt the sands that now shifted beneath her feet slowly drawing her to her husband's side one final time.

She snugged him up beneath his bed covers, as if preparing him for a long journey. As she lifted his arm to tuck it beneath the blankets, she saw his wedding ring. Her heart collapsed, but with an inner strength that would often fail her in the weeks and months to come, she sturdily met the duty of being the one to slip it from his finger. It let go easily; her sobs came in turbulent surges.

Wiping her eyes and studying his face, she drew her finger along the scar from when he fell in his office. It had healed well; it looked like no more than a wrinkle. The only wrinkle he'd ever earn.

She kissed him and held his hand. She would keep no memory of how and when she let it go.

New footprints disturbed the dust as John and Walt paced the corridors of the old hospital, the old man's tale nowhere near its end.

John stood at the slats of one of the shuttered windows. Looking out, he could see Rocky's diner across the street.

And his car. Out there, just a little over an hour before, none of this was true.

"It was a closed casket," John remembered darkly as he turned back to Dr. Bolger.

"Your mother let us make the arrangements," the old man said, girding himself for the fury he was not fool enough to think he was going to evade for long.

"Who did you bury?" John asked through grit teeth.

"We didn't bury anyone, John," Walt said patiently. "We ran this hospital, we could control things.

"Dave Stanton was a good friend of your father's and a member of my church. I trusted that he would help paper things over at his funeral home."

John became very still, forcing his breath to come in even waves. He was close to hyperventilating.

Above all else, the question assaulted his mind:

"You *controlled* things," he glared. *"For thirty years?!"*

His voice echoed down the hall of the dead building, followed by the skittering of creatures unaccustomed to the presence of humans.

Walt Bolger had been anticipating this moment since that December day in 1985. He had long resolved that if the day ever came that he had to reveal all to Larry's family, he would do it in a way that would cause them the least amount of trauma. For decades, he obsessed over this moment while praying it would never come.

He decided long ago that the family would need a gradual descent into their new reality; they would have to be allowed time for their ricocheting stabs of disbelief to settle, if only by degrees, before he could take them deeper into what he had done. And how it had been possible.

"Son, what I've brought you to is enough. For today," Walt said compassionately but firmly to John.

"We need to take the time for you to just accept that your dad is alive. I swear to you that you will have a full account of how this came to be, but when I tell it to you I need your mind to be snapped back from what I just put it through. Does that make sense?"

John just stared, his complete inability to comprehend seeming to have frozen him in place.

"You could have the police here in fifteen minutes," Walt said matter-of-factly but not without fear. The statement brought John to attention as the old man met his eyes. "They'd get the story from me and you'd have what you want to know, including that I will pay a great price for this.

"But I'm hoping that while we can, while it's just me and you and Larry, that you'll let me try to explain in a way that will do you—and your family—the least amount of harm," he said, pointing back to room 116. "That's the best friend I ever had in there. I don't want to hurt you all any more than I already have."

They stood together at Larry's bedside.

"When you're ready, I will tell you how we got here. You'll take all the time you'll need with him. We'll figure out what to tell your family. And then, if you choose to, you'll finally put this to rest. Larry's got places to be."

John flinched at what Walt was getting at. Walt pressed on.

"I'm leaving town, John. Hank Burch, who used to be an oncologist here, wants me in Phoenix to see what he can do for me."

John's mind roiled. "*I'll* let him die? *That's* why I'm here?"

Despite the gravity of Walt's situation, John began to protest.

"You can't leave me to——"

"John, I could have ended Larry's life myself, years ago, and you never would've known," Walt said sternly. "Did I make the wrong choice?"

John looked down at his father, withered and still. And yet: breathing in, breathing out. The same air filled their lungs.

Even in his frenzy to accept this, he could not deny that there was something massively profound here at his father's bedside.

The weight fully, squarely, settled upon John's shoulders as he began to take on the responsibility of believing his father's existence. But whatever fortitude it gave him failed when suddenly he thought of his mother.

"Jesus, my mother . . ." he moaned. "She'll never understand this." He ran the scene through his head and despaired. "This could *kill* her."

"One step at a time, John. We'll figure a way through this, one step at a time," Walt said sturdily.

"But it's time for you to start. Go home to your wife. Tell her about your day," the old man smiled gently.

Yes, John thought dumbly. *Robin was good at things like this.*

Walt stepped back to escort them from Larry's room, but John remained rooted in place. He slowly leaned closer to the bed, self-conscious but grateful for the opportunity to speak to his father.

"I'll be back, Dad," he whispered. "Okay?"

Ten

There was a private place where John and Robin could talk, but they hadn't been there in a long time. Back when they first found themselves arguing a lot about their marriage, Katie was old enough to listen in and perhaps extract traumas that she would internalize and let fester. They had an aging mutt named Wobble and a small park nearby, so they resolved to take their unhappiness there. Even in the dead of winter, all of a sudden Mom and Dad were *really* into taking the dog for a walk, sometimes for hours.

But the fights kept coming and maybe they walked poor Wobble to death, because before long the dog was dead and the walks faded away. John proposed getting a new dog in order to maintain their cover, at which point Robin wondered with exasperation if maybe the problem was not how to keep the fights going but why they were happening in the first place.

John couldn't fault her logic, but he had really come to like the walks. When they got through this bad patch, he hoped the family would go forward with a new dog. He'd walk it alone if Robin didn't want to join him.

John's mind had been agitating spastically when he returned home after leaving Walt and his father at the hospital. Katie was there, but Robin wasn't. John knew he couldn't unravel the way he needed to with his daughter in the house so until Robin got home, he had to act like nothing was wrong.

"Hey," he said with forced cheer to Katie as she sulked over homework at the kitchen table. "Where's Mom?"

"Work?" Katie muttered, her black-lipsticked mouth pinched by a chin propped up by a balled, black-fingernailed fist. Every day, the goth thing spread—the dark, mopey soul of a teenager, splashed across her body like an existential billboard. As much as John despaired at seeing his once-sunny child painted up like a sad, trendy corpse, he often wished he had had this fashion option when *he* was a sulky fifteen-year-old.

Kids these days, they could just buy their attitudes down at the mall. Their parents would pay for it.

"Dunno," John said in response to his daughter as he paced edgily. "Too late for Mom to be at work."

"Store?" Katie sighed.

"Hey," John said, way too brightly. "Let's list all the places she *could* be! My turn. Dentist!"

The front door jangled open; John whirled on Robin.

"Hey, hi, there you are! Let's walk the dog!" he announced tersely as he headed out of the house.

Robin stopped. They hadn't had a dog for over two years.

"Jesus," Robin whispered after John told her.

Larry Husted died years before they got together; she knew John's father only through reverent family stories that she silently suspected were a bit *too* reverent—the guy was a small-town doctor, he wasn't God. But her husband stood before her now, swinging wildly at an unimaginably raw trauma that had coldcocked him just hours earlier.

Her mind churned. *"How?"*

"I don't know," John said through his dazed struggle. "He said he'd only been in the old building for a couple years, but other than that he didn't tell me."

"He didn't tell you?!" There was a scolding in her voice. "How could you let him—?"

"He *said* he'd explain everything, after . . . After . . ." he insisted defensively before trailing off. *"Help me!"*

Her responding to his raw plea came automatically. In this precise moment, the best of what they brought to each other seemed to seep back in tentative rivulets. It ran sludgier, but there it was.

She found the right tone.

"So what are you going to do?" she asked.

"Who the fuck knows? In the entire history of dead fathers, nobody's ever had to deal with this!"

"Well, maybe there's been *somebody*," she instinctively

countered. John had never learned to love the way Robin brought an arbitrary contrariness to their marriage, often when she seemed to know it would rev him up.

His terse glare told her this was one of those times.

She sat silently and watched him pace. Over the years they had racked up hours of silence in this park, the two of them running out of words without ever getting to the nub of what was dying in their marriage. Those quiet stretches grew to be agonizing, neither willing to articulate the hard things that needed to be said.

Now, as John continued to pace and chew his lower lip frenetically, Robin finally grabbed him gently at the wrist.

"Hey," she soothed. "Sit."

He parked himself beside her on a picnic table. John felt stillness for the first time since he had crossed into room 116. He appreciated her bringing him to it.

But she knew there was work to be done.

"You have to tell your mother," Robin said.

"How?" he agonized, jumping up to pace again. "Does Hallmark have a card for this? 'Congratulations, turns out your husband's not dead!'"

"John . . ." she scolded. He shook his head regretfully; usually he knew when his humor went wrong.

"This could kill her," he sighed.

"You don't know that. When you were telling *me,* it sounded like as awful as this is, something has touched you in a way you need to share with her."

He exhaled deeply, rifling through the barrage of emotions he had been wrestling with the past several hours.

"I don't even think about him anymore," John said sadly. "I haven't for years. The whole time you've known me, I haven't gone to the cemetery once. I couldn't find his grave if you put a gun to my head.

"Whatever he used to be to me, he had just become a bunch of bones at the bottom of a hole. And, you know, that's what it was. That's what I knew."

Robin recognized his harsh dispassion as a defense mechanism. She knew he needed to sort this out his way.

"But all this time later, to just stand beside him . . ." He sighed, then the tears came. Robin held him. The silence of the park was broken for several hard minutes by John's sobs.

He finally pulled himself together and broke the hug with his wife.

"I have to tell her," he said resolutely. But with dread.

"Yes, you do. But you shouldn't have to do it alone. Tell Mike, make him help you with this. Make him do something decent for his family for once."

Robin had no affection for Mike. She spent years watching John try to forge some sort of relationship with his older brother, despite Mike's disinterest in anyone but himself.

Over the course of their entire marriage, she probably had no more than ten conversations with her brother-in-law that lasted over five minutes. Mike knew about eighties heavy metal, and dope, and how much better the world would be if everybody just smoked dope while listening to eighties heavy metal. Everything else—politics, culture, essential human connections—were of no use to Mike Husted.

But Robin saw right away that Mike might be the answer here.

"He won't feel this the way you do," she reasoned. "All you've ever told me was how he hated your father. He'll be able to look at this dispassionately and maybe know what to do. He could surprise you."

John scrunched his mouth skeptically. "You think?"

"Sure. He might have heard an Iron Maiden song that addresses this very thing."

She winked; he smiled. An echo of something good returned to them.

"But you can't tell either one of them until you know how the hell this happened," she said, bucking him up for what he had to do next. "You need to sit this old doctor down—first thing tomorrow—and not let him up until this all makes sense. Do you want me to come with you?"

John studied her intensity with fondness.

"I think you'd scare him."

"He *needs* scaring."

"I'll handle it," he said, hugging her. "This is for me to take care of."

Eleven

Walt invited him to his home when John called the next day just past dawn.

John had not slept all night. There in the silent darkness, he picked up a kind of radio signal that he now knew his father had been sending from across town. He thought of the moments in his life for which his father had been absent and his mind convulsed to think that Larry had been nearby all along. Although he hadn't; not really. Not in any way that could have engaged John and his family.

Nothing—not one damned thing—would have been any different if Larry had played a mute, meaningless role in his son's life over the past thirty years. Or so John reasoned in those first mad hours of acceptance.

The ornate Bolger house smelled of coffee, eggs, and bacon

as Walt led John back to the kitchen, still locked in a late 1970s fustiness.

Pleasantries were not attempted. Breakfast clotted on their plates. Walt picked up where he left off the day before.

"When I spoke to your mother that day so long ago about ending your father's life, he should have died the next day. Or the next week," he began. "We kept his feeding tube in; we would not starve him to death. But every day I came into the office, I knew with all my heart that it should be the day that he would finally let go. He *had* to let go.

"We had crossed some very bad lines, John. We knew that."

"Who's 'we?'" John asked darkly.

"It was me, and three others. Friends of your father's. They're dead now. Your business now is just with me."

John silently, sternly commanded the tale to continue.

"We had put our careers in jeopardy; we had exposed ourselves and the hospital to enormous legal risk. And the only way what I am about to tell you makes any sense—*the only way*—is if you believe that at a time of so much grief and uncertainty, we were trying to do right by both your mother *and* your father."

The old man's earnestness was compelling; John had to give him that. Walt, sensing John's willingness to hear the whole tale before lashing out, cinched up and carried on.

"They think that before long, computers might make it possible to repair the brain," Walt began. "Computer chips now restore hearing and eyesight, control pacemakers. It's just a matter of time before maybe they can be used to regenerate cognitive function."

John jolted at the news; Walt moved quickly to correct any misunderstanding.

"It's too late for your father, John. Years and years too late," he said tersely. "But I am telling you this because I need you to understand the conversations your father and I had right up until the day he had his stroke. Look . . ."

John had given serious notice to a meticulously stacked pile of thick manila folders on the kitchen table. Tabs were color coded, with piles of folders sorted accordingly. Walt opened the first one and slid a copy of the local newspaper toward John. The date in the headline was February 21, 1985. The day Larry had the stroke.

"See," Walt urged. "This is the story I told you about, the newspaper article your father and I were discussing."

John saw the short newspaper article about William Schroeder, one of the first artificial heart recipients who crashed an early barrier by spending a whopping fifteen minutes outside his Louisville hospital.

"Every day back then, it seemed there were stories like these," Walt said eagerly. "They were miraculous times, and for young doctors like me and your father—so dedicated and so damned full of ourselves—we knew we were blessed to be there on the cutting edge. We wanted to lead the way on some of this."

John flipped through one of the folders. It was full of articles from newspapers and densely written medical journals, dating back to the fifties. Jagged handwriting filled the margins.

"That was your father's file. That's his writing," Walt marveled.

John absorbed the soft throb tickling his heart as he saw his father's unfamiliar scrawl.

"Remember, this was the eighties. Computers hadn't been available to us all that long. And they were nothing like what we have today.

"The medical journals, they knew what was coming," Walt continued, fanning another stack of medical stories. "Everything was going to get smaller, computer chips were going to get faster. With what they were promising, anything seemed possible. And so much of it came true!

"In the mid-seventies, they refined a chemotherapy drug that took the cure rate in testicular cancer from ten percent to ninety-five percent. Saved tens of thousands of lives. But it came just a few years too late to save your grandfather. Larry's dad. That haunted him.

"Seeing how technology was moving things forward so much faster, he became obsessed with losing control of his own care. He needed to know that if he could no longer make decisions for himself, the rest of us—the doctors he trusted with his life—would fight to keep him viable if there was any chance of recovery."

Walt produced a lone manila envelope with just one document inside. He slid it to John. It was a legal agreement, with Larry's signature at the bottom.

"He wanted all of us to sign one," Walt sighed. "But none of us took it as seriously as he did. Bob Schurmer, his lawyer, drew that up. It's giving us permission—it's *ordering* us—to not let him go."

John stared at the document, queasy at the degree to which his father had taken this. He wondered about the state of Larry's mind. His faith in medicine and belief in his own powers bordered on the obsessive.

John jabbed his finger at the signed agreement with incomprehension. "Why would anyone even think to—"

Walt held up his finger to silence him, anticipating just this moment.

Five separate stacks of folders were set apart from the rest, each bulging with material. Walt slid the first of them into play, the name *Schiavo* etched neatly on the tab.

"You remember the Terri Schiavo case?" Walt began.

Of course John did; it had only been a few years before. A woman in Florida fell into a coma and she hung on for years. Eventually her husband wanted to let her die, but her family didn't. John remembered being thoroughly disgusted by the family's intervention. He thought it was ghoulish and profane to keep a hollowed-out shell of a human being alive simply because technology made it possible, and *God* commanded it.

"That case all came down to *this*," Walt urged as he touched Larry's signed order.

"The Schiavo thing was a few years ago!" John cried impatiently. "He signed this in . . . *1976!*"

Per the script he had spent decades crafting for just this moment, Walt slid forward more stacks of evidence. It was almost as if he were constructing a barrier between himself and John.

"Karen Ann Quinlan was twenty-one years old in 1975 when she mixed alcohol with prescription drugs and fell into a coma that transitioned into a persistent vegetative state," the old doctor recalled from memory. "Irreparable brain damage, just like your father. After a few months, her parents—good Catholics—wanted to let her die. But her doctors—and the courts—said no.

"Your father watched the Quinlan case closely. He was *mad* at this girl's parents. After only *four months* they were giving up on her and trying to shut down her ventilator. Four months! Because Karen wasn't able to tell them she wanted them to keep fighting for her."

The old man laid his palm across Larry's signed decree as a silence descended upon the kitchen. John recognized the need to meticulously read this document with the same care that his father had drafted it.

He read aloud his father's command: "'I order that all actions be taken to sustain my life, until it is the consensus of the doctors to whom I am entrusting my care that there is no current or pending medical measures that could provide a reasonable expectation of restoring me to a cognitive state of being as defined by me to be a state of mental and physical ability, notwithstanding grave and perhaps permanent diminishment of function that could result from my impairment.'"

John's eyes bore a hole through the mournful old man. "He's saying, 'Once there's no hope, *you have to let me go.*'"

Walt stared at his coffee cup. John angrily balled up Larry's agreement and brandished it at the old man.

"He trusted you to let him go!" John shouted.

Twelve

Walt stood slowly from the kitchen table and wandered away when John's anger hit its peak. He thought the old man had walked to another part of the house merely to let the tension subside, but when he didn't return John followed. He found Walt standing alone in a dusty bedroom, empty aside from a hospital bed and walls adorned with images of the Bolgers' Catholic faith.

"Within days of your father's stroke and continuing all the way to your reunion with him yesterday, I have known that to most eyes he appears dead in all ways other than the air in his lungs and the blood in his veins," Walt said solemnly. "To be a life not worth saving."

John stood among the portentous religious imagery and immediately sensed where this was leading.

" *'Sanctity of life'* is a phrase that has become such a charged expression over the years," Walt continued. "I know for people like you, who don't hold to the word of God, it's within your capacity to decide which lives don't measure up. Don't quite deserve a chance, especially if they're just going to be in the way."

John's temples began to throb. The air in the room turned icy as it grew thin.

"My wife and I, we didn't live that way. We truly had no expectation that your father would hang on more than a few weeks, maybe a few months. But the path for your father was never ours to choose.

"If it was God's will to keep Larry alive, then it was our duty to minister to him. No matter the sacrifice," he said stoically, gesturing to the empty bed. "This was his home. For twenty years."

John's mind roiled as he stared at the bed.

"Terri Schiavo lived for fifteen years in your father's condition," Walt said. "If her family had had their way, she could still be alive, knowing the care they would have provided her. If the patient is fed and hydrated, if disease and infection are treated effectively, if their environment is kept as sterile as possible, a human life is a very resilient thing.

"But their care is unrelenting, often without insurance. Few loved ones can be expected to take on such a burden. Marie and I accepted the task as a blessing, and as a test of our faith."

John went to a window and stared out, his thoughts overwhelmed. Terri Schiavo *had* hung on for years, that was one of the surreal elements of the story. That *happened*.

"I still had my practice," the old man continued, "so it was on Marie to set Larry up here and tend to him. Changing his feeding supply, repositioning him to avoid bedsores, keeping him clean and sanitary—it's all simpler than you'd think, but it's constant. And she committed herself to him, a hundred percent.

"She loved that man, John. If nothing else, I hope you'll believe that. She gave him such tender care, I really think you would have been touched by that."

John turned away from the window. Brutal truths continued to pummel his comprehension of all this.

"Your wife and my mother had been best friends," John whispered bitterly. "My mother was *across town,* and the two of you said nothing.

"She thinks her husband is dead!" John hissed.

Walt joined John at the window. "Son," he began softly, "the moment I committed to this, the moment *I lied* to your family about your father, I put myself at terrible risk—legally, professionally. Morally. And the longer it dragged on, the more I had to lose.

"I don't expect you to give a damn about any of this, but that's where I found myself," Walt said plainly. "Marie and I pulled back from your mother—we pulled back from pretty much the whole town—so that there wouldn't be a risk of being found out. That's how much we believed in what we were doing."

The old man sighed.

"Then Marie died. May 2004," he said quietly. "That left

just me and Larry. For maybe a year I tried to take it all on myself, but it damned near killed me.

"So for a good while I brought in hospice nurses. They were young, fresh out of nursing school; I told them Larry was my brother. They weren't going to question old doc Bolger.

"But as it dragged on, the agency started asking questions. I was surprised they let it go as long as they did.

"But the time finally came when Larry couldn't live here anymore."

The old man heaved a weary sigh.

"That was the closest I came to letting him die. God had given me this test, and it looked like I was finally going to fail," he said. "But then came this."

He had the Schiavo file again.

He reminded John that 2005 brought the closing chapter in the Schiavo firestorm. The Bolgers, virtually trapped in their home to hide Larry's presence, had spent the previous six years monitoring the endless fight over Terri Schiavo's life. They drew strength and validation from the faithful who filled their TV screen all day and night, forcefully sharing their belief that even the most stilled life was a gift from God. Marie Bolger died praying that that poor girl down in Florida would be spared by being delivered to her family's care.

But a year after Walt lost his wife, no further legal challenges could prevent Terri Schiavo's husband from ending her life. The faithful—including George Bush and the social conservatives in Congress who had outdone themselves with sanctimony and indignation—were outraged when Schiavo finally died in the spring of 2005, fifteen years after the stroke that silenced her.

"Not even the pope could stop it," Walt said, putting on his glasses to read.

"'Even our brothers and sisters who find themselves in the clinical condition of a "vegetative state" *retain their human dignity in all its fullness*,'" the old man read meaningfully from the newspaper account of the pope's official declaration. "'The loving gaze of God the Father continues to fall upon them, acknowledging them as his sons and daughters, *especially* in need of help.'"

He lowered his bifocals and trained his gaze on John.

He shook the newspaper article dramatically. "This was the burning bush, and it was talking to *me*."

John said nothing, because there was no debating faith this deep.

"I had shown weakness, I was about to give up, but then I heard that my mission was not through," he declared. "For Larry, and for the sacrifice that my wife had made, I was charged with finding a way forward. And by this point, I figured whatever I came up with, God was going to see it through."

Thirteen

Walt Bolger had seen patients abandoned to the hospital's care several times in his nearly forty years at Holt Memorial. Maybe the patient had no family to begin with, or relatives simply stopped coming around when estrangement or dark family secrets exposed an utter lack of interest in their afflicted "loved one." The families dumped the cost of care on the hospital, which in turn billed the state for as much government assistance as possible. Several balance sheets counted on the infirmed dying sooner than later. Most did.

At the time Walt made his move, the hospital's B wing, a dreary and crumbling corridor, already hosted two unclaimed patients trapped in perpetual sleep. He convinced himself that if he could slip Larry into a room on the wing, he could fake a file that would disguise his identity.

The only trick would be getting him tucked into a bed. Walt saw a way.

Almost since the day it opened, the emergency room at Holt Memorial at four o'clock every Sunday morning hosted a swamp of wobbly humans spun loose from what daytime folk considered proper behavior. Even in the best of times, working-class bars in small Wisconsin towns encouraged Saturday night binge drinking that routinely set the standard for an alcohol-abusing nation. The Bush economy had sent the dollar to record lows as the seeds were sown for the economic freefall that would come at the end of the decade. Jobs were going away, and angry and aimless adults suddenly had less money with which to spend more time drinking.

When bar time came, and dizzy, bitter adults were flushed out onto the streets to weave home while dodging their equally bombed children, carnage was as sure as the dawn.

The gamble that Holt City made in building the new hospital had accomplished at least one thing. With the shiny new facility up and running, smaller rural hospitals within forty-five minutes in all directions soon went out of business, taking their emergency rooms with them. Now every carcass pulled from the glass and goo of a drunken car crash, every frowsy party girl whose evening concluded with her tipping over and shattering her skull upon the sidewalk outside her favorite bar, stumbled or was rolled into Holt Memorial's ER.

Added to this was the growing immigrant and working poor population, which had no choice but to use the emergency room for basic health care. They could be found in the ER throughout the day, waiting for hours to be seen, but it never failed that the direst health crises erupted in the dead of night.

As Walt had gambled, this four a.m. slurry of humanity in the emergency room cleared the way for Lawrence Husted's return to the hospital he built.

Larry barely weighed eighty pounds when Walt came for him. With a wheelchair borrowed from the hospital, it was only a slight struggle for Walt to ease Larry from his bed and roll him to the garage, where he laid him on a thick nest of comforters he had stretched out on the backseat of his Cadillac. Even at 3:30 in the morning, it was warm and humid outside; as this was Larry's first time outdoors since 1985, it was a good night for him to be taken for a ride.

The scrum surrounding the ER entrance was just as Walt needed it to be. The wounded came by ambulance, car, or forms of deliverance they would have no recollection of the next day. Friends and family smoked grumpily out front alongside those who had been treated and released with nowhere to go or no one to take them.

Walt turned off his headlights and drove around back, where the old, abandoned hospital sat silent and spooky. Since 1982, few souls had ventured back here. Overgrown brush in surrounding fields walled off the dead building from the world.

The dark was absolute; Walt grimaced and gasped as he

fumbled blindly with Larry, easing him out of the car and into the wheelchair. For one awful moment, the chair began to roll and Larry nearly slipped through his hands to the pavement.

With Larry safely bundled into the wheelchair, Walt rolled him toward the glow of the emergency room entrance. From a safe distance away, figures were already visible in the shadows. They huddled together with a bottle or a smoke; Walt kept moving, careful to not draw their attention. He hoped he was home free when he encountered a young man of about thirty, zipping himself up as he stepped unsteadily from behind a tree.

His clothes were worn and ill-fitting; he looked as if he had gone without a bath for weeks. As he flinched sheepishly at being caught relieving himself, he projected a vulnerability that Walt found encouraging.

"Evening," Walt said genially.

"Hi," the man replied. Standing closer, Walt thought he might be in his twenties.

"Everything okay?" the old man asked.

"Yeah," he said unconvincingly, looking toward the ER. "My girlfriend . . ." He trailed off worriedly as he lit a cigarette.

"She's in good hands in there," Walt said gently. "They'll take care of her."

The spindly kid seemed to find some peace with this. He fidgeted as he nodded to Larry, his chin dropped forward onto his chest. "He doesn't look too good."

"Yeah," Walt said with concern. "I need to get him inside."

He hesitated just slightly, and then produced his wallet.

"I wonder if you'd do something for me," he said casually as he produced a hundred dollar bill. If Walt had misread this kid, he was about to be mugged.

The kid just stared at the money longingly.

"I need you to roll my friend into the ER," Walt said. "Once you're through the doors, there is a row of chairs to the left and then beyond them there's a corner that is hidden by some plants.

"I need you to park him in that corner. I need you to not be noticed," Walt said plainly. "Come right back, and this is yours."

The hundred dollar bill seemed to glow in the predawn darkness. Having lived the hardscrabble life Walt suspected, the kid had probably been in enough dodgy situations in his young life to not question someone else's crooked scheme. But finding it in such a well-groomed old man at four o'clock in the morning felt like a trap. He studied Walt warily.

"You've been in there, right?" Walt asked, gesturing toward the ER. "It's a madhouse. You'll be in and out in thirty seconds, and no one is going to give a damn what you're up to."

The kid gave Walt one last careful look, and then stepped behind the wheelchair to grasp the handles.

"I'm going to stand right over there," Walt said firmly, "so I can see you all the way to the front door. Once I lose sight of you, I expect you back here—alone—in no more than a minute."

The kid swallowed nervously and nodded as he began to push Larry forward.

"Hold on," Walt whispered sharply, grabbing the kid's elbow. They both watched as a cop walked out of the ER and pulled out of the parking lot in his squad car. The coast was clear.

"One minute," Walt repeated, and then moved to watch anxiously as this total stranger took momentary care of the friend he had devoted his life to protecting.

Fourteen

"'Morning, Diane," Walt smiled sleepily to the lead ER nurse as he strolled through the front doors with the sun rising behind him. After the kid had returned from delivering Larry and disappeared into the night with his money, Walt had gone across the street to Rocky's and picked nervously at his breakfast until he knew the ER would be clearing out.

Every conceivable body odor hung in the air, undercut by disinfectant and rubbing alcohol. The last untreated patients slept uncomfortably in waiting room chairs as a janitor mopped up a pool of vomit.

The gaunt, sixtyish nurse, up all night and long ago hardened to the carnival of injury and despair that was her responsibility, reacted with the instinctive fear of a snap inspection at seeing Walt Bolger so early on a Sunday morning.

"Dr. Bolger," she said with a curious, husky rattle. "What brings you into my torture chamber this time of day?"

He smiled as he approached the admitting desk. "I have a patient up on six who had a bad night. Judy asked me to come in and see if I can do anything for him, get him to eat something.

"Rough night?" Walt asked with well-earned empathy as he looked around the waiting room.

"Fellah brought his special lady friend in around two thirty when their night of passion hit a snag. We took one of those Sesame Street puppet things out of her rectum," she drawled matter-of-factly as she tended to paperwork. "Plastic, maybe eight inches tall. Really big head.

"It was still smiling when it finally yanked loose. She wasn't."

Walt smiled sympathetically, then nodded toward the corner. "What's the story with this one? Someone admitted him yet?"

She looked to the other side of the waiting room and saw Larry slumped over in his chair, hidden behind a ficus.

"Oh, Jesus," she sighed. "Bonnie! Bring the cart."

A bleary-eyed young nurse emerged from the exam rooms pushing a rolling intake unit. She followed Diane toward Larry, while Walt trailed behind.

Diane reached Larry and studied his face closely as Walt held his breath. He thought Diane's time at Holt City dated back to Larry's reign there. If so, she didn't recognize him.

She looked around the near-empty lobby as the nurse

methodically began to check Larry's blood pressure and other vitals.

"Mark," Diane called, "did you see who brought this man in?"

The janitor shrugged.

"Check the bathrooms, send security out to the parking lot," she instructed him. "They probably just got tired of waiting and went out for a smoke."

Her frustration rising, Diane went through the pocket of Larry's thin robe but found nothing.

"How is he?" she asked the nurse, who had just taken Larry's pulse.

"He's fine," the young nurse said with surprise. "Blood pressure steady, temperature normal. Somebody's been taking good care of him."

Diane turned to Walt, her wry attitude gone. "I'm sorry, doctor," she said soberly. "We'll take him back, give him a thorough workup. If no one claims him, I'll call the police and hope that he matches up with a missing persons report."

She stepped behind Larry's chair to wheel him to an exam room.

"Hang on," Walt said. The red folder he had slipped down the back of Larry's robe was visible by just an edge. He pulled it out and read from its meager contents:

"'My father's name is Peter. I have done all I can to help him for almost twelve years. He doesn't die and I cannot afford to help him anymore. I'm sorry. Please take good care of him.'"

Walt looked to the only other page in the file, where in a handwriting he had labored to fake he wrote all that was needed to be known about Larry's care.

"No last name," he said convincingly, checking both sides of the pages and the file folder. He feigned contemplation for a moment as he reread the instructions.

"Let's admit him, as a John Doe," he said, adding with a smile. "*Peter* Doe.

"Put him on the B wing with the others, get a drip going. Looks like he's been in this chair for a while, so make sure his pressure points are treated. I'll check in on him later."

For all her gruffness, Walt knew Diane cared about her job. "I try to monitor everything that goes on out here," she said defensively. "But when it all hits the fan, it's just too much to stay on top of.

"If this turns into a big investigation . . ." She trailed off with concern.

"Tell you what," Walt said with a comforting smile. "Let's just keep this to ourselves."

He squatted down with his hands on his knees to study Larry closely.

"I think the best we can do is make our friend here as comfortable as possible. To look at him, I can't imagine he'll be with us for very long."

With Larry settled onto the B wing with the hospital's other unclaimed patients, Walt provided his friend's care while tending to his diminishing medical practice. Nurses stuck on weekend and graveyard shifts were glumly content to do the rest for Larry, barely bothering to learn his false name, let alone questioning his identity. The hospital's nursing staff was either young and fresh out of school, or old and going through the motions. They monitored his feeding supply, changed his diaper and warded off his bedsores with all the engagement they gave watering the potted plants in the break room.

It was the same rote, antiseptic attention that Walt and his wife had provided in their home for over twenty years. Now sustained by expert, government-financed indigent care, Larry's rugged constitution ground on in the B wing for another seven years.

God abided.

Fifteen

It would be a 2012 meningitis scare in the B wing that prompted Larry's final desperate move into the old hospital.

A steady flow of the unnamed or unloved had come and gone from the increasingly dreary B wing, with old Peter Doe the only constant. The compromised immune systems of the patients on the row required that they be moved out until the threat could be assessed and with vacancies up throughout the hospital, it was decided to resituate the disenfranchised among the regular population and leave them there.

In the case of Peter Doe, however, administrator Dean Durning decreed that the time had finally come to transfer him to a county facility that could deliver his minimal care more cost effectively. With government funding being rationed more tightly, Holt City could no longer afford such charity cases, especially one that refused to check out.

Walt's plot was unraveling. But after all this time and such an extraordinary commitment, he was desperate to keep his friend from dying anonymously and alone in a wretched county hospital that would welcome his prompt death as a bookkeeping necessity.

As he bore down on Dean Durning's office, a long cardboard tube under his arm, he still had one last card to play. As with every new mad knot tied into his endless scheme, he had had years at Larry's bedside to cook it up.

To the hospital's administrator, Walt Bolger had just been one of those legacy cases who kept modest practices well past retirement age seemingly for lack of anything better to do. Durning would encounter the old man sporadically in the hospital's corridors, and occasionally he was obligated to reverently recognize his place in Holt Memorial history at fundraisers and other events, but Walt was primarily just one of those dusty old men whose portraits were on display in the lobby. When he barged creakily into Durning's office one morning in the midst of the meningitis scare, he assumed it was to finally announce his retirement.

Within minutes, it was Durning who was ready to quit.

"We can't!" Durning cried weakly after Walt bluntly told Durning who Peter Doe was, and the macabre, flagrantly illegal acts that brought him there. Durning's mind raced to keep up, but he could only blink dimly as Walt proceeded to announce the legal and media hell storm that was about to befall his hospital if they didn't form an immediate, unthinkable alliance.

As he would a few years later with John, Walt brought evidence of Schiavo and other high-profile right-to-life cases, this time emphasizing the ugly and relentless public protests that came to overwhelm the hospitals where the stories played out. The hospitals in these past cases weren't guilty of anything, Walt stressed. They just had the misfortune of being the place where the stricken had been allowed to settle while strangers furiously batted around their fate.

It would be a whole other kettle of fish, he prosaically threatened Dean Durning, if Larry's story came out.

Walt and the others carried out their unconscionable plot as employees of Holt Memorial. Walt—the ringleader who kept Larry in his home for two decades, essentially a kidnap victim—was *still* on staff. Dr. Lawrence Husted, beloved figurehead of the struggling hospital and life-giving legend to the town, had been residing on the B wing right under the administrator's nose for seven years. The man's family was betrayed for *decades*.

Worse, if the tussle about what to do with Larry went public, and the Right-to-Lifers and Let-Him-Die-ers arrived to set up camp, and the satellite trucks rolled in behind them, and the cell phone videos of shoving matches and prayer circles started hitting the internet, the hospital would be found guilty long before any court ruled on it. At best, it would be a PR disaster; more likely, it would result in a legal judgment that would shut the hospital's doors for good.

The chill sent down Durning's spine shook loose his resolve.

"We will terminate the patient," Durning announced abruptly with terse, unconvincing authority. He knew he was crossing into taboo legal and moral territory.

"This is an untenable situation," he insisted. "I cannot risk the solvency of this hospital. I cannot risk the care of the patients who *need* us to be here, because of this insane plot of yours.

"We will terminate," he concluded firmly. "I will see to it myself if you won't."

Walt met his glare with easy, menacing calm.

"Son, I am a dying old man," he began with unsettling resolve. "I have given thirty years of my life to that man. He and I have come too far together for me to let him go now.

"If you push me, I'll bring the whole damned world in on this. By the time I would be held accountable, Larry and I will be dead. You'll wish you were."

Durning swallowed hard; he knew he was boxed in. Before he could continue flailing for another solution, the frenzied old doctor unfurled the contents of the tube he had come armed with.

These were the blueprints that he and Larry had pored over for years in the early eighties as the move from the old hospital to the new became reality. In the plans drawn with great optimism all those years ago, the B wing where Larry had spent the past seven years was a short tendril that stuck out from the new hospital's north face. In the blueprint, the wing came to a dead end, with nothing on the other side but Wisconsin countryside. The old building was never intended to stay around.

In reality, the short wing from the new building joined with the long-abandoned hospital. When it became clear that the original building was never coming down, the passage was kept open for a while so that the empty building could be used to store records and discontinued medical equipment. But by the time Dean Durning came along, it had been padlocked for years.

"The B wing's empty for the first time practically since this hospital opened," Walt said decisively as he drew his finger to the blueprint. "We'll finally wall it off, like we've done everywhere else.

"Larry will stay behind in the old building. I will assume full responsibility."

Durning gazed at the blueprint, his head spinning.

"The wing will be closed at both ends," he said doubtfully.

"Let me worry about that."

The old man's insistence was as convincing as the threats that he had promised would befall Durning if he stood in his way.

The conspiracy was on. The hospital administrator already doubted his sanity.

"I am agreeing to this," Durning concluded resolutely, "because I know you can't handle this on your own. A man a third your age could not provide him the care he needs. In these circumstances."

Walt's shoulders sagged at the reality of this.

"There's going to come a point—*soon*—where you and I will bring this to an end," the administrator said resolutely but not without compassion. "We will do it quietly, and humanely. And it will be done."

Sixteen

The Bolger house was silent. With Larry's move into the old hospital explained to John, Walt's story had reached its end. At some point in the telling, when John stood to stretch his legs and allow his mind a moment to pause, he found himself back in the room in Walt's house where his father had spent the first twenty years of his not-quite death.

John still had dense and unsettled memories from his childhood of the emptiness that his father left behind when he died, the spaces in the family home that Larry would never fill again. As a boy, it felt to John like Larry was never around because of his commitment to his job. But when his father was gone for good, the hole he left proved that he had been a commanding presence in the house all along.

John felt the same lingering sense of his father in the Bolgers' spare room that he did in those first few weeks following his father's death, when John would stare with still-ravaged emotions into his parents' bedroom, or his father's den, or the kitchen where the family came together for meals:

Dad was here, and now he's not.

Walt stood in the doorway and watched John struggling to process it all. After living alone with it for so long, Walt had told the tale and he was at peace with how it all added up. Having sworn an oath to stand between his friend and a death that his church would call murder, he had met every challenge and endured every sacrifice while awaiting Larry's natural demise.

Walt drew closer to John as he prepared to let Larry go.

"I want you to tell me what you felt yesterday, in that first moment with your dad," Walt said softly, breaking John's reverie. "What you felt in your heart, that split second before your head caught up and demanded answers."

John relived it again. Walt watched as the emotions began to surge.

"There *you* were," Walt continued in a near-whisper. "And there *he* was. And you two were together. Again."

John was set upon by torrents of emotion yet again. Walt moved to John and held him as he cried.

"That *moment,* John," Walt whispered. "That was the *life* I had to protect. Was I supposed to throw him away? Because he was too sick to be who he used to be?"

Walt accepted the raw, cathartic rush of John's crying as the response he had longed for. They held each other and leaned into the flood of emotion together.

Walt finally broke the embrace. Tissues were at the ready,

and tears and flowing noses were mopped up for the work left to be done.

"My job is finished now, John," the old doctor said with a fatherly sturdiness. "That moment I brought you to is yours now. And unfortunately, everything that made it possible."

Seventeen

John drove through his old neighborhood, headed to the old family house to break the news about Larry to Mike. Back in the seventies, when his parents moved here, Applewood Drive was the main corridor through a historic section of town that for generations had been where the upwardly mobile of Holt City settled. The houses, built in the early twentieth century, were all large, imposing, and as sturdily constructed as the lumpish German food that sustained the immigrants who built this small Wisconsin town.

It remained the well-kept and serene heart of Holt City, but more hardscrabble neighborhoods were squeezing in from all sides. The town had suffered mightily with the shutting down of the GM plant in nearby Jamesville, followed by the domino-like collapse of seemingly half the businesses downtown. While John's old neighborhood remained crisply

Caucasian, he never failed to note that in the ethnic face of the town was shifting dramatically.

As he turned onto Abbott Street, he saw the cozy house where he had grown up. It was grand but not ostentatious: four bedrooms, spacious living areas, rich cherry woodwork throughout, and a covered porch that looked out over what had once been a large, neatly landscaped yard. In its day it was a blond brick showplace, but when Rose's finances began to suffer it never made sense to pay a regular service to keep the place up. John—and Mike, almost never—tried to make it over to mow the lawn and repair window casings and door frames that were finally giving up the fight to nearly a century of Wisconsin winters.

John tried numerous times to get Rose to consider moving to an apartment, but she wouldn't hear of it. Besides, the house was the largest investment she had. Unloading it while the town was in the dumps would be foolish. All the family could do was hope that Holt City would grow healthy again.

As he approached his old driveway, he heard the familiar, muddy rumble of live rock and roll played way too loud. Inside the steel and glass of his car, he suspected its source. He just could not believe he was hearing it.

He hit his head on the low ceiling leading down to his mother's basement, as he did every time he went down there as an adult. His skull aching, he was primed to explode when he rounded the corner into the rec room to find Mike, shirt-less and shrieking into a microphone. A doughy guy with thinning hair cranked out a stiff-but-credible rendition of the Crüe's "Kickstart My Heart" on a cheap Strat copy, while a kid of about fifteen laid down a forceful beat on the drums. His mind already scrambled by the events of the day before, John could only stare uncomprehendingly for a moment.

When Mike saw his brother, he threw himself into the song, invigorated in a way John hadn't seen in ages. His voice wasn't as strong as it had been in his glory days, but it had earned a convincing rawness with age and hard living.

The song came to a clumsy finish, and Mike and the gui-tar player hooted and high-fived proudly. John saw the teen-aged drummer behind them twirl his sticks idly while he rolled his eyes. He was young and ferociously talented. These old farts he had somehow fallen in with were a joke.

Mike beamed at John. "Whatja think?"

The silence—during which John did not say a lot of things, including, "Hey, guess who's not dead anymore?"—stretched on forever.

John finally reacted. "You have got to be fucking kidding me."

"Check it out," Mike said eagerly, handing John a flyer. "Theatre of Pain, the hottest Crüe tribute band in Chicago, is looking for a new Vince Neil.

"Their current guy killed a kid with his car, but his blood alcohol wasn't that bad and the kid was high and the singer has a good lawyer, so he might skate. But if he's sent up, they've got gigs booked through the end of the year, and they'll need someone to step in right away. Can you believe it?"

"What?" John asked, reasonably enough.

"Their manager was a *huge* Gravel Rash fan back in the day; he says we got high together once in '91. I got him on the phone and I said, 'Hey, my name is Mike Husted, I used to be . . .' and the dude just freaked. 'Mike Husted? From Gravel Rash? *Fuckin' A!*'"

"What?" John strained irritably.

"They did almost fifty gigs last year. They're bringing down almost a grand a show!"

John clucked doubtfully. "A piece?"

Mike's enthusiasm faded slightly. He had no idea.

"Dunno. Think so. So, hey, you dissin' Taggert, or what? He's helping me work on my chops."

John squinted in the dim basement light and stifled a cruel laugh. Jay Taggert, Mike's primary partner throughout his rocker days, was now almost completely bald, with a paunch and apparently a bad knee that forced him to plop down painfully on his amp. Unlike the leather and studs of the past, he was wearing a Dave Matthews Band tour shirt and sandals.

John had nothing but foul memories of Taggert, who treated him like shit every time he was anywhere near the band. Once, when he was sixteen, John came down the basement to find a girl giving Taggert a blowjob while he sat on the washing machine. John was late making his shift at Taco Bell because he had to wait to get his uniform in the dryer.

"Hey," Taggert snickered at John. "You got old."

John said nothing, just looked to the drummer with curiosity.

"That's Todd. He's some kid from the neighborhood," Mike explained. "I'm paying him with beer."

"And pot," the kid added.

"Yeah, right," Mike drawled. "Got you covered, junior."

He turned to John. "So, sweet, right? You've been on my ass about gettin' a job, so how cool is this?"

"But only if the current fake Vince Neil killed a kid," John said dryly.

"Well, yeah. But, you know . . ." Mike crossed his fingers.

It was a coping device, John allowing himself to be distracted by this idiocy instead of breaking the news about Larry.

"They're not going to pay *you* a thousand dollars a show," he insisted. "That has to be for the whole band. You could probably get the *actual* Mötley Crüe for *two* thousand dollars."

"Hey," Mike protested. "Don't fuck with Mötley. Nikki Sixx is clean now and they're gonna go back into the studio. Mick Mars had some health things goin' on but—"

"Shut up!" John finally could hear no more. "Come upstairs, we have to talk. You guys go home."

Taggert started packing up his guitar with a scowl. "Jesus, when did you become such a dick?"

"When do I get my pot?" the kid demanded.

"He'll leave it with your mom. Get outta here!" John snarled as he headed upstairs, bumping his head again.

The TV was on when John entered the family room ahead of Mike, his mind so thoroughly distracted from what he had come to lay on his brother that he wasn't sure he could refocus. It didn't help that a typical Jerry Springer freak show blared from the set (today's topic: "I'm *Happy* I Cut Off My Legs!!!"). John knew that this was the sort of crap Mike sat around and watched all day when he was supposed to be out looking for a job. Except for *Days of Our Lives,* which Mike watched with his mother while she made him grilled cheese sandwiches and soup.

John sat on the La-Z-Boy and reacclimated himself. On shelf after shelf, new family pictures fought for space among decades of old snapshots. The same snazzy photo of Larry in his blue suit that was on display in the hospital's lobby peeked out from behind a drawing of a unicorn Katie had done in first grade. A class picture of Mike at age seven showed him beaming behind a gap-toothed smile, achingly angelic.

Rose hadn't redecorated the room since John left home. The carpet was wearing well but was outdated. The ornate, textured wallpaper was pulling away in spots, and the cherrywood trim was dusty and cobwebbed up along the ceiling. John hated sitting in here, not just for the complicated memories it contained but for the decline it represented.

Mike sauntered in with a cigarette and an unrinsed can of

SpaghettiOs for an ashtray. He flopped himself onto the couch with the weariness of a coal miner back from the mines.

"Don't smoke in here," John lectured.

"She doesn't mind."

"She wouldn't tell you if she did. She just puts up with stuff more and more rather than bother anybody."

"You know, she's a lot tougher than you let on," Mike said. "You baby her, so she plays up a lot of this memory stuff. I talk to her like an adult, and she holds it together fine. You and this doctor of hers, you gotta stop being in such a hurry to write her off."

"She has an appointment in a couple weeks," John said through grit teeth. "You can take her, tell him yourself."

"Yeah, well," Mike said as he picked cigarette ash out of his chest hair. "Unless I'm out with the band or something."

"Do you even know where she is right now?" John asked with irritation.

"She's at lunch, with one of the ladies," Mike shot back, proud to be caught paying attention. "The one with the big ass and the mole."

John stood abruptly, determined to not have *this* fight right now. He opened a window to clear the air of cigarette smoke, and then sized up the room for some sort of setup to the revelation he had come to wallop his brother with.

He pretended to idly peruse the bank of family photos until he got to the formal portrait of Larry. "Do you remember when this picture was taken?" he asked casually.

"I don't know," Mike shrugged. "There was some kind of hospital brochure or something they were doing. The morning they took that picture, he was struttin' around here like he was fuckin' James Bond or somethin'."

John smiled, perhaps sensing slight nostalgia in Mike.

"You know, I'll bet he was around forty-five in that picture."

"Yeah?" Mike replied aridly.

"And now *you're* forty-five," John said slowly. "So, like, there's some emotional connection there. If you think about it."

Mike rolled his eyes. "Whatever, dude."

John pushed on. "He'd be almost eighty now, can you believe it?"

"Yeah, and probably still ridin' my ass every fuckin' day," Mike yawned, his attention drawn to the TV. The Springer show went to commercials, where an oily lawyer intensely promised millions for anyone lucky enough to have a lawsuit to bring.

"When my job fired me illegally, Jackie Gergleman got *me* one-point-six-million dollars!" one of the lawyer's satisfied customers boasted.

"That's the way, man," Mike sulked bitterly as he poked his cigarette toward the television. "Get the right fuckin' lawyer and the right fuckin' corporation to sue, and you could never have to work another fuckin' day in your life."

Mike was so worked up he dropped his cigarette into the can. He fished it out and took a drag, despite the spaghetti sauce. "Win me a lawsuit like that, and I could tell the whole world to kiss my ass."

John processed this, and his universe shifted as he cradled

the picture of his father. Across town there sat a hospital with a secret in its dark corners, and a decent, if crazy old doctor who broke any number of laws to sustain it.

Would it move Mike—as it had John—that their father was still around to radiate some kind of indefinable touch? Or would he be on the phone to TV's Jackie Gergleman in a flash, looking to sue for millions? He'd have a slam-dunk case, no question, and it would outrage Larry Husted to the core—John felt confident of that. For no other reason, John knew he would share nothing with Mike that day.

Suddenly, there was no point in John being there.

"So, what? You kicked my band out so you could ask about a picture?" Mike asked.

"Uh, yeah. Katie's doing a school project, about the family. This was the last good picture we had of him, so she needed some detail."

"Whatever," Mike said as he stood languidly and walked to the mirror across the room to study his long, thinning hair. "I'm gonna have to dye my hair blond, like Vince. Maybe get some of those extensions. You know anything about that?"

"Um, no."

"Maybe Robin does. Think she'd help me with that?"

"She'd *love* to help you with that."

"'Cause, you know, it's for my job."

"Your thousand-dollars-a-night job."

"Fuck you," Mike grumbled as he headed back down to the basement.

Eighteen

"He's fine," Rose said dismissively as she sat across the booth from John at Rocky's.

"You don't have to put up with his smoking, or the band," he said. "It's *your* house."

"He tries to smoke outside when I'm home. And I like having the music. It reminds me of when you were boys. He needs to get his chops together."

John sighed to hear Mike's bullshit echoed back through their mother. Of all the concerns she should have for her eldest son, his *chops* were way down on the list.

"He needs to find a real job," John stressed. "He's forty-five years old."

"He could be Vince O'Neil, any day now," she said hopefully. John stared at her sadly—how much crap had she rationalized over the the past thirty years to accept the wreck of a life Mike brought upon himself?

"Even if he could make money from this, which he *can't,*" John said, "he's going to be back in bars, hanging around drugs. It nearly *killed* him last time."

Rose shivered and withdrew, and John knew that he exposed her to blunt talk she was no longer able to process. As her thinking grew more scattered and her memories more elusive, he saw that she became easily upset at uncomfortable truths.

Surely her mind retained bitter shards of Mike's rock-and-roll crash. She watched as the Gravel Rash dream died so gruesomely, leaving Mike broke, uneducated, and in prison before he was twenty-five. But those dark recollections—along with the details of her husband's death—were haphazardly filed in a drawer that dementia was fast welding shut. John saw that she could retrieve traces of memory, but the essential connections that make a memory vivid or even cohesive enough to understand were lost.

Blurting out a biting reference to Mike's downfall just sent her mind churning for details that she knew she should possess, but were never going to come. As a result, John found that talks with his mother most comfortably stayed rooted in formless chitchat: old family friends, local gossip, past Husted glories and minutia.

The unfailing sameness nurtured her. Ordinarily, John was content with indulging whatever frivolous topics brought his mother solace, and that was the expectation when he had called her the week before to schedule lunch at their usual spot. Back before Larry came back.

Rose loved Rocky's. The older waitresses still doted on her as Lawrence Husted's widow; even the younger ones knew her as a regular and treated her with cordial deference. Rose still expected respect for her standing in the community, even if it had faded over the years. At Rocky's, it was as if Larry Husted never died. When Rose walked in, respect was paid.

So there sat John, the hospital looming over his mother's shoulder, her husband alive within. John ate nothing. His stomach roiled with acids and anxieties that scoured his insides.

This was not remotely the time to tell Rose the secret. This was just a lunch date.

The dark conversation about Mike quickly dissipated. Small talk loomed.

"So what did Walt Bolger want to talk to you about?" she asked, picking at the cottage cheese beside her BLT.

John froze; *this* she remembered.

Then, for not the first time he went easily to hazing up the truth. Her condition sometimes demanded it, and conveniently made it easier to justify. Facts didn't always stick, and John couldn't count on the memories crucial to her full understanding. If the goal was to keep her calm—and the reality was that she might not remember what she was told anyway—sometimes a well-intentioned lie did the trick.

Lying in bed at four that morning, dreading this lunch, John spun such rationalizations easily.

"He wanted to tell me that he's leaving town," John said.

She waved this away. "He's been talking about leaving for years. He's never going to let that hospital go. He's got to be over seventy years old and I hear he's still hanging around there."

"He means it this time. He wants to make sure you're going to be okay."

"Tell him I'm fine. I've got you, and Mike. And, you know," she said defensively, "all old people have problems remembering things. It's not the end of the world."

He felt her shutting down this topic of conversation. It broached unpleasant realities.

"Well," he shrugged. "I think he's just trying to be a good friend."

"I know," she conceded with a tolerant sigh. "He's just an old worrywart."

They said nothing for several moments as Rose searched for memories in the coffee shop, then she turned to catch John transfixed by the hospital across the street.

"Penny for your thoughts," she said.

He squirmed. "Just thinking about Dad. Guess it was seeing Dr. Bolger the other day. He told me some stories." John smiled at some of the tales Walt had shared.

"I don't think I want to know what those two got into when they were around each other," she sighed with fond disapproval. "They could be like a couple of little boys. Walt Bolger really loved your father."

"Yeah," John said. "I got that."

He stalled. He knew the question that needed to be asked,

but here was the thing: This was a family that almost never opened up about deeply personal things. John and his mother were close enough; Mike was Mike. Rose and Robin got along fine. Katie was as close as any teenager to her grandmother, which was typically not close at all. On holidays, or for random reasons, they all came together and smiled and inquired about the inanities of each other's lives.

But the pain and the sorrow and the joy and the nagging anxieties that each experienced, which each continued to wrestle with, sometimes for exactly the same reason—do families really talk about such things?

Still, on this day, John needed to know. He really needed to know.

"Do *you* ever think about Dad?"

Rose shifted awkwardly. A raw, naked emotion was unexpectedly spiked and demanding a response. *This* was why families stuck to talking about the weather and how the Packers were doing, John thought.

"Of course," she said with an edge. Was her answer true, John wondered, or was this the tone a widow takes when she is forced to admit that after thirty years the honest answer is, "Not really."

John had admitted to Robin that his father had long ago faded from his mind. A photograph or one of the hoary family myths running in endless rotation brought Larry back just long enough to reburnish his vaguely recalled presence in John's past. But little of Larry reached across the decades to coalesce into a meaningful memory.

Still, Larry and Rose had *history*. They lost their lifetime together, but the time they did have, when their lives were young and their futures uncharted, had to have a left permanent mark on the spouse left behind.

For John to presume otherwise would be to accept that if he vanished that day, Robin might think nothing of him thirty years on. Or that he could so easily stop thinking of her. A marriage had to count for more than that.

But *could* Rose remember? She was beginning to have trouble remembering her granddaughter's name; what thoughts remained of a marriage severed three decades ago? Without knowing what she still felt about Larry, how could John be sure that she would be able to cope with the unthinkable secret he was keeping from her? If he strung this out for another year, could he ever really know?

On the other hand, if John walked her across the street right then, how could he ever undo the trauma he caused if it turned out he'd made a terrible mistake?

These were the questions that gnawed at him.

He looked past his mother to the hospital. He and Larry were alone in this. For how long, John had no idea.

Nineteen

"This is not acceptable," Dean Durning said sternly from behind his desk, confronting John and Walt.

It was the happiest day of his professional life when a few weeks earlier, Walt Bolger told him it was finally—*finally!*—time to initiate the endgame for Larry Husted. For two years, Durning's stomach had roiled as he endured the situation on the other side of the B wing wall.

His impulsive gesture to accommodate Walt for what he assumed would be a few weeks grew to mock him as Larry lived on and on. Walt's way in through the dead hospital had so far provided perfect cover, and when the crafty old fucker started hiring an undocumented nurse to cover more and more of Larry's treatments, Durning knew he had been conned.

It would take mortality to finally draw this holy mess to

a close, and it turned out to be Walt's. When Walt told Durning about his terminal prognosis and his intent to leave Holt City to tend to what remained of his life, Durning was appropriately regretful but silently elated. He assumed that on his way out of town, Walt would tenderly let Larry go and take it up with God when the time came.

Instead, the administrator protested mightily when Walt insisted on telling John Husted everything first. Durning knew nothing about John Husted, but he was very familiar with his older brother from school. The whole town knew that Mike Husted was in and out of jail for the past twenty-five years and a bum. There was no way he could be trusted with the truth.

"John's different," Walt assured him. "I've known him since he was a boy. I trust him to help us bring this to the proper end. For all of us."

Once again, Walt Bolger was backing Durning to the wall and using mad logic to extract his compliance. Telling all to Larry Husted's son came with incredible risks, but so did the threat of mutually assured destruction that Walt continued to blackmail the administrator with every time he suggested that Larry's time on the B wing had to end.

Over the past two years it galled Durning to believe so, but every damned decision the old doctor had made on behalf of his friend had been the right one. So he agreed to allow John Husted into the circle, and he prayed that Walt's gamble would work. He shook John Husted's hand on that day when Walt first brought John to the hospital to break the news about his father, and he trusted that it would all be over soon.

Which was why he was apoplectic when after only a few days of contemplation, John called a meeting in Durning's office to announce that he wasn't going to take action any time soon. Larry was sticking around.

"No!" Durning snapped. "No more!" He turned to Walt for support. "Tell him!"

"John," Walt said gently, leaning forward for emphasis. "I told you, we're both prepared to be as patient as we can be as you work your way through this. We understand that we've placed you in an extraordinary position."

John snorted at the understatement.

"But this *does* have to come to an end. The hospital cannot continue to keep Larry on here. And I *am* leaving."

John bore down grimly. He was not a forceful man, but the madness of the situation imbued him with a righteous sense of purpose.

"I will not end my father's life until I know for certain what I need to do about my mother," he declared firmly. "I do not know when I will have an answer for that. It's kind of complicated," he sneered icily. . . .

He met their eyes with simmering indignation. "For right now, you don't need to worry about my brother. I'm not sure he won't turn this into something we're all hoping to avoid. But my opinion might change on that because that's his *fucking father* lying there, and I'm not sure it's my place to keep that from him."

He laid his glare into Walt. "Somehow, in ways I cannot begin to get my mind around, you have kept my father alive and kept him a secret for thirty years. If it takes another month, or another *year,* that's the way it's going to have to be."

Durning nearly jumped from his chair. "But—!"

"Until that day comes, if anything happens to him, I will destroy the both of you *and* this hospital," he said darkly. "My father put this place up, and I will not hesitate to bring it down."

John shot from Durning's office with an agitated head of steam and no place to go. He left the building, headed for his car, but just kept walking.

He found himself at the edge of the hospital's land, standing against a meager cornfield that still portrayed Holt City's rural roots. He paced and ran scenarios and wished he had learned to smoke, because all the scenes he saw in movies in which the hero's brain boiled at some desperate challenge always seemed to require a cigarette.

He wondered if it was too late to start smoking. And then he wondered if this was really what he should be wondering about.

He finally turned and was not surprised to find Walt Bolger, waiting respectfully to continue the conversation.

John did not look away; Walt took this as an invitation to come closer.

"A lot of what I said in there was to throw a scare into that asshole," John said tersely, nodding toward the hospital before looking the old man square in the eye. "But not all of it."

"I know," Walt said.

"I *will* do whatever I have to do."

"You're going to do this your way, John. I knew that when I decided to bring you into this," Walt said.

"But I want you to remember one thing," the old man continued. "This town *needs* this hospital. It helps a lot of people. It's never been the success your father and I hoped it would be. It's always struggled."

The old man swept his arm toward the building.

"One by one, we've been shutting down whole patient wings as folks have left town or decided to go to Madison or Milwaukee for what they think is better care. But our neighbors, this is where they want to be.

"If all this with Larry gets out, between the lawsuits and the bad publicity, it couldn't survive."

John heard the regret in his voice.

"Your anger is with me, where it should be," Walt said. "But God's in the process of taking me beyond your reach. Don't punish others who had nothing to do with this."

A breeze blew across the cornfield. An ambulance gave a short, urgent blast of its siren as it rolled up to the hospital's emergency room.

"You *can't* keep this going on your own," the old man implored plainly.

"I'm not talking about another thirty years," John pleaded. "I'm talking about the time I need to make this okay. For my family."

Walt smiled wistfully at John's determination. "Son," he

RAISING THE DAD   115

said firmly, "you have *no* idea the commitment your father requires."

"I'll learn. And if I get it wrong, if it's more than I can handle . . . At least I'll have tried."

Walt studied him sadly. "*This* is why I was afraid to tell you."

"Well, you did. And now we're here."

Walt saw John's resolve back in Durning's office, but he was getting in way over his head. John had to see that.

"Meet me back here at three o'clock tomorrow morning," Walt finally said, encouraged to see the surprised look on John's face. "Park behind the Taco Bell. Stay away from the streetlights."

Twenty

The dim light of Larry's hospital room seemed even more cloak-like well past midnight. The silence was absolute, despite the fact that a life was being saved right before John's eyes.

He and Walt stood out of the way as a Hispanic woman dispassionately performed her job. She was compactly built, anywhere between forty and fifty-five years old depending on how much of her worn look came from hard living.

She performed her duties wordlessly, gently dabbing lotion into Larry's arms and then opening Larry's diaper. John recoiled at the lack of dignity afforded his father and at the unexpected sight of his gray, withered penis. He stirred to protest as she began wiping him, but Walt silenced him with a stern glare. This was the raw, clinical reality that Walt and the nurse knew. If John was really going to take this on, he had to accept it.

Before John could even bother to keep his eyes averted, the nurse slipped a new disposable diaper onto Larry with one seamless motion and began lotioning his ankles.

"Over time, bodies in this state train themselves to eliminate waste on a kind of schedule," Walt whispered. "The biggest concern is pressure sores. Moisture increases the risk. The diapering has to be dealt with immediately."

The nurse continued to apply lotion with firm but delicate motions, allowing the cream to absorb into the skin before carefully blotting away the excess. Larry's skeletal frame offered no challenge for her as she lifted and cradled his body. There was almost a ritual to it, an anointing of the sick. She paid special attention to Larry's heels, ankles, and elbows.

"Any bony area has to be watched closely—the back of the head, the base of the spine. Anywhere that is subjected to constant pressure," Walt explained. "If the tissue does not get enough blood, it dies. Then infection sets in."

She lightly massaged every inch of Larry's body, then she effortlessly moved him into a different position. She exposed the incision around the IV tube in Larry's stomach. She wiped away a small amount of leakage, and then she changed the supply bag that hung on a hook at the side of the bed.

"The only life support we supply is food and water," Walt said. "He's always managed to breathe on his own.

"If he gets a fever, we bring it down. If there's an infection, we cure it. Gloria recognizes every fluctuation and knows what to do."

John studied the nurse with fascination, then watched as she opened Larry's mouth and held a small suction device in one hand while brushing his teeth with the other. The procedure struck John as even more invasive than the diapering process, and it made no sense. He turned to Walt uncomfortably.

"You don't want to know the disease that would penetrate through the gum line if you didn't brush regularly," Walt explained. "It would be lethal for Larry."

It was an arduous process; Gloria did the job with sullen precision. She then wiped Larry's mouth and tucked in the corners of his sheets before neatly arranging her supplies. The used diaper went into her tattered handbag.

The entire treatment took about five minutes. Not once did Gloria meet John's eyes or deviate in the slightest from her duties. She was like a spirit, moving among John and Walt in a detached universe she shared only with her mute patient.

As she went to make her exit, John impulsively met Gloria at the door.

"Thank you," he said softly. What he witnessed moved him powerfully.

For the first time Gloria was pulled from her routine. She looked with concern to Walt, who smiled easily.

"*Éste es Larry hijo de, Juan,*" he said. Gloria's sullen face registered a trace of surprise, then she nodded respectfully to Larry's son.

"This is Gloria," Walt said, completing the introductions.

John smiled gently, but the woman was eager to leave. John was an intrusion into a rigidly regimented course of action that did not welcome deviations. And there were secrets here that an outsider might bring down upon all of them.

Once the door closed, John turned on Walt for answers.

"Gloria has been with me for almost a year," Walt explained matter-of-factly. "She's a trained nurse, from El Salvador."

"She's illegal?" John asked. Walt nodded.

"She knows how to not be seen," the old doctor said. "She's been the least of my worries."

John tried to process this. What he observed was eerie and beautiful, this choreographed ceremony to keep his father alive. But what it suggested boggled John's mind.

"How often . . . ?"

"Pressure sores should be addressed every two to three hours. I have pushed the limits by seeing it done about every four hours, with immediate treatment if there's inflammation. But what you just observed still has to happen six times a day, every day. Around the clock."

John was dumbstruck. "Jesus . . ."

"She's here every night, at eleven, three, and six. I still try to be here during the day but as it's become more than I can physically handle, Gloria has taken on more and more. She's got an apartment a couple blocks away," Walt said.

"What you just saw is the extent of the treatment. It's simple, but it is relentless," he continued. "You say your job allows you to work on your own schedule, maybe you could cover the day shift.

"You might need to work on your upper body strength, though. Larry looks like he's wasted away to nothing, but manipulating him—several times a day—takes more strength than you'd think."

John looked to his father. The miracle of him still being alive had become clearer.

"But I guarantee you that your marriage and your career will not survive if you try to do this full-time," Walt said. "Right now, I am paying Gloria two hundred dollars a day. Cash."

John gulped as he tried to do the math.

Walt pushed on.

"You can buy the nutrition drip at Walgreen's. If he needs medication, Gloria gets it through the black market in Chicago. It's quality medicine, but it's expensive."

John saw the price soaring. "But, it . . . It's just going to be for a while."

"That's what *I* thought," said Walt.

The insurmountable weight of it all sent John back to his father's bedside. The nurturing perfumes of the lotion still hung in the air. John knew his father was clean and safe. Despite the atrophied contortion of his body, Larry seemed at peace. And John, despite it all, felt a kind of peace standing beside him.

"Go ahead," Walt said softly as he approached the other side of the bed. "Ask him what you should do. *I've* been asking for years."

The idea struck John as mawkish, but Walt's nurturing smile encouraged him. John stepped closer and gently stroked his father's gray, matted hair.

"How about it, Dad?" he murmured awkwardly. "You're kinda leaving me with a lot to figure out."

"See?" Walt smiled down on his friend. "He's no help at all."

Walt brought the blanket up to Larry's chest, and then tenderly began manipulating the joints in the fingers of his left hand. "Your boy's got a lot on his plate, old man. I'm trying to give him good advice, but you Husted men can be stubborn sons of bitches."

John took his father's other hand and began mirroring the massage procedure Walt administered. Walt feared that this physical connection was exactly the thing that would make it hard for John to let go, but he knew from years of experience that these simple intimacies with Larry had a powerful allure.

"Not too hard," Walt tutored softly as John caringly kneaded his father's hand. "We just want to keep the blood flowing. That's it. Good."

Twenty-one

"What do you want me to say?" Robin said tersely across their kitchen table. This is what she said whenever she wanted to say what John didn't want to hear. She'd been saying this a lot the past several years.

"I don't know," he sighed. "I just know I only have one shot to do this right."

Her empathy was not a question. For all their problems, this was deeply sensitive stuff. Which still didn't make it anything they could handle right now.

"Right for *who*?" she asked. "I know you have to figure this out for your mother. Mike can go to hell, as far as I am concerned. But where are *you* on this?"

His silence red-flagged the conundrum. It was now almost two weeks since John found out about his father, and he was stalling on doing anything about it.

"He's *never* coming of out this, right?" Robin demanded. "I know this Dr. Bolger told you this, but you believe it, right? This isn't about you holding out hope that he might still come around?"

"On the morning of February 21, 1985, my father told me to make sure that I shoveled the driveway before he got home from work that night," John said. "Those were the last words he ever spoke to me, and I don't expect that to change."

"You don't *expect* it?"

He pushed back at her grilling. "That will not change."

"So he'll be just there, beyond communication, beyond reach, for who knows how long. Like a goldfish."

"Jesus!" John recoiled.

"You cannot put me in this position, John! I know what you're doing. You're forcing *me* to make all the coldhearted arguments *you're* afraid to make for yourself," she said. "Fine, I'll do that. You're suggesting we get into Katie's college money, shoot a hole through our finances, so that you can take over the expense of keeping your father alive. The father who, up until a few days ago, you were content with being dead. And who is never coming back, not really."

John winced. Robin kept at him.

"Do you have any idea what your mother's care is going to cost us when the time comes? Her insurance is not going to keep her in the sort of home we want for her. Not even close."

He drew himself inward, and trusted her to understand.

"You can't know, Robin," he said quietly. "Unless it was your father, you can't know what it felt like to be in that room. To feel . . . *something* that we were sharing. I can't let that go any sooner than I have to."

She took his hand. No matter where this marriage was headed, that she took his hand right then . . . He appreciated it, more than she could ever know.

But she still had to speak the harsh truth.

"We can't afford this, John."

"I know." He hung his head. "But I need us to make it work. Just for a while. Please."

She squeezed his hand to signal him to look to her. And to really listen.

"For a while," she said evenly. "*A little* while. We have a responsibility to Katie's future. And your mother's. What you're hanging onto—and I swear I understand what you're struggling with—is the past.

"You're getting to touch something powerful, in a way no one ever has. Be grateful for that. But when the time comes, I am trusting you to do the right thing for *this* family."

Twenty-two

The small plant John bought sat on Larry's bed stand. He spent some time picking it out, wanting it to fit in with the simple but warm décor Walt Bolger had shaped over the years. Seeing it now in the room, it looked puny, insubstantial for the circumstances—entirely the wrong statement to make. This was why men don't bring each other flowers.

He had come to observe Gloria's eleven o'clock visit; he would sit with his father until she came back at three. She was still apprehensive after Walt explained the situation to her, but John believed she wasn't going to protest working for him going forward—she was making good, tax-free money for a few minutes work. If she worked other jobs during the day, she probably earned a better living than John. She would take his money just as she had Walt's, and hope that Larry continued to have a long, secret life.

Seeing his father's treatment a second time drove home the methodical simplicity of it. The diapering and tooth-brushing still made John squeamish, but he quickly saw the parallels. As a hard-charging doctor in the early seventies, Larry Husted may not have been the most evolved father in the world, but John chose to believe that he diapered and brushed John countless times when he was small. John certainly did it for Katie.

What's a little spit and shit between family? It all washes off.

If Larry got sick, Gloria would take care of it. Or maybe that's when John would tell Gloria to not come back. If Larry got sick, maybe John would just sit and let nature take its course.

Until then, there would just be the routine: lotion the pressure points (gently, never rub), brush the teeth, change the diaper, change the IV bottle, reposition the patient. Wait and repeat. It was important work, but it was only difficult for its frequency and the need to remain unseen. After watching Gloria that second time, John felt almost cocky about his ability to take over.

"*Gracias,*" John said as Gloria left, using his high school Spanish for the first time in his adult life. If he ever needed to tell her that he had a burro named Pepé, he remembered how to say that, too.

He meant to find Katie's English-to-Spanish dictionary and take it for his own. Based on her grades, it wasn't doing her any good.

"How do you say 'flunk' in Spanish?" he asked Katie recently.

"Do you know they don't even *have* sarcasm in Spanish?" she responded glibly.

"Is that true?"

"Sure."

Once Gloria slipped out, the density of the solitude in the room pressed in on him. The lateness of the hour didn't help; John's thinking always got wispy and weird when he was sleep deprived.

Unable to find an acceptable position on the chair near Larry, John slid it closer, causing a scraping sound that rattled the still. He instinctively looked to his father with alarm.

"Sorry," John whispered.

Gloria left Larry turned toward him. Eyes closed, his face drawn taut by the ruinous toll of this unnatural existence, John nevertheless recognized himself in his father. Every time one of Larry's friends or colleagues encountered John around town, they all made the same observation: *"You look just like your father!"*

He studied his father's face. If John currently resembled Larry at forty, then here was his face at seventy-seven.

If I had spent the past thirty years plugged into a wall, John thought to himself mordantly.

Larry's hair was unwashed and speckled with dandruff. Clearly hair care did not have the same urgency as dental hygiene, but was it ever washed? This was not three decades of hair. Who cut it? How often? He added this to the list of questions he wished he had asked Walt. There were finer points of "Larry care" that hadn't occurred to him in light of the grimmer realities he was going to be addressing.

John brushed the hair back from Larry's temple; he didn't approve that it was so brittle and dirty. He'd find out how to do the shampooing and make it a regular part of his care. He used to love doing that when Katie was little.

Drawn in close, the time was right for a private word with his father. Not because he believed Larry could hear him, but because he hadn't spoken to his father since he was thirteen and never expected to have the chance again.

He cleared his throat and instinctively made sure no one else was around to hear.

"I shoveled the driveway," John began awkwardly. "You probably don't remember, but that last morning, when all this started, you told me to shovel the driveway. So I did it after school, before homework."

The absolute vacuum into which he spoke mocked him. He winced and scolded himself: *You open with* that?

Oh, well, he reasoned. Maybe specifics weren't all that important to start.

"Haven't *stopped* shoveling, every time we get snow. If I don't have Mom dug out by lunch, I hear about it. Still trying to get Mike to do his share, but . . ." he trailed off. No point in getting into *that* yet.

"And I have to do my own driveway. We're on Kern Street, right down from where the Fredericks lived. Katie—she's fifteen—says shoveling's not a job for girls. No grandson. Sorry."

Would Larry care that he had no male grandchildren? John decided he would. From this point forward, Larry became pretty much whatever John projected on him.

"But I have a snowblower, so . . ." John shrugged, not even interested in his own story. The lateness of the hour lubricated that part of him that encouraged his thoughts to ramble to odd places. "I figured you've been lying here, wondering how the driveway turned out."

He leaned back; exhaled self-consciously. The chair pinched his spine, defied him to settle into one spot for more than a few minutes. He wanted to prop up his feet at the foot of his father's bed, certain that this position would be the most conducive to keeping the vigil, but he instinctively recoiled at the casual disrespect.

He couldn't help using humor to take the edge off the burden that fell on him, but the full weight of reality never left him. His father had this profane stasis forced upon him for longer than the mind could grasp, and no one would ever know if the best intentions of Larry's closest friend had turned out to be a torture sentence.

The shittiest of hands was dealt to the gnarled body before him. Solemnity was due.

"So . . ." John exhaled, already feeling spent. He coughed weakly, then settled back into the chair. Maybe that was enough talk for now.

They had all kinds of time.

Twenty-three

The ground had shivered beneath eleven-year-old John's feet, the dragon-like skip loaders gouging into the earth, swinging around abruptly as if tapped on the shoulder, and then emptying the soil into dump trucks to haul away. For almost a year, since his father came home with an expensive bottle of champagne and celebrated with his family the final go-ahead on the new hospital, the cornfield alongside old Holt Memorial took on the relentless bustle of a life-sized ant farm.

Young John was not conscious in the slightest of the ordeal leading up to this: the fevered pursuit by his father and his doctor friends to get the project approved, the tension between his parents as Larry's commitment to his patients and the new hospital left his mother feeling abandoned and overburdened in raising their sons. John just knew whenever he was allowed to come by the construction site, burly men in hard hats and the musky funk of BO and cigarettes treated him like a prince.

Scores of local laborers earned top union wages bringing the new hospital to life, and the public grandstanding of Dr. Lawrence Husted throughout the project's evolution made him a hero to those now prospering as a result of his efforts.

Johnny Husted, who hung timidly at his father's side and recoiled at the bone-shaking clamor of heavy industry, was welcomed by men on the construction team who were so unlike his crisp, well-spoken father. John was lifted up into the cabs of cranes and bulldozers and allowed to shift the levers, and escorted down into the enormous hole in the ground that would one day house the new hospital's boilers and generators.

Standing below ground, the din up above muted by the cold, moist denseness of the earth, John was handed a flat rock by a squat crewman with a lazy left eye. "It's an arrowhead," the man said with dramatic flourish. "Finding 'em by the dozens down here. You hang on to that, for good luck."

John did, for years. Over the subsequent decades, he would sometimes see a short, rough-hewn old man with a go-funny eye around town and wonder if it was the same guy. If getting your father back from the dead counted as good luck, John figured that had to have been some kind of arrowhead.

Once, John's fifth grade class came to the work site for a tour. For an hour or so he was a celebrity, the kid who not only helped get their class sprung from school for a whole morning, but who was hailed by workmen who greeted him by name. Even Kelly Hogan, for whom John longed with a chaste desire so all-consuming that he worried something was wrong with him, stood close to him at the lip of the new hospital's pit for fear she might fall in.

Later that day—and in silly, unprovoked bursts of memory that announced themselves intermittently well into adulthood—John wished he had produced that arrowhead that was never out of his pocket.

"Here," he could have said to Kelly, telling her the story of the Indians who once lived there, embellishing the tale with the fertile imagination that had already begun sending transmissions. He could have offered it to her with a somber flourish, and she would have accepted—how could she not? And in the transaction, her fingers would have brushed his hand. That indefinable *something* that overnight seemed to be radiating from pretty much all girls, but in great, woozy ray gun blasts from Kelly Hogan, would be exchanged skin to skin. There would have been a *connection*.

And as they passed each other in the hallway, the next week and maybe here and there up through senior year, maybe she'd give him a glance. Maybe just a look of acknowledgment, a remnant of the moment they shared at the edge of the great hole in the ground. Something none of the other plain boys in the hall got.

John could have built upon the arrowhead moment. A week or so later, he could have found himself passing her in the hallway. He could have caught her eye, and he could have asked, "So. How's that arrowhead doing?" But something

much more clever *("How's that arrowhead doing?"???)*. Something delivered with a sly, loopy wink. Like Bill Murray in
Meatballs.

"Hey!" John could have begun with mock urgency. "The
school is surrounded by Navajo, give me back that arrowhead
or we're *doomed*!!!"

The fantasy version of her, who would love all things
about him if she would only *give him a chance,* would have
laughed. And that might've been it. A laugh, and she'd move
on. But now they had reaffirmed the arrowhead as something
they shared, just the two of them. It was the grain of sand in
the gullet of the oyster of love. Who *knows* how it might
evolve?

Another year, and now they're in junior high. And they're
in a class together, maybe two or three classes. And that sometimes cruel tyranny of alphabetical seating would deliver
Kelly *Hogan* to John *Husted* with the same glorious inevita-
bility it had throughout grade school. Years later, John would
wonder about that. Was that all it took to be swallowed up
by that first, all-consuming crush? *Proximity?* If she had been
Kelly *Zipperer,* would she have meant nothing to him? Was
love really that random when you were eleven?

Who cared? She was Kelly Hogan, and the back of her
head was his to gaze upon obsessively for the whole school
year. He would stare at her long, black hair—impossibly
black, like an infinite void that could consume men's souls—
and fixate on the mole on the back of her neck that would be
exposed for tantalizing seconds when she tossed her hair this

way or that. It was just a little brown fleck—prepubescent John couldn't begin to understand why it transfixed him so—but it was a secret about Kelly Hogan he convinced himself no one else possessed.

Least of all Kelly Hogan.

Who knows what the back of their neck looks like? John reasoned incisively. As he charted the back side of her upper torso and head throughout seventh grade science—during which he learned alarmingly little science—he came to believe that at least in this very specific instance, he knew Kelly Hogan even better than *she* did. And while even John was wise enough to know this was an avenue of seduction never to be attempted ("So, um, did you know you have a mole on the back of your neck?"), it was information he held tight to.

Eric Arndt, stuck there in the first row between fat Carly Abdul and Rich Baderstein, didn't have a *clue* about what Kelly Hogan had going on, mole-wise. This was the bond John and Kelly shared.

And they could have had the arrowhead. He should have given her the arrowhead.

Instead, on that day so long ago, as she moved away from the hole in the ground and toward him, John moved away from her. Not in full, she's-got-cooties retreat. Just an instinctive keeping of distance, as if something desperately desired and now unexpectedly within reach could contain unseen peril if one weren't careful. Best to stay a few paces away to size up all angles before committing to a plan of action. That felt safe.

The moment passed; Kelly Hogan moved on. Life played out from there.

Staring now at his father for hours in his hospital bed, John strained to remember if he ever tried to confide in him about Kelly when he was a kid. His dad had been there in the same house during those years John ached for her, and moped over a dropped fly ball in Little League, and had his consciousness expanded by the sheer *awesomeness* of *The A-Team* when it came on in '83. He just had no recollection of sharing any of it with his father.

Which was not the experience he knew with his own daughter. Before Katie started withdrawing as a teenager, John seemed to be privy to every scant fluctuation in her existence: teacher conferences were never missed, soccer games were attended ritualistically, friendships and their bitter breakups (followed by immediate reconciliations) were reported upon by their daughter in long, breathless accounts.

Robin was more likely to hear about boys and crushes and looming puberty vexations, but John's head sometimes spun at the amount of insight he had into his daughter. What he didn't get directly from her, he picked up in carelessly left open social media pages or overheard cell phone conversations or mistakenly forwarded text messages. With way too little effort he knew way too much about Katie. Lately, it was becoming a curse.

But in those fragile few years before Larry died, when John crept up on puberty and started driving himself inward, John couldn't imagine his father knowing in the slightest what was going on in his son's life. The man worked all the time, and when he was home he worked some more or seemed irritated by being kept from it.

When Walt Bolger told John about his father's sense of humor, about how moments before being struck down he declared himself down with Daffy Duck over Donald Duck, John felt betrayed. The father he knew was distant and stern and rarely *fun*. Turned out he saved that for others, outside the home.

In the early eighties John and his grade school friends were fixated mostly on *He-Man and the Masters of the Universe,* but there *were* quantifiable differences between Daffy Duck and Donald Duck. John had *opinions* on this subject. If he had thought it remotely possible that his father did, too, this is something they could have talked about.

Having come to consensus on Daffy as the superior cartoon duck, maybe John would have felt comfortable opening up about his mortifying lack of athleticism. And how the growing meanness in Mike was making him sad. And about a girl at school with a mole on the back of her neck.

Maybe Larry *wanted* to have those conversations with his young son, but John's introversion turned him away. Quite possibly Larry tried, but John kept things bottled in and Larry stopped trying.

The trauma of Larry dying had blacked out much of John's

childhood; maybe he and his father were closer than he re-called. But he doubted it.

For decades, John clung to smudgy recollections of the one extended experience he shared alone with his father. It was the summer of 1979, when John was seven and Larry had committed to sharing Cub Scouts with his son. It was a sincere fatherly gesture only occasionally followed through on, but Larry did his best to attend a camp weekend scheduled for late August.

The Cub Scout camp took place over two nights; Larry and John made it for just the second. While all of John's friends and their fathers gathered on Friday and drove up in a caravan that inspired tales of boyish goofery that John would hear about for weeks, he and his father weren't going to get there until Saturday.

That one night in the wilderness, though, was magnificent. There was hiking on stony mountain paths, and swimming in the lake, and Frisbees and belching and almost assaultive laughter to the point of light-headedness. A picture of John and his father taken that Saturday, the two of them posing with mock machismo beside the four-inch sunfish that Larry reeled in, sat on the shelves of his mother's living room for decades. It was the first thing John brought with him to his father's room in the dead hospital to add to his collection of family memories.

Later, as fathers and sons sat up late around the campfire,

toasting marshmallows and listening to ghost stories, John felt a trance-like calm come over him as an uproarious day folded into the dense muteness of night.

He still held memories of his father, glimpsed through the smoke of the campfire, showing a relaxation John would never see again. As the men drank beer and passed around a silver flask, Larry unwound, laughing easily and sharing stories John spent years aching to remember.

When the hour got late and the wooziness of being up way past bedtime kicked in, a guitar appeared. The boys were obligated to hoot derisively as their fathers started to mangle Elvis Presley songs of *their* youth, but John watched in fascination as his dad joined in. He was shy at first; John watched his father's lips quietly recalling every word as he held himself back. But as the night got longer and the Pabst kept flowing, Larry ended up belting out those corny old songs as loudly as anyone.

The fathers finally shooed the boys off to their tents, and the men remained around the fire for another hour. Drifting in and out of sleep in the heated embrace of his sleeping bag, the day's activities having depleted him, John still recalled straining to listen in on the adult male voices whispering and laughing amidst the crackling of the dying campfire and the crisp hiss of opening beer cans. Which voice was his father's, buried in the soft murmur just outside the tent? Was it something Larry said that caused the others to laugh too loud, disrupting the silence of the slumbering campground? Was this the father he got to take home with him the next day, or would the serious and stern front draw back up by the time the weekend ended?

John was still awake when his father crawled unsteadily into their small tent. In the near total blackness lit only by the moon pressing through the trees, John watched as Larry slid into his sleeping bag and emitted an exultant sigh of contentment that seemed to unburden his soul. Father and son lay side by side, face-to-face. In the dark, through half-squinted eyelids, John studied his father's shadowed face. He reeked of beer and smoke and sweat and the pungent funk of teeth he failed to brush.

Larry's breathing was deep and satisfied. He seemed to drift off to sleep almost immediately. Or perhaps he lay there humming an Elvis song to himself.

Maybe the two of them, lying there inches apart, didn't know the other was awake and available to talk. For just a few moments, before they both drifted off to sleep.

Twenty-four

"*What the fuck, dude?*" Kurt snarled at Mike.

The band had just come off stage at the Olde 95 in Cicero, outside Chicago, and were crammed together in the storage closet that passed for the dressing room. Kurt played Mötley Crüe bassist Nikki Sixx and was the leader of the band. He was almost ten years younger than Mike and a really good musician. Theatre of Pain and teaching guitar lessons was the only thing standing between him and getting a real job.

"Learn the fuckin' words!"

Mike fought to meet Kurt's anger, but the cocksure character he played onstage melted fast. "He dropped a fucking beat! It threw me."

Rod, the drummer, just shrugged dimly at the accusation as he pulled off his wig and dug through his bag for a pipe.

Glenn, who played guitar, fidgeted edgily until Rod came up with the dope.

"Don't fuckin' pass it off on him. You haven't gotten through a set yet without fuckin' up the words!" Kurt shouted.

Mike felt himself give up the fight as D.J., the band's manager, came in with a wad of cash.

"This is fucked, man," Kurt snapped at D.J. as he pointed at Mike. "It's fuckin' Mötley, it ain't Shakespeare. If the dude's too fried to remember the fuckin' words—"

"Shut the fuck up," the manager sneered, peeling off some money and stuffing it into Kurt's hand. "Go buy some Midol."

The bassist stomped out of the dressing room. Rod sparked up his pipe as Glenn waited his turn. The woozy bonfire scent of the burning weed stirred something primal in Mike. His nights, like that smoke, traditionally drifted away with the first appearance of the intoxicants.

D.J. paid Rod and Glenn their share of the earnings, and took a hit off the pipe in return. He then offered Mike his pay, but pulled it away as Mike reached for it.

"You still got the voice, man, but you're makin' us look bad out there," D.J. said. "You said you were going to study up. The lyrics are all out there on the internet."

Mike squirmed. At forty-five years old, he had barely touched a computer, let alone the internet. Back in the mid-nineties, when everyone else his age was all about emails and chat rooms and web pages, Mike was beginning his prison stint. Once he got out, in between all the shorter trips to jail, it was all he could do to hang onto a place to sleep. Besides, computers were for assholes.

"Don't worry about me. Once I get 'em down, ain't gonna be a problem," he said. "Anyway, the acoustics in this shithole have always sucked. Nobody's gonna hear if I get the words right or not."

"The *owner* heard. We pack this place every time we play. Sell more beer for him than any other tribute act on the circuit. He ain't gonna fuck up his good thing with a Vince Neil who needs cue cards. So get it together."

D.J. frowned sternly and handed Mike $175, his cut after the rest of the band, D.J., Bob who helped lug the amps and drums, and gas were taken care of. Having gone long stretches when a spare twenty bucks felt like a fortune, the bills felt good in his hand. But he knew this was chump change. And even then, nothing was guaranteed.

The band had seven more gigs scheduled. After that, Mike could be out on his ass. He couldn't remember the words, and he didn't really look like Vince Neil. His gut was losing its rock star tautness, and he struggled to get the hair right. He overheard the bartenders laughing and saying that his hair, bottle blond and teased to ratty heights, made him look like an old whore. If Mike were just a guy in the crowd, checking out the new Vince, he probably would've said worse. He clocked a half-assed Jimmy Page in the head with a bottle of beer once when there was a hack Zeppelin playing the tribute band circuit.

D.J. and the others left the dressing room to break down the gear and see if any girls had stuck around. Mike felt a headache coming on in the wretched little room. The cushions on the two thrift store couches were slashed and duct-taped about a hundred times. Fist-sized holes cratered the walls.

Mike grabbed Rod's bag and rooted around for whatever he could find. That pot smelled fine and would've taken the edge off, but Rod disappeared with the pipe. Instead, he found an Altoids tin filled with an assortment of pills and some candy corn. He found a blue pill—maybe Adderall, but the markings were faded—and he washed it down with beer. The candy corn was stale.

It was 2:30 in the morning. It felt like he pulled something in his back during the show, but he knew that if he didn't help the band haul its crap out to the van it wouldn't help him keep the gig. After that, there was still a two-hour drive back to Wisconsin in his mother's car to the bed waiting for him in his mother's house. All to make 175 bucks.

The first serious talk about a record contract for Gravel Rash had come from Razor Records in the spring of '91, right before Mike turned twenty-one. An A&R guy named Eddie Kingsolver had been tracking the band for about six months, showing up unannounced at the band's gigs throughout the Midwest. Heavy metal was in one of its usual transitions, from the hair band glory of the Crüe to the seedy Hollywood grit of Guns N' Roses to the seething jackhammer barrage of Pantera and Slayer, and all of the record companies tried to stay ahead of the trends.

Gravel Rash was already something of a throwback; Guns N' Roses, its most obvious influence, had become a cliché for the band's dope-addled determination to plow their multiplatinum act into the ground. But Eddie knew that particularly in the dull-minded middle part of the country, there would always be a market for the kind of blues-based debauchery Gravel Rash traded in. Signed at the right price without a lot of perks, there was a buck to be made on Gravel Rash.

Mike Husted, the band's lead singer, was a genuine talent: charismatic, fearless, and possessed with a voice that wrung a kind of debased beauty from the sound of vocal cords straining to rip loose from their moorings. Eddie knew that Mike, along with the rest of the band, was seriously fucked up. He worked with young metal bands long enough to recognize the dope-and-excess template that reached backward from Guns to Mötley to Aerosmith to Sabbath to Zeppelin, ending in that great wellspring of rock decadence, the Stones. Most never find a career, many die seedy addict deaths while trying, but just enough bands beat the odds and make the Big Time to keep all the rock star wannabes playing the same deadly game.

Eddie knew that in the few months he was checking out Gravel Rash, heroin found its way into the band's bloodstream. When Eddie returned to Chicago that spring to take Mike aside and tell him that his bosses at the label were just tweaking the numbers before a contract was drawn up, he flew in from New York with a taste of Persian Brown meant only for the lead singer. The record company man was careful with these Midwestern bands—the dope in the hick markets was always weaker there, you could trigger an OD with the finer East Coast product—but he sensed Mike could handle it.

If the band took off, the dope would eventually have its way. There would be firings, interventions, and the predictable plunge into flaccid, unwanted music. Record companies gambled that it wouldn't come until sometime after the third album, after enough units were sold to clean up on a final "Greatest Hits" album to put a bow on the artist's career.

The label would move on to the next fresh new thing, and the discarded artist would spend his time between rehab and sad attempts at career resurrection, clinging to royalty statements and wondering where it all went. If he ended up dying young in some interesting way, his estate would see a bump in record sales.

But this was all just a best-case scenario when Eddie Kingsolver took Mike out for a four a.m. breakfast after a particularly fearsome Gravel Rash show at the American Legion Hall in South Beloit. The band did fewer and fewer bar gigs because of the size of the crowds they drew, and in that rundown theater the record company man saw glimpses of what could be—with some label reshaping—a credible arena band.

Mike liked Eddie. He was older—close to forty, it seemed to Mike—with that funny New York accent that Mike knew only from TV shows and movies. Eddie knew all about the music business, casually dropping the names of all the major acts he said he knew through the label. He seemed to really care about Mike, singling him out from the rest of the band and never blaming him when fuckups occurred on stage. And he got Mike high—really, really high. That showed how much he cared.

"How long you known Matt?" Eddie asked as Mike devoured a plate of pancakes. The surge from the sugary syrup rattled interestingly with the heroin bump Eddie provided him.

Matt Kirkwood was the second guitar player in Gravel Rash, behind Jay Taggert. Together with Kyle Lucht on bass and Terry Lemon on drums, the five had been Gravel Rash for nearly two years. It was precisely the sound and the look Mike honed since high school, and their ascent through the clubs to the point where Mike now sat across a table at Denny's from a guy with Razor Records was a direct result of the chemistry they had forged and the murderous pace they had maintained.

"Dunno," Mike pondered. "Matty's been with us for, maybe, a year and a half?"

Eddie shrugged as he lit a cigarette. "Throw a stick in any direction in New York, you'll hit a better rhythm guitar than him."

The slight to his bandmate knifed through Mike's fog. "Fuck, man," he flinched. "Him and Taggert, they're tight. Like Izzy and Slash, or Perry and Whitford. You pull him out, we're a whole other band."

"Maybe," Eddie said. "But you and Taggert are the franchise. You write all the songs. If we get a record into the stores, you two are going to see all the publishing money. It's not like splitting a grand five ways from Al's Bar on a Saturday night. You make the majors, things change."

"We're a *band*," Mike insisted weakly. He hated the air of big business that was pressing in on his rock-and-roll party.

Eddie cocked his head with a grin to lighten the mood. "Don't sweat it. But I know the label is considering some things. I mean, it's their money, right? So just promise me, you'll hear them out if they come at you with some ideas. Promise?"

"I guess."

"You trust me, right? I don't do business with people who don't trust me."

"I trust you," Mike grinned. He had no choice but to put his faith in Eddie. Despite his swagger and the years he had invested in his music career, Mike didn't have a clue what he was doing. If they offered him a contract, he knew he'd have to find a lawyer and he had no idea how to go about that. His mother was useless, and the adults he knew through his parents were all doctors. Like any of them would help Larry Husted's fuck-up son, anyway.

Eddie said he'd find him someone to look over the deal, and Mike figured that would be good enough. What mattered was that everything felt within reach.

"It's really gonna happen?" Mike asked, fighting the giddiness that strained to seep through. Big money was being teased for his ability to pose like an outlaw, so it wouldn't help to show that he was feeling like a little kid doubting the arrival of Santa Claus the next morning.

"It's happening now," Eddie said cockily through a swirl of smoke. "Believe it, it's happening."

Twenty-five

A deadline loomed for a grant John took on, knowing that getting it turned around in time was going to be tough. First True Home, a nonprofit that provided emergency housing for battered women, teetered on insolvency, and they were paying John five thousand dollars to quickly get a complicated federal proposal out in time. In his effort to prove to Robin that his commitment to supplementing the cost of Larry's care, John was glad to pick up the job. That would cover half a week of Larry's care right there.

He put his feet up, his laptop resting on his legs. He withdrew to "the zone," that fertile, fuzzy-edged place where his mind was set free to roam, and he considered the plight of a battered woman in need of a bed. In no time, his brain obediently dealt the words. Sometimes, his typing just felt like taking transcription:

"When a home becomes unsafe," he began, *"shelter becomes critical. For a night, for a week, or as a first comforting way station en route to a healthier, happier life."*

John shrugged. Grant proposals compete against scores of worthy causes, trying to sway a foundation manager or government drone charged with slogging through dozens of such appeals each day. The bad economy had gutted charitable giving at precisely the moment when nonprofits that served the most vulnerable needed the most help. The money was still there—sometimes in the hundreds of thousands for the right cause—but the odds of grabbing it were horrible.

The trick was to write right up to the line of compassion without crossing into schmaltz. John always started thick with mawkishness, but then pulled it back word by word. His job was ultimately to reduce human despair to a kind of strategic rhetorical exercise. His knack for emotional distancing was a plus.

John stretched contentedly. The proposal would be good, eventually. He felt the welcome call to really dig in when the winsome peal of "Over the Rainbow" broke the silence. As John reached for his phone, he regretted how the song now instinctively made him set his jaw before taking a deep, calming breath.

He used to love "Over the Rainbow."

"Hi, Mom," he said softly. Rose didn't understand caller ID, let alone custom ringtones. It was some kind of magic trick, her son always knowing it was her on the other end.

"Can't sleep?" John asked.

"Did you remember to . . . ? *Shoot!*" Rose cursed with frustration.

The words stopped coming to her early on, the first sign that something was wrong. Rose could maintain a conversation with her usual verve, but then would skid to a halt as a trapdoor opened and the words fell away. In the beginning, she'd recover and carry on, but over the past year the occasional lost word became entire thoughts. She would embark upon a sentence, then have no idea where she was headed.

The abrupt silences that came to complicate John's relationship with his mother were clumsy and strained. If he tried to help her by guessing at the word, she'd bristle. If he didn't try to help, she'd bristle. He came to let the silences stretch on until she chose how she wanted to proceed. It was important for her to maintain as much control over her life as she could.

"Why did I call you?" she finally said impatiently.

John took another deep breath. "I got you in with Dr. Kelly in a couple weeks. Was that it? I put it on your calendar last time I was over, remember?"

John heard the rustling on the other end and knew she was surprised to find it written right where he said it would be. Her defeated tone told John she knew that this thing she forgot was another thing she once knew.

"No, that wasn't it."

John rubbed his eyes. "Did it have anything to do with Mike?"

"Is he there?" she asked eagerly.

He looked around the room, as if it was remotely possible. "He's got one of his band things. You won't see him until morning, remember? Mom, he's forty-five years old. You can't stay up all night worrying about him."

"It wasn't that. I remember now. It had something to do with . . . *Shoot!*"

"Mom, you need to go to bed and stop stressing about these things. If it's important, you'll remember it." This was an expression Rose used throughout her life, whenever anyone had a harmless lapse of memory. John in turn came to employ it, but he realized for the first time what an awful thing it was to say to someone with dementia.

"You sound tired," Rose said. "Everyone else in bed?"

John squirmed in his chair and stared past his feet, propped up on Larry's bed.

"Yep," John said to his mother, despairing at his deceit. He put in regular work hours at the hospital between his father's overnight treatments. Cell phone reception was acceptable in the dead wing, but the lack of even an old school dial-up connection freed John from the time-wasting lure of the internet. It was actually the ideal place to get serious work done.

"Why are you working so hard all of a sudden?" Rose asked. "Are you and Robin having trouble with . . . ? *Shoot!*"

"Our money is fine, Mom," John sighed. "We've just got some expenses, and we need to start thinking of Katie's college fund."

"You know I'm going to help you with that, when the time comes."

"I know. We appreciate it," he said, knowing that there was no guarantee that Rose's money would sustain herself, let alone her granddaughter's education.

No one anticipated Larry dying so young, so John's parents failed to pay into premiums for long-term health care back when they would've been a bargain. The plan Rose paid into now was okay, but she was as physically strong as she was mentally frail. Her body could soldier on for years after her mind gave up the fight, and that would get expensive. Sometimes at night, John wondered how this would all work out.

"It's late," he said quietly. "Promise me you'll get some sleep."

"You, too."

"I will," he said. "I have some things to finish up here, then I'm turning in. Goodnight, I love you."

"Love you."

He looked at Larry, sleeping in the shadows. His father's breathing remained ragged and labored, but Walt said that was normal. He told John to be alert for any changes in the sound and to inform Gloria immediately if he had concerns.

The vital signs monitor kept track of Larry's status with a hypnotic sameness. But as Walt warned early on, it was not uncommon for Larry's heart rate or oxygen level to shoot high or dip low for a moment, causing the unit to beep and the display to go from green to red before normalcy was returned.

"Your vitals would do the same if we hooked you up to that thing," Walt explained. "That's just being alive."

For the first several nights, John fixated on Larry's every

breath, anxiously noting the slightest variation until he realized that such intense scrutiny would quickly drain him. He had to keep reminding himself that ceasing to breathe—one of these days; maybe tomorrow—was the only obligation Larry had left.

Twenty-six

John could handle the new obligations in his life only because his days were his to schedule however he wanted. Next Step required his presence at development meetings and to sit in with the staff often enough to stay in touch with the nonprofit's mission, but he did his grant writing from home and as he chose to attend to it. This is why, despite the fact that there was work due for both Next Step and his freelance clients, he was asleep on the couch at four o'clock on a Thursday afternoon when the phone rang.

"Is she there?" Robin asked sharply when he answered.

John's heart raced, his mind sludgy from sleep. Wandering away is a serious concern for Alzheimer's patients.

"Who? Mom?" he asked.

"Katie!"

He sat up on the couch and shook off the fog. This was the time of day when he'd normally be keeping an eye on their daughter. Unless something special was going on, she was supposed to be home every day after school.

John looked at his watch; he'd been asleep since 2:30. As the napping became a regular thing, he came to count on Katie coming through the back door to wake him up. He always shot right up and composed himself, not wishing his daughter to know he snoozed while the rest of the world was at work.

John went to the kitchen: no backpack, no homework spread across the table. He called up from the bottom of the stairs hopefully.

"Katie? You home?"

Nothing. He cursed his carelessness, and girded himself for Robin's displeasure.

"I guess she's not here. Did you try her cell?"

"She's not answering," Robin said. "You need to come over to school."

John looked at his idled laptop and the pile of neglected work. "I really need to—"

"*Now,* John. Leave a note for her and tell her she is not to go *anywhere* until we get home."

Robin hung up. John had been considering a custom ringtone for his wife, just so he'd always know it was her calling. Something she'd find funny, like maybe the B-52's "Love Shack," which they flailed about to at their wedding. Robin knew that he already used this trick to screen his mother's calls and she'd be pissed to know he did the same to her, but John figured she would never find out because she'd always be on the other end when the phone rang.

It felt like the perfect plan, but John still tested it for flaws. He didn't need to push Robin's tolerance any further.

As clumsy a strain as the Larry situation brought to their marriage, things really became awkward after John brought Robin to see his father.

It wasn't a move he was eager to make, wondering if Robin would find the invitation ghoulishly inappropriate but impossible to turn down if she thought it important to him. On the other hand, this was the father-in-law Robin never met. She was complicit in putting their family's finances at risk to keep him alive, and she had been placed in the horrible position of saying nothing about it when around Rose or Mike. Or their daughter.

John recognized Robin as a partner in this whether she was enthusiastic about it or not. If letting her see for herself what he was committed to helped, he wanted to bring her in. If she preferred to keep her distance, that was fine, too. But it felt like he needed to make the offer.

"What would we *do*?" she asked when he clumsily brought it up about a week after she agreed to help keep Larry going.

"You'd just meet him," John said before correcting himself, Larry being beyond making new acquaintances. "You'd *see* him, for just a minute. We wouldn't have to stay."

"I won't pretend to talk to him," she said bluntly. "And I

don't want you making conversation for us. 'Hey, Dad, here's the wife!' That would be too . . . Just, no talking."

"Okay."

"What if we get caught?"

John smiled. "Honey, you don't need to do this. I'd really understand."

"He's your father. As long as you're doing this—we're doing this—I should at least meet . . ." she drifted off, dismissing the convolutions with an exasperating sigh. "I should have a look at him."

"Okay," John said, loving her for trying to figure out how to make this work.

She sized up the jeans and T-shirt she wore. "I have to change."

By the time John led Robin into room 116, the lovingly preserved tableau clashing with the haunted house rot she stumbled through to get there, Robin regretted her decision. She thought she could distance herself enough from the creepiness of it to play a part in her husband's ordeal, but as her mind strained to take it all in she realized that there would be no fault in finding this more than any wife should be expected to handle.

A Christmas card photo of her with her family from several years ago sat on Larry's shelves. Robin squirmed at seeing herself reduced to a prop.

And then she saw Larry, emaciated in his perpetual nap. Robin immediately saw the resemblance between father and son, rendered on Larry in a near death mask of what John might be reduced to one day. Would Robin still be his wife by then? Would disease or body failure bring *her* to the same tragic state of diminishment?

Tangles of time—past, present, and future—spun through the room in ways Robin hadn't anticipated. The power John said he felt standing in his father's presence struck her in entirely different ways.

Robin felt the unspoken pressure to extend a hand to make contact with Larry's waxy skin, or to straighten his straw-like hair. It would have been the compassionate thing to do, if only for John, whom Robin felt anxiously desiring some sort of bonding moment between the two. But this scheme was too grotesque, this sad form in the bed too much a stranger. She came to have a look, as she said she would. But it was not in her to offer more.

Uncomfortable meeting John's eyes, she sized up Larry's room. The new Tom Perrotta novel John was struggling to find time for at home waited for him beside a comfortable-looking wingback chair. A box of Cheez-Its, some cookies, and a case of bottled water were situated beside the chair along with the pair of slippers Robin hadn't noticed missing from their house.

John had described the process of tending to his father, but she also knew there were long hours to fill in the middle of the night, when he wasn't home sleeping beside her. When he wasn't there to confront Katie as Friday and Saturday night curfews were broken.

What he created for himself here was cozy, like a den. Robin couldn't help desiring such a refuge for herself.

There was a dense and brittle silence at Larry's bedside, John and Robin seeming to have jointly realized that there was nothing for them to discuss. Robin worked up to announcing her desire to leave, but sensed some sort of protocol required her to stand dutifully for at least a few more minutes.

The unwieldy quiet bore down on John, made him squirm with discomfort. Some gummed-up cell of his brain suggested to him a mood-lightener.

"See, Dad," he said, leaning over his father with a proud, man-to-man smirk. "I did all right."

Robin recoiled. *"Jesus, John!"* she protested, rushing from the room.

There was no way she'd find her way out of the old building on her own. A rat up her pant leg would not make things any more comfortable between the two of them now that Robin had met the old man. John bolted to catch her.

When John arrived at the high school after Robin's call woke him up, there were fire trucks in the parking lot. Inside the building, teachers and parents who were looking angry and sad grouped together at the periphery of the main commons. As John approached, he smelled the smoke and felt the dampness of too much water where there should have been none.

Rounding the corner, he saw that the commons—where he spent hours as a student—was drenched. One whole wall, where banners and artwork were always on display, was charred black. The fire began to reach elsewhere before the sprinklers in the ceiling did their job. But the student projects situated throughout the room were turned into soggy clumps of papier-mâché and poster board.

John saw Robin standing with Debbie Sterling and Johnette Griff, Robin's two closest friends in the math department. The uneasy look John detected from the two of them as he approached his wife put him on immediate alert.

"What happened?" he asked. Robin quickly took him by the elbow and led him to an empty classroom, closing the door behind them.

"Why don't you know where Katie is?" she began.

"She . . ." John stammered. "I don't know. I was busy, I lost track of the time."

"I trust you to be with her after school."

"I am! I just . . ." John insisted defensively. He fought to keep this tamped down. "Do you want to tell me what's going on?"

She dialed down her anger. Besides her concerns for her daughter, she was saddened that her school was attacked.

"A bunch of kids came running in from the parking lot, started tearing things up in the commons, and one of them set a banner on fire. It was a bunch of those *fucking* goths."

John knew that Robin's emotions had to be raw to show such contempt for any of her students. Even the shitty ones.

"It could have been really bad," she said fearfully.

Once upon a time John would have hugged her at seeing her so distraught, but she was really mad at him. He would have made things worse if she took his consoling as insincere or designed to lessen his guilt. That's how he read the moment, anyway.

Hugging came with complications when a marriage wasn't working the way it should.

"And you think Katie was with them?" John asked doubtfully.

"I don't know," Robin admitted. "It was the same crowd she's always texting with, Johnette saw someone running out that could have been her."

"I really don't think it was," John said softly. Robin just shook her head wearily.

"Well, you would *know,* wouldn't you, if you had been paying attention," Robin said dryly. John knew that this was a subject that was not going get resolved right then.

"What do you want me to do?" he asked, punctuating each word coldly.

"I don't know," she sighed. "Check that Starbucks they always hang out at. Go to the mall. If Connie Frederick is working at Foot Locker this afternoon, she might know something. Just try to find her."

"Fine," John said.

"But don't go home without me. If she's there, we need to deal with this together. I want to be there."

John knew what she was saying. She didn't want him having a first crack at their daughter, to help her get her story straight if he decided for himself that she was innocent. He resented the charge, but he just turned and headed out.

"Fine."

John and Robin came through the back door at 6:30 to find Katie at the kitchen table doing homework. This in itself was a confession of guilt, a fifteen-year-old's limp attempt to deflect parental wrath by pretending to be more conscientious than all three knew she was.

Posing herself with her schoolbooks like the diligent student they kept wanting her to be was the right move. She knew her dad, in particular, would be impressed.

"Where were you?" Robin asked before even closing the back door.

"I'm sorry," Katie pleaded openly. She wore layers of black and her understated makeup still had a hard-edged severity. "Gretchen had to return something at the mall and she said it'd just be a few minutes, but we ran into some friends. And then we missed the four twenty bus. I tried to call you, but my phone was dead."

"None of your friends had their cells? They've taken out all the pay phones at the mall?" Robin asked. Katie looked to John for backup, but John clearly was not going to get in the middle of this. His silent head gesture to Katie said, "Don't make this any worse."

"I said I was sorry, okay?" Katie sighed petulantly.

Robin took off her jacket and set down the schoolwork she brought home, seeming to idly move on to regular business while keeping her eye on her daughter. Now that Katie locked herself into her "look at me doing my homework without being asked" pantomime, she had to sit there and actually do it.

Robin took on a studied nonchalance. "Did you hear what happened at school this afternoon?"

"Yeah," Katie said, a tone of wonder and disapproval in her voice. "I mean, it's all anyone's been talking about." Her phone was on the table beside her. John saw the usual scroll of incoming texts.

He listened hard to Katie. He was not as clueless about his daughter's changing behavior as Robin thought he was, but he wasn't going to apologize for giving her the benefit of the doubt until they heard her out. Still, he was already on guard for the crack in her story that would break his heart.

"Anybody talking about who might have done it?" Robin asked.

Katie kept her eyes on her paper. "Just some kids," she muttered, pretending to concentrate.

Robin drew closer. "Were you with Brendan or any of those other kids you're always texting with?"

"I told you," Katie sighed, the tension escalating. "I was with Gretchen at the mall, and then we met some other girls, and then I came home on the bus."

"You weren't given a ride home?" Robin persisted. "You weren't riding around with any of your goth friends?"

"No one calls us *goths* anymore," the teenager sulked.

"Answer my question!"

Katie slammed down her pen with righteous rage. "They

didn't do it! *God!*" She pointed to her phone. "Everybody's already saying they're guilty and they weren't even there!"

Robin sat down in the chair beside her. "How do you know?" she asked.

"Because they just weren't!" Katie insisted bitterly. "You don't even know them! Just because you don't like the way they look doesn't mean they're guilty of everything!"

Katie rose to storm out; Robin grabbed her wrist.

"Sit down," she said firmly. Katie threw herself back down, radiating raw contempt. John saw this fury in his little girl, and it drew fine razor knicks across his heart.

Robin spoke evenly. "How do you know where your other friends were after school if you were at the mall with Gretchen?"

Katie appeared cornered. "Fine! Call Gretchen if you think I'm lying! She'll tell you where I was!" she shouted defiantly. It was a classic teenager ploy, daring her parents to seek out the confirmation that she knew would blow her story. It was remarkable how often parents don't call their bluff by picking up the phone. It was almost as if they didn't *want* to know.

"We just want to be able to trust you," John said earnestly.

Katie turned on her father, just like that. Just to hurt him.

"Maybe you'd know where I was if you weren't sleeping on the couch all day!"

John recoiled as Robin processed this new information.

"It's not *all* day," John offered stupidly to his wife, blindsided to find himself on the defensive. "Sometimes, if I'm—"

"I know you're out all night, *Dad*. I'm not stupid," John's daughter continued, delighted to lay bare a parental secret. "Nice how you expect me to be perfect when *you're* not."

John's mind ping-ponged for a response.

"Your father has been taking care of your grandmother at night," Robin shot back at Katie reflexively. "She's having real problems, which you would know if you cared about anyone but yourself."

John turned to his wife—a lifeline was the last thing he expected. Her glare back at him quickly disavowed him of any sustainable truce. It appeared Robin was merely prioritizing her anger on the fly.

John's head spun. His daughter just betrayed him, and his wife—at least for the moment—lied in his defense despite being dangerously unhappy with him.

His inability to respond seemed to stretch on for minutes. Seeing her father struck dumb, disillusioned, and exposed, Katie felt a little girl's ache of empathy that her teenaged peevishness quickly suffocated.

"Whatever!" she sneered as she fled the kitchen and raged up to her room.

John's eyes followed her up the stairs. He turned to Robin, who was looking at the couch in the living room.

Now that it was just the two of them, Robin found nothing left to say. She shook her head wearily and headed up to their room with her grading work.

Twenty-seven

Where once there were babies lurked spiders and rats. As John swung his flashlight through the nursery in old Holt Memorial, the creatures skittered grumpily into the dusty dark corners. The return of Larry Husted's boy violated decades of peaceful rot.

With hours to kill between Larry's treatments and desperate for a distraction from his writing projects, John began exploring the old building within the first couple weeks. He didn't stray far at first, rattled by the creepiness of the world he had passed into. A living hospital was unsettling enough, its coldly institutional offer of salvation constantly mocked by the ghosts of those who insisted upon dying no matter what the gauzy brochures in the lobby promised.

But a shuttered hospital spoke only of death: the death of patients not saved, and the death of the dream that took flight when the building's doors first opened. Back in 1922, when the hospital opened, there had to have been another eager young man just like Larry Husted, inspired by the cutting-edge medical care of his day and impatient to get to work healing the sick.

Now what was once cutting edge was a blighted ruin too burdensome to tear down. The shiny and new never hear the knowing titters of the dustbin.

Larry walked these halls as an ambitious young doctor, only to eventually declare them obsolete. And now he was the building's last living patient. Maybe that's why he refused to check out. Someday a new Larry Husted would come to tear down *his* hospital next door. Larry, like the building itself, refused to let time do away with him.

When John began to feel bold with his strolls away from Larry's side, he started to venture up to the higher floors. First he just aimlessly poked around but after enough deep four a.m. reveries at his father's bedside, John became fixed on a destination. When his flashlight refracted off a large, dust-clouded window partitioning off two separate rooms, John knew he had found the nursery.

Feeling a time-traveler's sense of disorientation and awe, he stood on the baby side of the viewing window. It was a small room, with space for about a dozen cribs laid out in neat rows of four. John drew a grid in his head and paced off each square, standing for a moment in each. Somewhere within this private dance, he figured he stood upon the very spot where his newborn self once lay, swaddled and cranky. If baby John had already begun hearing from that pesky new brain of his, he might've been reflecting on the previous nine months and his violent, wet ride into the world, and thought, *What the fuck?*

This recollection of events then caused John's brain to issue him an image of his mother's vagina and his passage through it. *Thanks, brain!*

John grimaced, then stepped to the other side of the viewing window. Now he stood where his father once stood. John stared into the abandoned nursery through the glass, choosing to believe that Larry once pressed his hands to the window with awe as he beheld his son. He wondered if forty-three years later a fingerprint expert could find a trace of his father's presence here buried beneath the layers of evidence left behind by decades of anxious fathers.

But an expert wasn't required to prove Larry's presence here; his existence was everywhere in the old building. And he waited there still. John looked at his watch. It was just about time for Larry's six a.m. treatment, and then John would go home to wake his wife and daughter to begin their day. John sent out his latest Next Step grant the day before. His out-box momentarily empty, he looked forward to catching up on his sleep.

Twenty-eight

John and Mike sat in the doctor's waiting room, Mike fidgeting between put-upon sighs. Standing out in his downmarket rock star wear (scuffed boots, ripped jeans, a cheap leather vest over a Quiet Riot T-shirt), he drew the attention of a little girl fascinated by his tattoos. She leaned over the row of chairs behind him and he was oblivious as she intently sounded out the word inked into his right shoulder.

"Tits!" she finally pieced together proudly. As she was right next to Mike's ear—and no more than seven years old—this made him jump.

The girl smiled as Mike struggled to make sense of the moment he shared with her, until she nodded to his shoulder. A cartoon cat salivated there, its eyes popping out of its head with a Tex Avery *ba-boiinng,* as the tastefully austere caption explained: *Tits!!!*

Mike got this one at nineteen, when he and Taggert hitched to Detroit to see Anthrax. He couldn't recall the inspiration for the design; he was so high that night that he didn't discover he was inked until the next afternoon, when he regained consciousness beneath the seesaws outside an elementary school. But someday soon, when the little girl in the waiting room learned about punctuation marks, she would understand that three exclamation points in the context of a cat viewing tits suggested that these were tits that exceeded commonplace expectations. Or the cat just really liked seeing tits.

Mike covered up his shoulder grumpily as the girl's mother pulled her away with a mortified scowl. John, who watched this from the corner of his eye, shook his head with a goading smile.

"Nice."

"Fuck you," Mike whispered, betraying just the trace of a blush. The mother heard this, too.

"Time was," Mike said cockily, "chicks were all about the tats. *You* wouldn't know."

"Who's going to hire you looking like that?" John shot back.

"I have a job."

"That's not a job!" John insisted. "You have no health insurance. They're barely paying you. After gas and dope—"

"I'm not using!"

"Fine. But you can't be making any money."

"What do you think we could get for the house?" Mike

asked abruptly in a tone that suggested he had been considering this for a while.

John was dumbstruck. "We're not selling the house! Where would she live?"

"She doesn't need all that room. We'd find her an apartment. Or maybe . . ."

"What? She'd move in with me?"

"Some families do that," Mike said piously.

John stammered at Mike's nerve. "That is her *home*. She doesn't *want* to move," he said. "Besides, nothing is selling right now, especially those old houses on the east side. The place is falling apart, thanks to us."

"Maybe we could—"

"I can't believe you," John whispered through grit teeth, a long-suppressed rant rising to the surface. "Find a lawyer to sue somebody. Kick your mother out of her house. Anything to keep you from getting a goddamned job like the rest of us."

"*I have a job!*"

"*That's not a job!*"

A nurse stood before them awkwardly as their spat spilled into the waiting room. "You two can come on back now."

John and Mike were led into the examining room, where Rose sat demurely opposite Dr. Kelly. A button on her blouse was not done up, exposing her bra. There was no script provided to a son to alert his elderly mother that she was showing skin, so John grabbed the only remaining chair in the cramped room and averted his eyes.

"Well, the good news is that your mother is *physically* doing great," the doctor began blandly, consulting his notes. "Her blood pressure, all her vitals, the blood work—she's fit as can be. I'm seeing a little osteoporosis, which is to be expected, and I'm seeing just the earliest signs of cataracts, which we'll want to keep our eye on. But we should be very happy with what we're seeing here."

The doctor smiled to the brothers and stifled a double take as he beheld Rose's oldest son. He focused his attention on John as he flipped through Rose's file.

"You remember when I saw Rose about a year ago I had her take a little test for me, just so that we could begin tracking these memory issues we were concerned about. It took some convincing but I just had her take the test again, and I'm seeing some things we need to discuss."

Rose looked defeated as the doctor preceded to talk as if she wasn't in the room.

"For instance, I asked Rose how many different kinds of animals she could name in thirty seconds," the doctor continued. "Last time, she named eighteen. Today, she named eleven. That was a little disappointing."

The doctor had a dry, insensitive tone. John shrugged to his mother with an understanding smile and then turned to Mike, hoping to see him offering similar support to their mother. Instead, Mike was deep in thought, probably testing his own animal-counting skills. John could tell by his brother's dim twitching that it wasn't going well.

"And I asked her to draw me a clock showing five o'clock," the doctor said, putting the two drawings side by side. Last year's drawing was shaky but showed five o'clock dead on; this year's was more like 3:05, with an extra hour hand bisecting an edge of the ragged circle before being scribbled out.

Rose bristled defensively. "I never *could* draw. I have to pay a doctor to tell me that?"

The doctor pushed on. "And, well, there are six or seven things we test for. And in all areas, we're seeing a diminution of cognitive skills that we need to be concerned about."

"Can you say for sure it's Alzheimer's?" John asked. Mike saw his mother recoil at the word.

"I would say it's dementia," the doctor said. "Alzheimer's is a form of dementia. There are distinctions, but even we can't define them too clearly.

"These things can always level off, and we have her on medications that have shown great results in slowing down the process in other patients," he continued. "But just going by the testing, we need to recognize that the disease is advancing at a pace that is on the high side of the scale."

The doctor's arid assessment of the situation brought a leaden pause to the room. John felt the usual push to step up and tend to his family's business. But Mike spoke first. "How fast are we talking?"

"It's impossible to say," the doctor replied, turning his attention to Rose. "You are physically strong, Rose. You're still engaged with life, with your friends, and your two sons here. You have challenges ahead of you, but I have every reason to believe that things don't have to change for you for a good long time. Will you trust me on that?"

He smiled and squeezed her hand. She appreciated his kindness, but then he immediately returned his attention to her sons. "The changes you've been seeing will continue. You need to monitor them and determine when things have advanced to a point where it's not safe for her to be on her own."

"She's not alone. I'm living with her," Mike said firmly.

"That's terrific," the doctor said. "Still, there will come a point where she'll need more help than you can provide.

"There are some excellent memory care facilities in the area, but the best of them have long waiting lists. It would be prudent to start checking them out, see where Rose would be comfortable, and get her name on some lists."

The doctor consulted her file. "Her long-term health plan is . . ." he said, wincing just slightly as he saw her coverage. He put a hopeful spin on it. "There are many fine places that will work with you with this type of insurance."

John, Mike, and Rose processed this as the doctor closed his file and stood. "You should schedule her for six months, and we'll see where things stand then. Call if you have any concerns before then. Sound good?"

He winked and made his exit. The three Husteds didn't seem ready to leave. Mike finally broke the pall.

"I got twenty-one. Animals."

"That's *good*," Rose said, impressed.

"What I did was, I just pictured a zoo," Mike boasted. "All the animals you'd see at the zoo. Bears. Elephants. Tigers."

Rose admired the ingenuity. "You remind me of that trick next time I come," she said conspiratorially. "I'll fix his little test."

"Giraffes. Rhinos. Bears," Mike continued sagely, as John handed his mother her purse and moved his family toward the door.

Mike kicked the floor when he remembered an animal he missed. "*Penguins!* Fuck!"

"Michael."

"Sorry."

John rolled his eyes with honest bemusement. His mother was just about through the door before he pulled her back.

"Um . . . You need to . . ." He pointed shyly to the un-done button on her blouse. "Sorry."

"Oh, for heaven's sake," Rose clucked at her son's awkwardness. She fixed herself up and followed Mike out. "I would have never thought of penguins."

"Zebras," Mike said.

"Bears," John contributed sarcastically under his breath.

"Bears," Mike tallied.

Twenty-nine

John felt a distant sense of déjà vu as he drove Rose and Mike home from the doctor. John and Mike coming together for the sake of their mother, despite the differences that at times left them strangers, was not without precedent. John sneaked a look at his brother in the backseat and wondered what he remembered.

It was late spring of 1990. John was a high school senior, his grades and his social life drifting unpredictably on the teenager graph between Under-Performing and Tolerably Proficient. Mike was burning up the Midwest club circuit with Gravel Rash, pickled primarily in whiskey and coke and absent from his family for months at a time. And Rose had lost herself in the only sustained relationship she would know following Larry's death.

Since the brutal blow of losing her husband five years

earlier, Rose gave in to an emotional skittishness that made her an awkward burden to the friends who were determined to keep her strong. No one else in their social circle had had a spouse struck dead, and while divorce was prevalent it was not the same; even if it left them bitter and alone, there was time to adjust from being married to single. Larry Husted was unexpectedly plucked from their midst at an age when they were in their prime. Rattled by the bluntness of the loss and its portents for their own mortality, most of Larry's friends instinctively knew to close ranks around his widow.

Rose was at the tail end of a generation that rigidly built its social structure around couples, even more pronounced among the upwardly mobile medical community of Holt City. After a respectful period of time following Larry's death, Rose was besieged by friends determined to include her in Friday nights at the country club and cocktail parties every few Saturdays. When her grateful but consistent rejections stretched well beyond even a generous grieving period, her friends became more firm in their invitations.

In time, the Widow Husted tentatively returned to surroundings where she once was content to mingle decorously at her husband's side. Now she ached to feel so alone, and despaired at being the third wheel. After only a very few nights out, she began hiding behind her answering machine and returning calls only when too late to accept an invitation. If John took the message, she blamed it on her careless teenager for not telling her someone called.

Undeterred, Rose's friends moved on to matchmaking. John was fifteen when a bland, pink-skinned man first appeared in his living room, reeking of Vitalis with designs to escort his mother to the 7:10 showing of *Three Men and a Baby*. Bill Stiegletz—heir apparent to the Stiegletz Home & Appliance empire—dimly peppered John with questions about his grades, his sports interests, his girlfriend status, and all of the other lazy crap adults inquired about when trapped alone with a teenager.

In time, John would have bullshit answers ready for his mother's suitors ("My girlfriend has lupus, which *sucks*"), but on that first, awful evening John scowled sullenly at the flabby betrayal plopped down into his dead father's La-Z-Boy. His mother clumsily informed him of her impending evening out, insisting with a mortified quiver that it was not a *date* but simply a movie with a friend of a friend. But having only recently sat for the first time sweating in the living room of a girl he barely knew, John knew what a date looked like.

He watched with queasy disapproval as his mother finally descended from her bedroom, acting dithery and weird as Bill Stiegletz startled her with a formal peck on the cheek. As they moved for the front door, John refused to shake the guy's hand.

When Rose returned before ten, John was pleased that the date appeared stillborn. He stood at the top of the stairs for a very long time, making sure the sounds of conversation did not emerge from the living room. When all he detected were the solitary stirrings of his mother and her occasional sighs, John went to bed.

The new men friends kept filing through the living room

every few months, none making more than three appearances. One was named Vern early on, so this became John's generic tag for all of Rose's half-hearted attempts at companionship: John was free to jerk off to the soft-core porn-thriller on HBO Saturday night, because Mom was out with one of her *Verns*. The dates never ran long enough for John to figure out who in the T&A mystery had committed the badly plotted crime. But once he did his business into a wad of Kleenexes, he never seemed to care.

None of the men who came to call seemed to make his mother any less lonely or sad.

Until Don Huff.

He was a flourishing boat mogul, with stores in Madison and Milwaukee and a third up north that was his big earner. Ski boats, fishing boats, pontoon boats—Don Huff was "the man to see before setting sea." He appeared in his own TV commercials, bringing him a form of celebrity that drew well upon his sea-stiffened good looks.

When one Friday night in 1989 he materialized in Larry's La-Z-Boy, John was begrudgingly impressed. Don had a charisma different than the stiffs and businessmen his mother failed to bond with, and he seemed to be a genuinely nice guy. Rather than bore John with the usual inane small talk, he engaged him in a detailed discussion of Michael Crichton's *Sphere,* which John was reading and that Don could recall at length. Don listened earnestly as John expanded upon some plot machinations that he predicted would tighten the screws as he read forward, and when John made references to *The*

Terminal Man—an early Crichton book Don hadn't read—the teenager felt uncommonly smart. John's choice of college—Stevens Point, maybe with a business major—met with Don's approval.

After John saw Don elicit a sort of smile from his mother he didn't recognize, and when that smile endured even when Don went home, John decided to not be the typical teenager who might try to destroy the relationship just to be an asshole.

The dates became a regular thing. Don, only tangentially connected to the doctors' clique, easily joined their ranks. Rose went out most every Friday or Saturday night, either socializing with her usual crowd or making new friends in Madison, where Don lived.

Upon returning home, there became sessions where Rose and Don settled into the living room with the lights low and God-knows-what taking place. John tried like hell to be out every weekend when his mother and her new boyfriend were in, but it was impossible to wall himself off from it completely.

On nights he wasn't able to make plans, he'd hole himself up in his room, sealed off by headphones plugged into a movie or his tunes, the volume loud enough to obliterate the living room thoughts that made him squirm. When he went out with his friends or had a date of his own, he never knew what he'd be returning home to. Far too many times he'd creep in through the front door, perhaps a bit high, only to find that his mother's date was running longer than his.

"John?" his mother would call from the dark of the den.

"Yep."

"'Night."

"'Kay."

"Things good, kid?" Don Huff would usually pipe in chipperly from his unseen perch, seeming to need to establish his presence.

"Yep."

Racing up the stairs to his room one time, John heard his mother giggle. Either she and her boyfriend shared a laugh about him, which was confusing to John, or Don made a move that elicited a girlish titter from his mother. Which was . . . *really* confusing.

But most of the time, John didn't have a problem with Don. He'd come over for dinner once or twice a week, and John was regularly invited to eat out with the two of them. It was strange walking into restaurants and watching people do a double take at the celebrity in their midst. Waitresses never failed to smile more broadly for Don, and customers often gave him a familiar nod. Don was always gracious to anyone who acknowledged knowing him from his ads, but he otherwise seemed oblivious when diners at other tables would nudge their companions to sneak a look. Nevertheless, Rose came to feel a certain thrill at becoming a regular fixture at Don Huff's side. John did, too.

Fortunately for everyone, Mike was gone for weeks at a time that spring. He had hooked up with a booking agency in Chicago, and now the band's tours spread farther and farther beyond the southern Wisconsin/northern Illinois axis of clubs that they were outgrowing. While still seedy and depraved caravans of getting high and *rocking out,* the tours took on a more professional feel, with paid roadies, decent gear, and a secondhand motor home that kept the party on the road and out of profit-depleting hotels. Venturing as far from home as Syracuse, Kansas City, and Akron, Gravel Rash won new fans and defied the record industry to ignore them.

Mike's stays at home usually came unannounced and lasted only until he could seduce another female fan into letting him move in rent-free. Engaging his brother only when unavoidable, John suspected the nerve-pixilated, nose-rubbing twitch of a raging cokehead. Mike's tattered rock clothes hung from his needle-thin body, he was never not deathly pale, and he usually stank of stale liquor, sex, and body odor. For his chosen profession, this was business attire.

Rose was offended by her son, but was unable to turn him away when he needed somewhere to stay. Given the late hours that Mike kept and Don's reluctance to wade into such a complicated dynamic in this new relationship, it was not hard to keep them apart. But as summer approached and a meeting between Mike and Don became unavoidable, John suggested to his mother that it be over dinner, in public, where maybe both men would be constrained from displaying what was assumed would be mutual distaste.

The setting was a Friday night fish fry at the Sunset Supper Club. This provided a sure way to hide him from the disapproving eyes of Rose and Don's peers, who would be starting their weekends over cocktails at the country club.

Mike grumpily rejected Rose's first several requests to finally meet the new man in her life, until John stepped in.

"He's all right," John said sheepishly in defense of Don, provoking Mike's derision for acting like a mama's boy.

"He's a fucking tool," Mike scoffed while building himself a sandwich in his mother's kitchen. He mocked Don's TV ads. " 'I'm Don Huff. For all your boating needs, come suck my dick and I'll set you up with a shitty ass rowboat for you and your whole gay family!' "

John shook his head at the predictability of his brother's act. "Asshole."

"Pussy," Mike countered.

"She likes him, okay? He makes her happy."

"So did Dad. Her record for picking men is for shit. Don't mean I gotta give a fuck."

John stared at this repellant stranger who darkened his house. The decision was not hard to use whatever it would take to deliver to his mother a civil, if strained relationship between the son she no longer recognized and the man who made her smile.

"She used to fight with Dad about you," John began. "She *defended* you."

"Bullshit."

"They went at it, just a couple days before he died. I listened from my room. He wanted you and the band out. Didn't care if you ever came back, didn't care if you froze to death on the street. He was sick of the noise and the dope and *you,* and he said if you weren't moving out, he was. And she said *you* weren't going anywhere."

"Bullshit," Mike said again, not quite as sure. "She never stood up to him, for me or anything."

"She said that she wasn't going to be forced to choose between her marriage or her son, but right then she knew that you needed her more. It got really mean. I don't know if they were really talking to each other again when he died."

None of this was true. One afternoon John heard Larry say he was sick of having the band in the basement and Rose said she didn't mind, and Larry growled *fine,* so long as it was when he was at work—that was the extent of it. John balls out lied about the rest. It felt like the right move at the time.

Mike shivered at an alien sensation as affection for his mother slipped past his hard-ass perimeter. John saw it happen.

"She slipped you money for the band, even when Dad was still around to bitch about it," he continued. "And then when he was gone . . . Fuck, man, she propped you guys up, even when you were being such an asshole."

"Those were loans," Mike protested weakly. "I'm payin' it all back."

"Bullshit," John said, driving his pitch home. "What's she gonna have after we move out? Are you such a skeevy fuck that you want her to be alone for the rest of her life? What did she ever do to you?"

Mike's silence proved the point.

"Then just be okay with this," John concluded. "Meet the guy and don't be a total dick about it. Do that for her."

Mike gave a mocking sneer to deflect any hint of compliance. "Fag," he drawled.

"Ass pus."

So it was that John, Rose, and Don sat and pretended to not keep glancing at the front door of the darkly paneled supper club. Mike sullenly agreed to join them there, but insisted on driving himself. He was coming straight from band practice, he said, but obviously he just wanted his own escape vehicle if things got too uncomfortable. John wished he thought of that.

The chime of the front door finally brought with it a look of confused joy that broke across Rose's face. John was puzzled when she stopped talking, and then understood when he turned and saw what she saw.

Only Mike's atrophied posture remained as he slunk into the restaurant. He had bathed, his long, frizzy hair tied into a clumsy ponytail. It was one of the first really hot days of spring, but he wore ill-fitting slacks and a mismatched, long-sleeve shirt. John realized why and was amazed: Mike hid his tattoos to mute his image. He looked like a dope dealer forced to supplement his income by working part-time selling car stereos at Best Buy.

He sank self-consciously into the open chair as Don extended his hand with a smile. "You must be Mike. I'm Don Huff."

Mike couldn't help being impressed by the boat guy on

TV sitting there in front of him, nursing a Bud. "What's up?" he said, avoiding eye contact.

"Well, we were just all eyeing the all-you-can-eat fish fry," Don said, trying to read the menu without the glasses he rarely wore. "But dinner's on me, so order up whatever looks good. Looks like you could use a good meal."

Mike might have taken this as a shot, until Rose gently grabbed his wrist. "You look very nice tonight," she beamed.

"Excuse me, miss," Don called out, friendly but with haughty undertones. "The rest of our party has arrived, I'm guessing he might want something from the bar."

The waitress, who was young and not at all pretty, did a double take as she recognized Mike.

"Oh," she stumbled. "Sure. I mean . . . Hi!"

"'Sup?" Mike grinned silkily. "Jack. Straight up."

"Great!" She scribbled in her pad, brushing her hair back nervously. She turned and flitted off quickly to get Mike his drink.

The boat tycoon and the rock star sized each other up. Fruitful topics were going to be hard to come by.

"So," Don began, "your mother tells me that your band is really taking off."

"We're playing our asses off," he replied with a cavalier cock of his chin. "Breaking big all over the Midwest, workin' our way out from there. Finishing up on a demo, and then hope to do some showcases in New York by the end of the year."

"That's a tough business you're trying to crack," Don said

sagely, one professional to another. "Even if you get your foot in the door, there's a lot that could go wrong."

Mike vacantly ran his thumb along the edge of a butter knife. "We think we'll be okay."

John watched his brother grin vacantly behind glassy eyes; he probably coked up just before he headed into the restaurant.

"Just be careful," Don continued. "If anyone offers you a deal, make sure you have a good lawyer go over the contract."

"Yeah, whatever." Mike reflexively dismissed Don with a scoff. "But . . . thanks."

The waitress returned with Mike's Jack Daniel's, spilling over the brim as she anxiously set it before him. "Are you all ready to order?" she asked brightly.

"I think the rest of us decided on the fish fry," Don said. "Mike?"

"Gimme the T-bone, medium rare. And another one of these." He drained the glass and handed it back to her with a seedy wink.

The waitress departed, and the four of them felt the awkwardness descend. The silence pressing in, Mike slouched farther into his chair, sniffling and brushing invisible cobwebs from the end of his nose.

"Looks like *someone* is catching a cold," Rose smiled.

John graduated high school and the "summer of Don" commenced. Long weekends to Chicago, Lake Geneva, and other upscale destinations became routine for Rose and her boyfriend, and John overheard talk about a West Coast trip in the fall.

By then John was sleeping with Becky Allerang, his girlfriend since the beginning of their final semester, so it was beyond stupendous to have the house to himself for days at a time. Mike was always on the road or crashing with a fan, and John took full advantage: sex in his own bed, parties as the urge arose, sleeping until midafternoon—the bachelor idyll of a minor league playboy. John earned decent tips bussing tables at an Italian place downtown, and college loomed in the fall with only slight foreboding. Life was just too good.

When one afternoon in early July John woke to find Rose and Don in the kitchen, legal-looking papers spread across the table and Rose signing her name wherever Don pointed, John noted mostly the smell of fresh cut grass breezing in through the window screens and the fact that they were almost out of toaster waffles.

He and Don remained civil over the summer, although the rapport they shared in the early days of his mother's relationship cooled. Don Huff was a self-made man, relentlessly focused on his business, and after the early glow of courtship with his mother faded, John saw that Don could be a prick. Toward the end of the summer, John took Don up on his offer to work at the Madison store, hosing down boats that had been on the lake for a test drive to earn extra cash for school.

Out of Rose's presence and master of his empire, John observed Don as a brittle and petty boss, yelling at his employees with a red-faced sneer. When Don let loose on John for failing to flush sand from an anchor winch, wrecking the motor, John walked out and decided he was done. Over breakfast a few days later, John met Don's lecture about John not honoring his commitments with a dark scowl. College could not start soon enough.

When his mother's calls stopped coming to his dorm room in the weeks leading up to Thanksgiving break of his freshman year, John took it as a relief, not a warning sign. It wasn't until he returned to Holt City for the holiday weekend that he learned that the feds raided Huff Marine, exposing tax fraud going back years. Prior to the market crash of '87, Don wildly overextended himself in the store up north. When his stores started failing, he claimed sold assets on his taxes that he had actually just moved to another set of books. This false shift in his tax burden gave Don a cushion to retain the image of solvency, as did his habit of forging manufacturer rebate payments that were supposed to go to his customers.

But as his debts kept mounting, Don started asking friends to lend him large sums of money, supposedly just to artificially inflate his asset sheet while he courted a new partner. This is what John came upon that July afternoon, his mother smiling contentedly as she signed away a substantial amount of the money Larry left the family. A woman in Middleton gave Don even more; he was sleeping with both of them.

A third woman, who knew better, started making the calls that would bring Don down.

John was not quite nineteen when he returned home to this.

College had been excellent. Classes were going well, dorm life was a blast, and the week before coming home a pretty sophomore from St. Paul slipped her hand down his pants while snuggling beneath a blanket with *The Simpsons* in the common room.

John would never hear directly from his mother what Don Huff did to the family; the extent of Don's deception and the financial mess Rose got them into would come through country club friends who knew John was coming home for the holiday.

Frank Kirschner, a lawyer who occasionally filled out a foursome when one of Larry's usual golf mates couldn't make it, sat John down for a talk in his office that Monday morning after John asked school for a hardship leave. Rose would be able to keep the house, Mr. Kirschner said with a positive smile that failed to calm John. He was horrified to hear that losing the house was even a possibility.

But the money she gave Don was gone for good. He was headed to prison, and some of his customers were suing him over the stolen rebate money. Between that, back taxes, and lawyer bills, there would be nothing left.

"The money your dad left you all, what's left of it, is invested well," Mr. Kirschner assured John. "So long as your mom stays healthy, I really don't see any reason why she can't maintain the life she's been living for a very long time. We'll just have to keep an eye on her expenses. It will mean some adjustments."

John's mind was racing so he didn't notice at first as his mom's lawyer slid a sheet of paper across his desk. When he finally focused on it, he saw a list of college scholarships and emergency financial aid information.

Two weeks later, Rose was still mum about what happened, and John was still not comfortable leaving her to get back to school. She slept all the time, and there was a leaden sadness about her when she got out of bed that made the old house go gray. Still a teenager, John didn't know how to draw her out, to encourage her to unburden herself and let her know he didn't blame her for anything—even though he did. He talked to the financial aid office at school, relieved to hear that his mother had paid his tuition through the school year. But after the spring semester, paying for school would be a challenge. He filled out student loan applications and scholarship requests to make it work, but they weren't going to cover everything.

John slept fitfully in his old room one night when he heard a noise. He bolted awake alertly; because his mother wasn't keeping normal hours, she often got up in the middle of the night, wandering aimlessly through the dark house. When he would sit with her, she said that her bed wasn't as comfortable as it used to be.

John sat in the dark to listen for the source of the noise. When he heard a male voice followed by a female titter, he stomped for the stairs.

Mike was in the kitchen, giggling through an obvious dope fog as he prowled through the refrigerator. A slutty, leather-clad club chick sat at the kitchen table about to light a cigarette when John burst in, not self-conscious at all in his T-shirt and tighty-whities.

"No!" he whispered fiercely. "No fucking way!" He yanked the cigarette from the girl's hand.

"What the fuck?" Mike shouted as the girl tried to process where her cigarette had gone.

"Shut up! It's three o'clock in the morning. Mom's asleep!"

"Gimme my cigarette!" the girl protested.

"You have to go," John insisted to her before turning to his brother. "She has to go. We have to talk. Why didn't you call me back?!"

"You're not my father," Mike scoffed as he grabbed for the cigarette. John shoved him back, grabbed the phone, and slammed it to the table.

"Call her a fucking cab and get her the fuck out of here," he hissed. "We have to talk."

The night was bitterly cold. John knew that getting dressed and dragging Mike out into it was the best way to sober him up. They both shivered sleepily as they walked the neighborhood.

"Fuck," Mike said bleakly, the reality of what John told

him seeping in. He angrily shoved John off the sidewalk, the frozen grass crackling beneath his feet. "Fuckin' Don Huff, I *told* you the guy was an asshole!"

"I know," John said quietly, rejoining his brother as they walked. It wasn't like what his mom was suffering with, but John was betrayed by Don, too. And he felt that, somehow, he should have known better. Should have protected her.

"How much did she give him?"

John knew the question was coming. Mike would find out eventually.

"Almost one hundred fifty grand."

Mike stopped in his tracks. *"What???"*

"He said it was just for a couple weeks, just to make it look like he had more money in the bank. So he could . . ." John trailed off. "He conned her, okay? It's gone, and that's it."

Mike still didn't move. Their house loomed at the end of the block.

"So what's left?" he asked.

"Enough. There are some investments and her Social Security. There's some insurance but it sounds like it's not enough. We could sell the house if we have to."

A primal trigger tripped in Mike's head. *"Motherfucker!"* he snapped, running for his car at the curb. His fury would not be contained with the toxins still running through him. John strained to hold him back.

"You can't get to him. They're holding him until the trial. There's nothing we can do."

Mike took sharp breaths of the cold night air through his nose, shifting in place like an angry, doped-up bull. John wished more than anything he could set Mike loose on Don Huff, to for once let his brother's crude impulses be put to savage, satisfying use. But it wasn't possible.

Mike accepted this bitterly, then walked the rest of the way back to the house without a word. He was about to storm through the kitchen door when John grabbed him at the elbow.

"Hey," John whispered, pulling his brother back. Their mother sat at the kitchen table in her robe. They watched her from the darkness as she stared at a pile of unopened mail. A sigh eased into a yawn as she rubbed her eyes. She looked much older than her fifty-one years.

John watched his brother watching their mother. He couldn't get a read on where Mike's anger was being channeled, and he couldn't risk letting it be toward her.

"Don't let this be about the money," John implored evenly. "Not tonight, she's not ready." Mike headed inside, revealing nothing.

As the back door opened, Rose turned with muted surprise to see her oldest son. Mike had been on the road for over two months, but the weeks since Don was found out made time crawl through a deep sludge for her—it seemed Mike had been gone forever.

She stood and walked quietly to him, her arms outstretched. Mike felt his mother crying softly into his chest.

"Hey, Mom," Mike said tentatively, the silence of the kitchen broken by the wall clock that kept the time since they were boys. "What're you doing out of bed?"

"I wanted to see you," she sniffed. He gently broke the hug.

"You need to get some sleep," he smiled down at her. "We can talk in the morning."

"You'll be here?" she asked urgently.

"I'll be here. Drag my ass outta bed after you've got the coffee on, we'll hang out. Long as you want."

She silently commanded Mike to stoop down so she could kiss him on the cheek, and she went back to bed.

Thirty

At one time, it was a small gymnasium. Maybe when the hospital opened in the twenties, patients came to the dank room John stumbled upon in the old building for physical therapy. While too small for a regulation basketball court, a hoop still hung forlornly on a far wall. Its net was long gone, probably appropriated for the nest of the great-great-great-grandparents of the rats whose black eyes studied John from the shadows.

Whatever its original intent, the room was given over to storage long ago. Walls and walls of ancient file boxes created a haphazard maze of clutter, many of the cartons split open from age and the weight of the stacked containers. Some towers of boxes collapsed, flinging paper records haphazardly through the long-abandoned room.

The air was heavy with a musty, mildewed cloud of rotting paper, causing John to sneeze convulsively when he first came upon the room during his nightly explorations. When he encountered the door to the gym, sealed shut behind a heavy chain and padlock, the suppression of its secrets was sure to fire John's curiosity.

He finally returned one night with a bolt cutter to cut the padlocked chain, and he was disappointed to find that the room held merely decades' worth of medical records. Stretched before John were cartons and cartons of the meticulously kept details of lives and deaths no longer of much interest to anybody.

The faded scrawls on the crumbling boxes stretched back to at least the sixties. The farther the boxes stretched toward the far corners of the gym, the further back into time they reached. Sagging floorboards and the angry murmuring of immense-sounding creatures—he had met snarling, dog-sized possums and raccoons during his nightly tours—kept John from exploring too far into the room.

Grabbing randomly at documents strewn across the floor, he found densely packed records made nearly unintelligible by complexly coded medical jargon, the faint legibility of carbon-papered typewriting, and the usual middle-of-the-night mush of John's brain. Trying to read by flashlight, he quickly realized nothing could be gleaned from the dry, context-less hieroglyphics of the files.

It wasn't until several nights later that John's restless mind drifted back to those boxes he found. He sat with Larry, imagining his father's work there in the old building. Had Larry ever assigned a patient to room 116? Weren't the odds pretty good that Dr. Husted once stood in this very room—maybe countless times—dispensing medical miracles, long before he became its perpetual patient? John decided that he had.

He welcomed into the room the vision of his young, vital father, perhaps a bit cold with his bedside manner but bringing authority and care to someone whose life may have depended on him. Some of his patients most likely didn't make it. Maybe Larry stood there right in room 116 and watched a patient die, and then turned to find family members to give them the sad news.

Because of the rote veneration that amassed around the memory of poor, dead-before-his-time Larry Husted, sometimes it was easy to forget that John's father was just a guy who went to work every day and tried to help people get better and not die. If he came home from work a little cranky or withdrawn from his family, maybe he had his reasons.

But then it occurred to John that Larry's history in the old hospital didn't have to be left to his imagination. Stored in all those decaying boxes, reaching back to the time when Larry first came to town, had to be the record of Lawrence Husted's career. If Larry's personal life was a murky patchwork of family photos, selectively calcified memories, and whatever pretend history John was making up about his father, the details of Larry's medical service could probably be retrieved with fine specificity.

John borrowed work lights from his neighbor Burt, who tinkered with his late model Ford late into the night for years until his wife left with the kids and Burt switched his hobby to drinking in the dark. John also borrowed hundreds of feet of extension cords, patching them together and snaking them from Larry's room to the gym. The power beyond the B wing had long ago been cut.

When John fired up the lights, the rats and whatever else called the gym home stirred and spit in unified protest. Instantly, hairy blurs of fangs and infestation leapt from their nests, bouncing off John's ankles and causing him to hop and scream like a dowager with a bat in her wig. He tore from the gym and retreated to Larry's room, embarrassed and queasy.

It wasn't until after he gave Larry his final treatment and packed up for home that he remembered to unplug the work lights left burning in the gym after his hasty escape.

Driving home on empty, predawn streets, he shivered to think of those hot lights bearing down on a room full of dry paper and cardboard, sparking a fire in the dead hospital that would have exposed Larry for sure. John pictured the firefighters, following the trail of extension cords back to Larry's room and staring in bewilderment at the scene they uncovered.

Thirty-one

The next night John stopped at a secondhand sporting goods store on the way to the hospital, where he bought himself hockey goalie gear and the longest stick he could find. When the clerk asked him if he needed skates, John fancied a brief image of himself padded and blade-footed, towering over the gymnasium rats and severing heads and tails with mighty, sword-like feet. But he quickly realized he would just as likely tumble from the skates and be gnawed to death, leaving behind a hockey-costumed corpse his wife would be left to explain.

Immediately following Larry's eleven o'clock treatment, John suited up and wrapped his ankles, wrists, and neck in heavy lengths of duct tape to prevent rodents from crawling inside his several layers of clothes. Only after he sealed himself in and began to sweat did he realize that it might be wise to fire up the lights in the gym from the plug in Larry's room and let the rats adjust to the intrusion of light for an hour or so before he went in.

John plugged in the extension cord to Larry's room, then lowered himself stiffly into the chair beside his father's bed. He sat in silence, suffocating inside the hockey gear while watching the minutes tick off slowly on the clock on the bed stand. This would have been a really confusing time for Larry Husted to wake up to see what his son was up to.

Half of the boxes housed rat nests, many containing bubble gum–pink babies and a mother *really* unhappy to have her brood menaced. The first lid that John disturbed burst open like a jack-in-the-box, the rat flying out and sinking its fangs into his chest protector and refusing to let loose no matter how much John clubbed himself with the hockey stick. After that, he learned to inspect each box for gnawed-out holes that indicated something living inside.

If the rats had taken over a box, the records inside were shredded and caked in decades worth of shit and piss. This simplified John's quest as he skipped over the infested boxes. He decided to concentrate on files from the latter half of the seventies—after Larry's rise to professional dominance began, before his work on the new hospital started to monopolize his time. If John found a box from those dates not full of vermin or black with mildew from years of water seepage, he'd carefully drag the box to the hall outside the gym. Despite grant writing projects starting to pile up, he knew he'd spend the next several nights seeing what was left of his father in those boxes.

The files were all frustratingly free of dramatic narrative. Meticulously noted numbers filled the forms—time of admission, body temperature, blood pressure, hourly notations of medications dispensed and urine passed—but it was hard to discern the *story* of the patient and the doctor. Nowhere—not once—was it recorded: "Dr. Husted burst into the room and, despite exhibiting a winsome air of regret at time not spent with his younger son, rolled up his sleeves to pull the patient back from the eternal chasm of death to the amazement of staff and the grateful embrace of humbled loved ones."

Not every patient made it. John began girding himself as he moved from file to file, wondering if line 25 on the patient form—the time of death line—would be filled in above his father's signature. John found eight deaths in the first box of files alone for which Larry was the attending physician.

Was eight a lot? John thought not, given the remarkable number of cases Larry probably took the lead on. The odds and the immutable appetite of mortality caught up to even the best doctors, but eight didn't seem alarming. And maybe subsequent file boxes would see fewer die. Maybe John just happened to peer in on his father during a bad patch.

In the six cartons of records from 1975 to 1980, Larry Husted signed off on twenty-three patients who died in his care. Of those, John discarded most into a pile that indicated circumstances beyond his father's control: car crash, gunshot wound, cardiac arrest. They were internal or external attacks on the body that did more damage than their doctor could rectify.

Of the twenty-three terminal cases, nine left questions. The dead were on the young side (five were children), and none had endured traumatic injury or system failure at the time of admission. Again, the medical terminology and alarmingly poor handwriting of the notetakers made certain that a layman like John would never make sense of what transpired.

Digging through Larry's past would have just been a few nights' diversion if not for one remaining file. It was much thicker than all the others, packed within a number of folders and bound as if intended for extensive reviewing. The powdery remains of a thick rubber band fell away as John retrieved the documents, and the top folder still had routing slips to the district attorney and Bob Schurmer, Larry's friend and lawyer. The date of a subpoena was stamped imperiously in a corner.

The pages inside had notes scrawled between notes, now in the more precise handwriting of lawyers. Words like *negligence* and *misdiagnosis* were discernible amidst the legalese. Questions from attorneys joined the initial questions of the doctors, and these seemed to press for answers. And a determination of responsibility.

John sat at Larry's bedside, looking from his silent father to the files closed tightly on his lap. And he began to read.

Thirty-two

The dead girl was Vicky Farragut. The Farraguts were one of those families that small towns seemed to breed so that everyone else had someone to look down upon. In the most generous terms they were a poor, rough-hewn lot. The numerous children were bullies and habitual flunkers whose parents sat pissed off and strange on their dirt patch front lawn for days at a time, surrounded by heaps of beer cans and cigarette butts. Randy Farragut was a Vietnam vet who came home broken in '68 and intermittently ran his father's Amoco station in what was becoming one of Holt City's struggling black neighborhoods. He was an angry drunk and a worse speed freak, and everyone other than his wife, Holly, knew to stay out of his way. Randy and Holly would eventually set loose seven feral little Farraguts upon Holt City; Vicky was their second, born in the old hospital the year before John was born.

She died in June 1980 at nine years old; John remembered when it happened. Not the details, but he could still call to mind the queasy, confusing waft of mortality that blew through the monkey bars when he heard about the death of a kid just about his age. Being a Farragut, the rumors on the playground were pitiless and fixed blame on the parents, which confused John even more.

In the days that followed, as Vicky's brothers and sisters started returning to school looking even more pale and vacant than before, John noticed that at least for a time the teasing stopped. At recess, most kids just stood in whispering packs and stared at them, imagining the funeral and a family worn raw by soul-searing crying and eventually a skeleton just about their size melting into the dirt out at Eastlawn Cemetery. Then they played keep-away until the bell rang.

Back then, at eight years old, it didn't take much to set John's mind to racing to keep him from falling asleep at night. The day he heard of Vicky's death, he recalled stirring in tangled sheets for hours. He now marveled to know that on that same night, just on the other side of his bedroom wall, the man who had overseen her death may have been awake as well.

Did the death of a child in his care keep Lawrence Husted up that night, or was his professional detachment so absolute that he slept with ease in order to be rested and on his game for the patients he would try to do better by the next day?

For the first time since John began massaging his father's unknowable past into behaviors he found pleasing, John stared at Larry in his bed and had no idea how his father might have reacted to the death of Vicky Farragut. And for the first time, he realized it was dishonest to invent his own answer.

"Did you know Dad got sued for malpractice in 1980?" John asked Mike idly while raking their mother's backyard.

"Yeah," Mike shrugged. "The Farraguts."

"Why don't I remember this?"

"Because you were eight and a dumbfuck. The old man tried to keep it from us, but *I* knew what was going on. I mean, he was on trial for weeks. It was on the front page when it was finally settled."

John was amazed that this all escaped him when he was a kid.

"God, Johnny Farragut sold good weed," Mike reminisced. "Got himself blown in half by a shotgun in Rockford, like in '87. Used the money I owed him for dope to help buy our first PA."

"What happened in the trial?" John asked impatiently.

"The girl died and her scuzzy parents said it was Dad's fault," Mike said, then scoffed cynically. "Like those rednecks had a chance against the great Larry Husted.

"But it went on longer than him and his lawyers thought it would, I know that. Larry was freakin' for a while, which was sweet to see."

"Where was I during all this?" John pleaded.

"Watching cartoons."

"That's not all I did!"

"Were you beating off yet?"

"No!" John said, mortified.

"Then you were watching cartoons. That's *all* you did back then. Once you started beatin' off you were in your room all the time, and then I could watch what *I* wanted to watch on TV."

"So what was he accused of? Why did it take so long to settle it?"

"I don't know, it was over thirty years ago!" Mike grumbled. "The kid had something wrong and they took her to the emergency room and he didn't take the time to figure out if she was allergic to something, and whatever he shot her up with killed her. Or that's what they said. The judge finally said it was bullshit."

"But not right away," John reiterated.

"Larry's nuts were in a vise for a while there," Mike sighed. "Good times."

Thirty-three

The *Holt City Gazette* had put the past several years of archives on their website, but John knew that the era he needed to revisit was going to send him to microfilm. He started spending his days—between tending to Larry and around his grant projects—at the library, piecing together the story.

Vicky's medical charts gave him a timeline to follow. He started with the date of her death and scrolled his way to the next day's *Gazette,* which included her starkly worded obituary: Randall and Holly Farragut's nine-year-old daughter Victoria Denise died at Holt Memorial, where she was admitted after several days of illness. Cause of death was undetermined. Vicky left behind five brothers and sisters. Mr. Farragut, the obit noted dryly, managed the Amoco station on East Becker Road. Funeral arrangements were unknown.

The date of the subpoena and the log of record requests as the files shuttled between lawyers' offices told John when the lawsuit was filed. The June 26 edition of the newspaper broke the news about the suit filed against Holt Memorial and Dr. Lawrence Husted.

The paper gave the story only two column inches on page three. John instinctively deduced that the paper favored the hospital and the highly regarded Dr. Husted over the lowly Farraguts, whose perpetual flaunting of the law and decent behavior was a staple of the paper's coverage. As John scrolled through day after day of old issues of the *Gazette,* he was bemused to observe how often a Farragut was caught driving drunk or selling dope or irking neighbors by dismantling junked cars on their front lawn at two in the morning.

John leaned into the eye-straining glow of the projector screen and tried to glean what he could from the short article about the lawsuit.

Vicky's parents brought her to the emergency room after days of either ignoring the fact that she ran a fever and had pains in her abdomen, or believing they could treat it themselves. When they finally brought her in the diagnosis was an appendix about to burst, but the claim stated that what should have been a routine procedure unexpectedly led to internal bleeding that killed her. The suit charged that Lawrence Husted, the attending physician at the time, was negligent in his treatment of the girl.

The paper reported that a lawyer named Henry Getch represented the Farraguts and was going after Larry and the hospital for $1.7 million. He pictured Randy Farragut salivating at such a sum in exchange for his daughter's life and knew he'd find that to be more than a fair trade. It was a tragedy and all, but he still had plenty of little Farraguts left over.

John was able to retrieve trial transcripts from the county archives. It all boiled down to the internal bleeding that killed the girl. As the ER physician on call when Vicky was brought in, Larry immediately diagnosed the inflamed appendix and removed it. He was concerned about low blood pressure that didn't right itself after the surgery, so he prescribed a blood thinner to flush the catheter and prevent clots. This was within accepted practice, but not a routine procedure for such a young patient.

The problem was that Larry failed to note in her admission records that for the four days in which her parents tried to treat her fever and stomach pains on their own, they gave her an outrageous amount of aspirin. This thinned her blood to a dangerous degree, which became lethal when Larry unknowingly compounded it. The little girl immediately began to bleed out and while Larry apparently struggled valiantly to save her, there was nothing he could do.

John squirmed at feeling pretty certain that his father fucked up. The nurses ask you all those questions at admission for a reason. The doctors need to know what they're dealing with. Larry's lawyer tried to divert blame—the admitting nurse should have alerted Larry, she should have pressed the parents for more specifics about the aspirin consumption instead of merely noting "high vol. asp."—but Getch, the Farragut's lawyer, insisted that it was ultimately Larry's responsibility to know the facts.

Henry Getch, in his late twenties at the time and probably no more than an ambulance-chasing gnat to a well-connected and prosperous attorney like Bob Schurmer, apparently scored blows Larry's lawyer had not anticipated. So after spending several days calling doctors and patients to publicly testify on behalf of Larry's medical skills, Schurmer turned his sights on the Farraguts.

The *Gazette* articles now deemed the story deserving of front-page attention as Bob Schurmer turned the trial into an indictment of Randy and Holly Farragut. The jury was all locals; they knew the Farraguts. And Schurmer didn't miss a thing: Randy's dope arrests in high school and, with greater and greater frequency after he returned from Vietnam. Holly's long list of petty offenses, like shoplifting, public intoxication, and fighting. And an endless string of police calls to the family's home, usually for noise or some boorish fracas, but often enough with concerns about the well-being of their children. Neighbors reported often finding little Farraguts straying into their yards in filthy clothes and helping themselves to fruit from their trees, seemingly unfed.

Henry Getch finally got the judge to rule the attacks on the parents irrelevant and out-of-bounds, but Schurmer got enough read into the record to set him up for the kill. He called Randy Farragut to the stand.

Schurmer focused on the four days leading up to finally bringing Vicky to the emergency room. How could the parents have allowed their daughter to writhe in pain for *four days* before getting her help? How could they have ignored a fever that spiked at 102? How could they not know that handfuls of aspirin *for days* were the worst thing to give a kid suffering from stomach pains?

Were they just ignorant, or was there some other reason they needed to keep their daughter out of the hospital? As John read he could almost feel the ice water in the lawyer's veins as he let go with the kill shot.

"Was it true," he began dryly, reading from a document, "that at the time that your daughter took sick, there was a civil action against you, ordering you to pay Kingston Auto twelve hundred dollars for car repairs you hadn't paid for? And that if you had taken your daughter to the emergency room, you risked having that order enforced if the police were brought in?"

"She was my kid, goddammit!" Randy said forcefully. "I wouldn't see her hurt for twelve hundred bucks!"

"But," the lawyer slinked, "if you and your wife could cure her yourself, with your aspirin, twelve hundred bucks could buy a lot of beer and cigarettes."

Randy's lawyer objected.

"No further questions," Larry's lawyer said as he took his seat.

The jury deliberated for almost three full days but when they came back, they cleared Larry and the hospital of all charges. The picture on the front page of the *Gazette* showed that after the verdict was read, Randy and Holly Farragut held each other and cried.

Larry Husted was in the background of the photo shaking his smiling lawyer's hand. Larry's back was to the camera, leaving John to imagine the emotions on his father's face.

Thirty-four

"Hey, what do you remember about this?" John asked Rose casually, having brought a copy of the *Gazette* article with him for a lunch of chicken salad in the old house. It was the front-page verdict story, the headline declaring "Physician, Hospital Cleared in Malpractice Suit." John was curious what his mother would remember from the event, now thirty-five years ago. He observed that distant memories, sometimes arcane ones, had a way of fixing themselves forever to the minds of Alzheimer's patients. While essential data and elemental knowledge from a half hour ago failed to find a home no matter how many times it was repeated.

John detected the unease as his mother was unexpectedly pulled backward in time. She stared at the photo on the front page, her husband visible but not quite there.

"That was your father," she said, her finger touching his

image. The details of the case began filtering back to her. "He was in trouble. Somebody sued him."

"I know," John said. "I read the story. It was that Farragut family."

The name triggered something complicated in Rose. She diverted her attention to the photo in the paper from Larry to the hugging, crying parents in the foreground.

"The Farraguts!" she recalled with a kind of wonder. "Do you know, back when I did my volunteer work for the hospital, we were dealing with them *all the time*? Those parents, they were just awful. And the children . . ." She stopped herself.

She studied the article as if to read it, but John could tell by the way her eyes fixed in middle distance that it was coming back to her through her own muddied recollection of events.

"We *knew* that little girl," she whispered.

"Vicky."

"Vicky," she said wistfully. "There were a lot of them. And then, after the trial, it just got worse. The *parents* got worse. One of them was always in jail or would disappear, for weeks at a time. But the babies kept coming. We were always taking up collections for them: food, clothes, toys—whatever we could get our hands on."

A fact returned to her. It still hurt. "After what happened, after the trial, someone decided I shouldn't go out to their house anymore to drop the things off. It was upsetting the *parents*," she said, an uncommon tone of derision in her voice.

"So I organized the drives, made the rounds of garage sales to get what we needed," she said, shaking her head with sad bemusement. "I kept buying back all the things we had already given them. The parents were turning around and selling some of it off to pay for God knows what."

"That was really nice of you to keep helping," John smiled. "Considering."

"Those children didn't deserve to do without just because their parents were so terrible."

He returned to the newspaper article. "So, what happened?" he asked tonelessly, without revealing his suspicions. "The Farraguts said Dad was responsible for their daughter dying?"

Despite the decades, a defense instinctively went up. It was a spouse's undiminished insistence on the truth of the matter.

"The jury found him innocent. *You* read the article," she said sharply.

"I know, but . . . If you really look at it . . ." John said, cutting himself off the moment the words left his mouth. The medical records, the court documents—Rose would have never seen what John had discovered, and they would have meant nothing to her if she had. Rose's man was innocent, and that was that. Retrying the case now to get Rose to let go of her undiminished loyalty would be cruel.

But maybe there was still something John could learn here, to shape this new perspective of his father he was discovering.

"Do you think he might have felt responsible, in some way?" John asked delicately. "I mean, I know the jury said he didn't do anything wrong. But . . ."

"Your father felt terrible any time he lost a patient," she said sternly. "Nobody else saw that, only me. And even then, he tried to not let it show. But I knew. Nights he'd come home for dinner, and then he'd lock himself up in his den. I knew."

She looked again at the smudgy copy of the old newspaper article.

"What kind of parent leaves their child to suffer for days? You don't treat a dog that way."

The law office of Henry Getch sat in a strip mall between a Domino's Pizza and an empty storefront that had once been the larger law office of Henry Getch. He was pushing sixty now, rickety-thin and his hair swept back and dyed black.

When John first called and asked if he could come in to talk about his work for the Farraguts thirty-five years earlier, Getch said he would have to charge John his hourly rate for the conversation. But as Getch became incensed at remembering the case, it appeared that having a chance to rail against it after so many years was reward enough.

"Your father killed that little girl," he said bluntly the moment John settled into the folding chair opposite Getch's desk. "Plain and simple. He *killed* her."

John flinched, instinctively rising to his father's defense despite his suspicions.

"You remember all this, all the details?" John said skeptically. "After over thirty years?"

"That was one of the first cases I ever tried. You know how many lawyers had to turn that family down before they got to *me*?

"You want me to tell you that Randy Farragut and that wife of his were saints, just some down-on-their-luck losers who couldn't catch a break?" Getch asked. "They weren't. They were assholes. They were shitty parents. But they brought that girl into the hospital alive and she died because your father didn't do his job."

The lawyer seemed to take satisfaction from watching John recoil. "Sorry now you gave me a call?"

John wasn't sure.

"He fucked up," the lawyer continued matter-of-factly. "It happens, even to doctors. *Especially* to doctors. That's why they have malpractice insurance. It wasn't *his* cash on the line. He should have just settled.

"But this wasn't about the money. It was ego. And reputation. His, and the hospital's. The town was already pushing back on the new hospital. The financing wasn't coming together. This wasn't the time for losing a court case. And there was no way your father was going to admit to doing anything wrong. So that *fucking* Bob Schurmer went and gutted the family, and your father let him. Everybody walked away, hands clean."

An uneasy realization rattled John as he absorbed Getch's venom: If John told Mike about Larry, and Mike *did* insist on suing the hospital and Walt, John was sitting across from a lawyer who had waited decades for another shot at them. Even a strip mall shyster like Henry Getch would be almost guaranteed the payoff of a lifetime, given the flagrancy of the acts and the shitstorm of attention that would surround the case.

"I hadn't lived here that long, I had no idea how the whole town spit on that family," Getch continued, surprising John with a sincere tone of regret. "I should have known. I should have never let that jury decide things. That was on me. If they could have found a decent lawyer, they should have sued *me*."

"Do you know what happened to them?"

"I had a trail of unpaid bills sent to them for years," he recalled hazily. "I think the last one bounced back from an address in Iowa. *Meth World* magazine named them Parents of the Year in 1997," he chuckled.

"Just between you and me," the lawyer belched moistly as he squirmed in his chair. "Your father probably did that little girl a favor."

Eastlawn Cemetery sat between the town and the interstate, along a busy stretch of road that had grown thick with mini-marts, big box stores, and fast-food restaurants in the thirty-five years since Vicky Farragut was buried there.

Vicky's headstone was small, surely the cheapest her parents could find. It read simply: VICTORIA DENISE FARRAGUT, 1971–1980. LOVING DAUGHTER. Here is where grieving Farraguts had stood, maybe cleaned up in secondhand clothing that John's mother and her volunteer friends had given them.

John winced at finding himself wondering how genuine the parents' sadness could have been when they seemed to care so little when these kids were alive. He remembered the picture that ran on the front page of the paper when they lost their lawsuit. If one chose to believe the parents were crying and holding each other over a lost payday rather than a dead child, they had a harder heart than John Husted.

John didn't know why he came to the cemetery. The bad TV movie version of this would have him bring a teddy bear or a single rose to lay on Vicky's grave, but he rejected the mawkishness of it with a queasy cringe. Coming here seemed like gesture enough.

As John stood at the grave and listened to the flow of the interstate a cornfield away, another maudlin movie scene coalesced in his imagination: Could Larry Husted have stood here once? All alone, for just a moment? To convey some silent sentiment to a little girl that he shouldn't have let die?

John decided he probably did not, and he left it at that.

Thirty-five

Between his lack of sleep and the emotional battering he brought upon himself on so many fronts—the unrelenting servicing of Larry, the truth he kept from his mother and brother, the escalating dysfunction at home, the ghosts of his father's past—John's mind was wobbly and getting worse as he arrived for another night of caring for his father. When he opened the door to Larry's room and saw a figure sitting in the shadows of his father's bedside, John's brain hazily grasped that someone else had stepped into his secret world. Or maybe he was asleep on the couch at home and a dream was commencing.

The air took on a queasy charge as John drew nearer to his father's bed. The closing of the door behind him clicked thunderously in the tomb-like room; the man at the bed didn't flinch. *This is a dream,* John comforted himself. *Just hover above it and see what freaky places it takes you.*

When the bland, smug face of Dean Durning looked up to greet him, John jolted abrasively into reality.

"He looks *better* than the last time I saw him!" the hospital administrator said with sleepy exasperation, pointing at Larry.

John impulsively pulled at Durning's chair to get him away from his father. "Get the fuck outta here," John seethed.

Durning jumped up but made no moves to leave.

"I don't think so," he said with simpering courage. "This is *my* hospital. This is continuing because *I* allowed it. But . . ." He pointed again at Larry. *"Why is he still here?"*

"I told you," John said, coldcocked by this unexpected demand to defend the situation. "Until I am ready to—"

"No!" Durning shot back. "It's been almost two months. I don't care anymore how hard it is for you to tell your family. They have to be told. Or they have to *not* be told, but you have to end this. That's *it*!

"And if you won't take care of this," Durning said darkly. "I will."

"Don't threaten me," John said.

"You're threatening *me* every day you're in here!" Durning shot back. "If this is exposed in a way we can't control, we're both going to be fucked. But your problem will be over. *I'll* take the fall for this!"

John struggled for a return volley as Durning exploited all the angles. "That *nurse* of yours would be on a bus back to El Salvador by the end of the week if this is discovered. I know what she has done for your father. Would he want that to happen to her?"

Because of their alternating shifts, Gloria had become a shadowy angel for John. He left her cash on the nightstand beside Larry's bed, she left language-hobbled notes for him when they were running low on the nutrition drip or lotion. Larry was always diapered perfectly when John arrived for the night shift, his skin oiled silkily and without a trace of infection.

Everything John was able to do for his father was what Gloria had scripted for him. If keeping Larry Husted ticking was some kind of mad miracle, Gloria made it possible. When this was over, she needed to slip away without consequence.

Dean Durning was just reinforcing what John already knew was true: This could not continue. Tell the family, don't tell the family—something had to be decided.

Bringing this to a conclusion would be right for everyone involved, including John, who was finding his mind going to some very strange places lately. As he spent more and more time with Larry, John feared some lines were about to be crossed.

Specifically: John wanted to put a pointy party hat on his brain-dead father. John would wear one, too. This made *sense* to him.

John relearned his father's birthday; it was coming up next month, on the sixth. Larry would turn seventy-eight. Larry had been denied thirty birthday parties, and John was certain no one, not once, thought to blow out a candle for him.

So on one of those long, late-night vigils at Larry's side, when John's brain rambled off on loopy tangents, he decided he wanted to put a pointy party hat on his father because the old man was due a celebration. He wanted to put a pointy party hat on his father just to bring some color and some lightness into this room.

Mostly, he wanted to put a pointy party hat on his father because it'd be really wrong but weirdly funny, and John wanted to believe that if Larry knew his son did it, he'd think it funny, too.

Walt Bolger told John a wealth of stories about his father; John was stunned and gratified to learn that Larry was a really funny guy. Walt thought Rose never really understood many of the things her husband found amusing, which is probably why John never heard about them. John had come to learn that wives just don't always know what's funny.

But his own sense of humor meant a lot to John. To know that he got it from his father was a gift he now knew to cherish.

So John sat there very late one night, staring at Larry and anticipating his birthday, and he thought, *Yes, I* will *put a pointy party hat on my father. I think this is something I will do.*

But then he thought, *What if* that *is the precise moment Dad decides to wake up?*

John really, truly knew that this wouldn't happen. But, he reasoned, if you had asked him six months ago if *any* of this could have happened, he wouldn't have thought that possible either. You never really know.

So just suppose: Larry Husted goes off to work in 1985

and wakes up three decades later in a strange little room, hooked up to tubes and staring at a guy who looks just like him when he was thirty years younger, with a pointy party hat on his head. Who could explain such a thing?

John would say to his father, "Yes, it *is* pretty odd, but I hoped you'd find it funny in a *Weekend at Bernie's* kind of way." But Larry wouldn't have a clue what *Weekend at Bernie's* was, so John would have to explain all *that*.

Then, what if *that* was the moment Larry finally died? *Really* died. Miraculously back to life after all this time, finally—for just a moment—there with his son to exchange a few words of compassion and wisdom, and they spent it talking about *Weekend at Bernie's*? Wearing pointy party hats? Like *that* wouldn't fuck a guy up for the rest of his life.

John found himself thinking about all this the other night. *A lot*.

So, yes, maybe it was time to let this end.

"A couple more weeks," he said weakly to Durning in his father's room.

"But—" Durning protested.

"Please," John said. "I understand. But . . . please."

Durning screwed up his spine. "I have a first year resident who is on thin ice. Talented kid, but screwing up too many times on procedure. If it comes to it, he'll do whatever I tell him to save his career.

"I will bring him here. He will withdraw your father's feeding tube and he will humanely tend to him until it is done. Then you, with or without your family, will be afforded as much dignity as possible to see that the dispensation of the body is discreetly managed."

John simmered at the cold efficiency of the threat.

"Two weeks," Durning said tersely, then left.

John drew closer to Larry, once again hoping to gain some unspoken guidance from him. But it was on John alone to act. His heart told him all along that he could not *not* tell his mother about Larry, but that he could not tell her and hope to still keep it from Mike.

So since Mike was going to know eventually, he was going to know *first*. For all that had gone dead inside his brother, John was prepared to gamble that Mike would know not to hurt their mother as she struggled to accept the truth.

For all he had been through, for all the damage he had done to himself and others, there had to be something decent left inside Mike Husted.

Thirty-six

On that day that Mike lost everything twenty-two years earlier, the morning elbowed its way in through a familiar dope afterburn. He wavered toward wakefulness, the coke and whiskey providing alternating surges of spikiness and immutable unconsciousness. As he fought off the daylight through still-closed eyes, he also felt the residual tweak of some pretty rank heroin.

The band had been dry for weeks, unable to score from their fans or local dealers as they played their way up the East Coast from Georgia, but the girl who brought him home the night before was connected. As he scratched himself beneath her sheets and felt her lying beside him, he assumed she provided the smack.

Most days on the road began like this for Mike, who hadn't yet turned twenty-three when it all fell apart. After tearing up whichever club Gravel Rash performed in, the lead singer had first dibs on the tail assembled backstage to carry the party into the dawn. Sometimes they went at it in the dressing room or on the bus, sometimes the girl had a hotel room if she and some friends took to following the band from stop to stop. And sometimes she just took him home.

Shit, Mike thought that morning as he fought to stay unconscious for another hour. He had to piss. He was going to have to get up, take a leak, and get himself back to the tour bus before it left for the next town. The girl usually drove him back to the previous night's venue to hook up with the rest of the band.

"Hey," he grumbled over his shoulder, jabbing an elbow into the girl passed out behind him. "C'mon, you gotta get me outta here."

His eyes were thick with sleep gunk; what the fuck did she give him last night? He rubbed them clean and then squinted in the morning sun piercing in through her window. The girl had dingy pink sheets and a pillowcase lined with hearts. The room was shabby and small. Mike vaguely remembered the house and the whole neighborhood being low rent when they stumbled in at whatever time that was. The place smelled like bologna and old onions.

He sat up and felt the full toxic headbutt from the previous night's party. His stomach sloshed queasily as he rubbed his forehead.

"Hey!" he growled, rolling to face the girl and finally seeing all the red. In the same instant, he realized that the dark matter caked into his eyes was her blood.

He swiped away the sheets to see a syringe drying in the sticky mess. Her skin cold and blue, her forearm still dribbled blood at the point where she pierced an artery. Mike bolted from beside her, standing cold, naked, and tattooed at her bedside.

"Fuck!" he whispered desperately, his body painted in streaks of red. *"Fuck me!!!"*

He pushed the girl at her hip, hoping for signs of life. "Hey . . ." He didn't know her name. *"Hey!"*

Mike's heart raced as the dope fog left his brain. He sized up the room, went to the window: it wasn't a house, it was an apartment. Four floors up. Just one way out.

His clothes were thrown throughout the room and tangled with hers. He found his tight, tattered jeans and tried to pull them on, hopping on one foot and then the other. One fake snakeskin boot was right where he needed it to be; the other finally turned up under her bed.

His shirt had ended up in bed with them; it was too bloody to put back on. He went to her closet and found a too-small yellow blouse that he wrestled to make fit. He spit into another of her shirts and tried to scrub the blood away from his face and arms.

Ready to bolt, he turned again to her naked body. He darted around to her side of the bed and touched his fingers to her throat. There was no pulse; not a trace of body temperature remained.

"Fuck *me!*" Mike whimpered, then tried to not rattle the doorknob of her room with his violently shaking hand.

He walked briskly and dead sober down the narrow

hallway. She lived a dumpy, just-getting-by life; the place was small and the door out was an easy reach. Only when near escape did he hear *Rugrats* jabbering from the curtain-cloaked living room. A boy of four or five sat in a trance in front of the TV, but he turned long enough to stare blankly at Mike from the shadows.

Mike ran.

The early morning sun was a bitch as he hit the sidewalk, trying to hold himself to an inconspicuous trot.

Her apartment building was on a main drag, the street already choked with people heading to work. Mike kept his head down as he bustled past dog walkers and blacks and Hispanics mottled glumly at bus stops.

When he came to a public park he hit the open field and broke into a fast jog. His mind was churning frenetically, his mouth parched.

It was *her* smack, he told himself. *Her* rig she killed herself with. Mike didn't like needles. He knew from the raw-nerved sizzle in his nostrils that he snorted some with her, but *no way* would his prints turn up on that syringe.

Just get to the bus, he commanded himself, his lungs starting to burn. Get to the bus, get out of town. Eddie and the label's lawyers would help him deal with whatever he was responsible for.

He reached another busy street and took the sidewalk east before stopping: he didn't know where he was. He couldn't remember the name of the club they played the night before, or where he would find the tour bus.

He didn't even know what town he was in. Passing license plates said Rhode Island.

He fell into a panicked spin, looking for landmarks that were never going to come. People began to stare at this lanky, tattooed scuzzball in a too-small yellow blouse and what appeared to be blood on his face. He caught their looks and fell back into his driven walk.

A liquor store. A rack of the town's free alternative paper. Mike stopped, feeling like a genius. He tore through the paper to the club listings. There was his Gravel Rash logo, hyping their show at The Station in West Warwick the night before.

The club was on a main drag, he *knew* it. Maybe the next one over. He could see golden arches two blocks down; that could be the McDonald's where they ate the night before.

He jutted into the busy street to get to the other side, but he misjudged the pace of the oncoming traffic. He had to hit a complete run to make the curb within the short break in cars. There hadn't been time to get his socks on. His cheap boots rubbed his bare feet raw.

And there was water in his ear, fucking with his balance. The sun beating down on him, cars beginning to honk, the other sidewalk still too far across. The more ground he covered, the farther the opposite side seemed to be retreating.

One car nearly clipped him as his legs began splaying clumsily. He instinctively tugged at his ear, trying to right his equilibrium. His finger came away, and the jolt at finding the girl's blood in his ear finally threw his legs into a tangle. He hit the asphalt hard, his face sandpapering across the grit as his front teeth snapped at the roots. His right leg twisted crookedly at the knee.

A car swerved to miss him, diverting another driver straight into a light pole. More squealing brakes, more sour metallic thumps as fender benders dominoed in both directions.

People leapt angrily from their cars to inspect the damage and ream out the long-haired dumbfuck bleeding and crying in the middle of the street.

An hour later, as a cop lowered him into the backseat of the squad car, bystanders clapped cruelly. It would be the last applause Mike would hear for a long time.

Thirty-seven

The girl was nineteen. Her name was Courtney. She had a long narcotics record and a reputation for running wild. She also had a four-year-old son, whom Mike met as he ran away.

The district attorney intended to make an example of the degenerate rock star who blew into town, shared *heroin* with the single mother of a small child, and then fled the scene, leaving the boy to find the body. The DA got $300,000 bail imposed as he began determining what all he could throw at him. He speculated in the press about reckless homicide.

The band didn't find out until they arrived at their next scheduled gig in Maine. The bus had waited in West Warwick as long as it could, but with another show that night and a five-hour drive ahead of them, they took off before lunch.

Scott, the road manager, stayed behind. Mike had done this a couple times before, passing out and staying in some girl's bed too long. Scott always managed to get him to the next stop by show time. But now Scott was waiting for a call back from Eddie Kingsolver to hear what they should do next.

When another show was canceled and Eddie still wasn't returning calls, Taggert finally called Mike's mother back in Wisconsin. The tour was dead: none of the clubs were willing to risk riots by putting out a metal band without its charismatic lead singer, and even if Mike made bail the DA warned him about leaving town.

But somebody ought to get him out of jail. The phone call rattled Rose, who only knew Jay Taggert as the sullen, long-haired boy who skulked in and out of her basement when not disappearing for weeks with her son's band. She had no idea how to proceed when Taggert suggested she wire $30,000 to a bail bondsman in Rhode Island.

John was twenty-one in 1993. Having scraped his way into his junior year of college, working third shift in a UPS warehouse and enduring so-so grades and a dismal social life as a result, he raged to hear that his mother had cut a check to Mike that was almost greater than his entire college tuition. It was the only time John ever yelled at his mother.

"What the fuck, Mom!" he shouted over the phone.

"John . . ."

"I mean . . . *What the fuck?* Are you paying for his lawyer, too?"

Rose's voice was tiny. "I don't know. The record company people, maybe they will . . ."

John stomped his way around the small off-campus house he shared. "Did he do it?" he demanded. "Did he kill this girl?"

"John," his mother gasped. "He's your brother."

"You don't have a fucking clue who he is! He could take every dime you have and *still* get convicted!" John sneered. In an instant, he knew he cut too deep. Rose spent years denying what she knew was true about Mike. Now it came crashing in on her, with big bills to be paid.

John churned in the silence, caught between wanting Mike to go to hell and not wanting Mike to drag his mother there with him.

"There will be a trial," Rose pressed on. "Nobody knows when. Mr. Kirschner, our lawyer, is making some calls, but he says Mike will need someone there, in Rhode Island. He'll get out on bail and hopefully he can come home until then, but when the trial comes we'll need to . . ."

John's brain roiled as he understood what she was saying. "*We?* I've got school! I've got a job! I can't go!"

"Fine, I'll go alone," she snipped brittlely. "I'll sit by myself, in a strange town, for who knows how long, while your brother is on trial for his life. Your father would be very proud of you for the choice you're making."

Rage and indignation xylophoned its way up John's spine. He spun furiously, fast-balling his phone into a Miller Lite sign on the living room wall.

Buried in Mike's contract with the label was a morals clause that in the best of circumstances would have been moot. If

Gravel Rash became a big earner, no amount of foul behavior would have caused the label to break its contract. If,
as was more likely, Gravel Rash amounted to not much at
all, the label would simply drop the band long before lurid
rock star behavior had a chance to inconvenience share-
holders.

Either the act would get so big that the label would for-
give them anything, or they would drop them by the time
their first album was going unsold for nickels on eBay.

So it was Mike's considerable bad luck to wake up in a
bloody bed before the first album was done. Gravel Rash
was not a priority signing at Razor Records, and no one
would stick their necks out for the likes of Eddie Kingsolver.
When word reached New York that the band's lead singer
was dumb enough to wake up with a dead junkie before he
even had a record out, it was just smart business to invoke
the morals clause and cancel the contracts. Eddie, who had a
roster of other acts to keep him in the game, didn't put up a
fight.

By the time the case came to trial, the DA's options were lim-
ited. Courtney's drug history, the dope-fuzzy nature of the
events, and the lack of Mike's prints on the syringe gave his
lawyer ample ammunition to slap down the reckless homi-
cide charge. Still, the defendant had shared hardest of hard
drugs during an evening of carnal degeneracy, and he fled
the scene rather than seek help for the deceased and her

orphaned son. A prison sentence of five years or more was threatened.

John agreed to travel to Providence with Rose for the opening of the trial. It was almost worth it, watching Mike led into court the first day, his rock star locks sheared off and his gangly frame wedged into a cheap suit.

Mike's swagger was gone, his broken slouch and sallow skin making him appear ten years older.

The DA came out firing, having stitched together a lurid account of Mike's sordid past. He tried to get past examples of statutory rape with young female fans introduced to the jury before the judge ruled them out-of-bounds. Mike's lyrics about drugs and fucking and talking about women as whores and playthings were read into the record. Rose, who could never understand the words her son shouted over the sonic maelstrom belching up from her basement, grew ill.

Mike's lawyer rigorously kept the focus on the law. He brought detailed attention to the time of death and the futility of medical intervention by the time Mike ran away. Yes, the defendant engaged in illicit drug use, but with a consenting adult whose own actions contributed to her death. Mike may need to bear consequences for the regrettable way he chose to extricate himself from the situation in an understandable moment of panic, but enough doubt existed about his role in the death of young Courtney to justify a severe penalty.

Sensing defeat, the DA offered a deal: no more than three

years at a medium security facility just outside Providence, followed by five years of parole back home.

Mike went in in 1993, and got out in a little over two years. He came home with an even stronger drug habit and a vacant sullenness that John suspected had something to do with violence he endured while behind bars.

Thirty-eight

With Theatre of Pain on a break, Mike learned enough about the internet to find a collection of Mötley Crüe lyrics, and he diligently tried to memorize the words. He got John to download the Crüe's hits onto one of Katie's tossed-aside, early issue iPods, and he spent hours walking the neighborhoods around his mother's house, blasting the music while—he hoped—working off his thickening gut.

Usually after *Days of Our Lives,* he'd strap on the iPod and walk until dinner. With the volume in his ears cranked up to stage levels, sometimes he got so caught up in the music that he'd let loose with lyrics right there on the sidewalk. During Crüe classics like "Same Ol' Situation" or "Girls Girls Girls," he would spontaneously start aping the histrionic stage routines. With his long hair hiding the headphones, even those who passed close by couldn't tell he was plugged in.

He was just a wild-haired, seedy-looking forty-five-year-old, gesticulating madly while shrieking about the need to shout at the Devil:

"He'll be the blood between your thighs!!!"

He learned how to lighten his own hair and tease it up so as to disguise the thinning parts. He recorded a Mötley Crüe concert on VH1 Classic and studied it like the Zapruder film, learning all of Vince Neil's moves. John always ragged Mike about his laziness, but he resolved to become the best pretend Vince Neil the tribute act circuit ever saw.

So it was a humiliating blow when D.J. called to fire him.

"What the fuck, man?" Mike demanded.

"Dude, it just wasn't working. We had a chance to pull this Danny kid out of a Poison act in Gurnee, we had to go for it. It's just a better fit."

"Poison is not the Crüe!" Mike sneered, genuinely offended.

"Dude, they really kinda are."

An awkward silence fell over them. Mike was planning to play his trump card under better circumstances, but suddenly this was it.

"All right. Well, look," he began, shifting gears quickly. "I was waiting to find the right time to bring you in on this, but . . ." He paused for effect. "I want to get Gravel Rash back together. I want you to manage us."

D.J. coughed.

"Enough with this tribute band bullshit," Mike said haughtily. "Gravel Rash never had its best shot. I still got the chops; you said so. So I couldn't remember the words to fucking Crüe songs? Watch how I still kick the shit outta 'Do Ya Like a Dog.'"

"Dude . . ."

"Taggert hasn't lost a fucking step. The band was always just me and him. We'll fill in with some kick-ass local guys, dust off the old set list. Start writing again. *The Rash is back, motherfucker!*"

"Dude," D.J. said with zero tact. "Nobody knows who the fuck you are."

Mike took the gut shot. "Bullshit! *You* did! The first time I got you on the phone, I thought you were gonna cum in your pants, you were such a Rash fan."

"Yeah, when I was seventeen. Everybody around here knew who you were when they were seventeen. Now they're, like, *forty*. They got jobs, kids. If their wives let them out of the house at all, they're gonna go see the real Ozzy, or a fake Crüe, before they waste time on some band that never even got an album out to help them remember who the fuck you were.

"And if they *do* remember you, they're remembering you at your peak. Time has fucked you up, man. And I've *seen* Jay Taggert."

Mike simmered to keep from getting sad.

"Look," D.J. said earnestly. "Thanks for filling in for us, we appreciated it. Hey, that Poison in Gurnee is still looking for a Bret Michaels. I could make a call, if you—"

Mike slammed shut the cell phone.

While licking his wounds with Taggert a few days later, Mike was offered a job. Taggert played with Cashmere, a steadily employed wedding band. Their set list ranged from the fifties to Kings of Leon, with enough white boy hip-hop and cow-boy hat shitkickers to play to the widest demographic possi-ble. Taggert, who took over his father's carpet store over ten years ago, considered it a sweet deal, pulling in some extra money with his guitar while also getting out of the house most Saturday nights.

The wife of their sound guy just had a premature baby and things were dicey at home, so Cashmere needed someone for the next several weeks. Taggert could tell that Mike was hurting from the Theatre of Pain thing, and he also knew Mike needed money. If the job lasted into the busy summer season, he could clear a few grand, easy.

The first job with Cashmere was at the Radisson in Dela-van, between Holt City and Milwaukee. Taggert insisted that Mike find himself a tuxedo, such was the level of panache that Cashmere brought to their gigs. After learning that renting a tux would almost eat up his whole take for the eve-ning, Mike asked his mother about the boxes of his father's things still in the walk-in attic space over the attached garage. The old man, with his cocktail parties and big fucking deals, must have owned his own tux.

"It'd be thirty years old!" his mother said doubtfully, sur-prised and skittish at the unexpected mention of those boxes of Larry's things. "Who knows what the moths have done?"

"It'd be fine for one night," Mike said. "I just need to take this one job to see if it's even anything I want to do. It's prob-ably bullshit."

"*Mike,*" she scolded.

"Sorry," he said, rolling his eyes. "Come on, will you help me dig through his stuff?"

Her resistance to revisit the past seemed to fade as her troubled, distant son asked for her help. He took things from her all the time, but she couldn't recall him ever asking for something.

"It might just fit," she said, stroking her chin and studying his narrow frame as she warmed to the project.

Mike brought in a folding chair and settled his mother into the attic, its chalky air made thick by the sun beating down on the garage roof. Mike marveled at the crap thrown in here: an old toboggan, the cage for a pair of gerbils John and Mike tried to raise when Mike was barely ten, his father's golf clubs. The boxes of Larry's clothes were stacked neatly in the center of the space.

Rose sat with silent apprehension as Mike pulled open the first box. She sighed as she stood and walked to the box, touching the fabrics lovingly. She brought the lapel of one of the suit coats to her nose and breathed in hopefully, but found nothing of Larry there.

Uncomfortable with the moment he was sharing with his mother, Mike dug deeper into the box. He stopped with a jolt as he came to a jade blue jacket that cut through the muted tones of all of Larry's other wardrobe.

"It's the suit. From the picture," he smiled. "The James Bond suit!"

She smiled as she took the jacket. "Oh, how I hated this thing. I thought it made him look like a gigolo."

The memories rode in like a warm breeze, and then Rose lowered the jacket back into the box.

"No, wait. This is it," Mike said with restrained enthusiasm, holding the jacket before him to estimate its fit. "This is hardcore."

"You said you needed a tuxedo."

"Nah," he said, warming to the image. "This'll be all right." He pulled it on over his mangy T-shirt. "What do you think?"

The sleeves exposed his wrists by over an inch, and the jacket hung loosely on his wiry frame. But the intense blue and the retro cut had a certain rock-and-roll flare.

Rose delighted in seeing Mike wearing anything resembling adult clothing. "It's not bad," she said, still unsure.

Mike felt her hesitation and thought he was being insensitive to her memories being stirred up here. "I don't have to, if . . ."

She straightened the lapels, then stood back to admire the view. "If this will help get you a job, your father would be happy for you to have it."

Thirty-nine

"That's not a tux," Taggert complained as the band set up in the empty ballroom. Taggert's tuxedo was black and spangled with red accents. He matched all the other band members.

"I'll be in the back of the room, in the shadows," Mike said dismissively. "Give me a fucking break." He was already one whiskey in, having charmed the bartender as she began setting up the bar.

"Cashmere is a first-class operation. People expect that of us," Taggert said sternly, his bald head turning pink with worry.

"This was the best I could do on short notice," Mike said. "I'll get us through this one, and by next time I'll have it together. All right?"

Taggert realized he didn't have a choice. "All right. We're

cool." He took a deep breath to center himself. "Are we ready to rock and roll?"

Tiffany and Brad, the bride and groom, were somewhere between twenty-five and thirty. The formative rock-and roll-years for themselves and their friends were the early 2000s. This meant a set list full of Matchbox Twenty, Nickleback, and Maroon 5—a bunch of pop rock wienies Mike didn't know by name but whose jangly, ball-less hits made his teeth grind.

The sound job was as easy as Taggert promised: knock back the volume if feedback bled through, keep the mud out of the bass notes, hit some simple lighting cues, and turn on the re-corded music when the band took its breaks.

The whiskey Mike kept cadging from the bar left him loose. The bartender had coke, too. While she was no looker and had a hard-living husk that wouldn't have been his first choice, Mike got signals that he might get into her pants when their jobs were through.

"Motherfuck!" Mike heard over his shoulder at the sound board while the crowd mingled during the first band break. "It *is* you."

A flushed, bleary-eyed guest in a tuxedo clutched a glass as he teetered before Mike.

"Mike *Fucking* Husted," he said in drunken wonder. "Gravel Rash rules!" He whooped too loudly, punctuating the declaration with the universal metal offering of the dou-ble devil horn salute.

"All right," Mike smiled cautiously, getting bad vibes instantly. The guy had the leathery skin and dark, dead eyes of a powder keg drunk. When you spent as much time as Mike had in bars, you recognized the sort of guy who routinely staggered along the razor's edge between being a fun drunk and a toxically evil fuck when he drank too much. He was obviously well on his way to the latter

"Saw you guys, like, a million times," his fan said proudly. "The Axe Tavern? Pokey's? Hard Franny's? You guys tore those dumps *up!*"

"We tried," Mike said curtly.

"What happened to you guys?" the drunk demanded. "You were like hot shit, and then you were fucking nothing."

Mike ground his teeth. "You know, whatever."

"Man, you guys *rocked,*" the drunk said obliviously. "Jay Taggert? Motherfuck! That guy could play like Slash and Eddie Van Halen *combined*! Hey," he boasted, "I caught crabs once from a girl he used to do. Didn't he OD or something?"

Mike couldn't help himself. "Nah. You've been watching him. That's him."

He pointed in the direction of Taggert, who just returned to the ballroom and headed to the sound board with a look of concern on his face. The disturbance caused by the drunk apparently made its way to the break room.

Taggert didn't have his hat on.

"Ewwww," the drunk cringed as he saw his one-time guitar hero approach. But by the time Taggert joined them, his fan worship returned.

"Jay Fucking Taggert. Motherfuck!" he beamed dizzily as he pumped Taggert's hand. "We mighta had the same crabs!"

Taggert looked to Mike with disapproval as the drunk suddenly grabbed Brad, the groom, and dragged him into their circle.

"Dude, do you have any idea who you got playing your wedding?" he slurred. It took Mike an instant to figure out that the drunk was an older brother. "These guys were fucking Gravel Rash!"

Brad would have been about ten when Gravel Rash was at their peak. "Cool," he said dismissively, taking his brother by the elbow. "Hey, Shawn, you need to have a seat and chill out. Please?"

Shawn yanked his arm away with an angry sneer.

"Hey," Shawn blurted toward Mike and Taggert. "You guys gotta play something. Together! *Gravel Rash!!!*" He whooped loudly.

Others started gathering to contain him. Some wore tuxes; more family members, probably all too familiar with having to shut down their sad, angry party clown.

"Shawn," one of them barked. "That's fucking *it*!"

Shawn took a drunken swing, missing by a mile. Acid seethed in his eyes; the shit was about to be unleashed. Taggert took control.

"Tell you what, man," Taggert said firmly, steadying Shawn at the shoulders. "Have a seat. Let your brother and his lady enjoy their evening, all right? In the last set, if everything's cool, we'll lay some Rash on ya. How 'bout it?"

Taggert looked past the drunk to Mike with a shake of his head: there was no fucking way that was going to happen.

But it was enough to defuse the situation. That puke-teasing pressure drop that inevitably hits all drunks announced itself to Shawn. He accepted Taggert's promise with a slurring *Gravel Rash Rules!!!* accidentally jabbed his aunt in the head with his flaccid devil horns, and allowed himself to be led to a chair.

"Thanks," the groom said to Taggert with a bit of an edge.

"It's all good," Taggert said to Brad with a salesman's smile. "You good? Come on, let's get this party going again!"

Taggert shared a disapproving grimace with Mike before gathering his band and heading back to the stage. Mike cut the recorded music, set the volume levels for the musicians, and went back to the bar.

The last two sets played out without incident. The music got sweatier and more credible as the old folks drifted off. Just past 1:30, the band wrapped up a hellacious version of Guns N' Roses' "Paradise City" and the singer started to announce their farewell.

"Aw right! Whoo!" he sweated. "Y'all have been a great crowd, thanks for rockin' with Cashmere this evening. Congratulations one more time to Tiffany and Brad, many beautiful years of livin' and lovin.' We got time for one more song, then we gotta—"

"Gravel Rash!!!" Shawn demanded boozily from the back of the room. He jostled the remaining guests as he elbowed his way to the dance floor. The singer squinted into the dimly lit room.

"So we're gonna leave you with . . ." he tried to continue. Shawn was suddenly at the front of the stage.

"Gravel Rash, motherfucker!!!"

His brothers tried to pull him back, but the glassy-eyed rage with which Shawn yanked away indicated his fury was back for one last encore.

"We don't know that one, brother," the singer smiled slickly. "But how 'bout you let Lenny Kravitz take us home with 'Are You Gonna—' "

Suddenly Mike was on the stage, weaving with determination toward the microphone. The next day, he would swear he was just trying to help.

He grabbed the mike from the singer. "Aw right!" Mike shouted. "Let's do this thing!" He still wore his father's blue jacket.

He turned as he had so many times to Taggert, waiting to count them in. But Taggert was already in his face. He knew in an instant that Mike was high.

"Get off the stage," he said grimly as Shawn teetered excitedly at their feet at the front of the low stage.

"Rash! Rash! Rash!" Some younger revelers, new to binge drinking and impressed by Shawn's blotto panache, started egging him on. Tiffany, herself pretty drunk, began to glare at Brad for allowing his brother to wreck her reception.

"C'mon," Mike said into Taggert's ear. "The dude is about

to blow. We lay a little 'Miss Mercy' on him and he'll shut the fuck up. You'll be a hero."

"Miss Mercy" was a Gravel Rash original, a raucous Chuck Berry–style raveup. Gravel Rash had had a bunch of them, but "Miss Mercy" *rocked* and without the endless guitar soloing that had been its trademark it could be over in under three minutes.

Taggert looked to the angry bride—his client—and he made the call.

"Chuck Berry, in A" he said tensely to his confused band. "Follow me."

Mike tauntingly nodded Cashmere's singer from the stage and posed at the mike stand as Taggert counted them in.

"One, two, three, *four*."

The band locked in from the first driving note, Mike eagerly anticipated the first lyrics, and Shawn hooted gutturally as he recognized the song.

And then he vomited great goopy globs of wedding cake and Chicken Kiev all over the dance floor. The boyfriend of the bridesmaid took the chunkiest hit, and he spun Shawn around and punched him brutally in the jaw. One of Shawn's brothers went for the bridesmaid's boyfriend, hooking him by the neck and yanking him to the floor. The song came to a ragged end as the first beer bottle flew. Mike never got to sing a word.

"Hey!" he shouted into the mike above the tussle. The whiskey and the coke and the adrenaline had the room beginning to spin. "What the fuck, motherfuckers?"

Cashmere's singer came back to the mike to take back

control of the room. Mike drunkenly shoved him off the front of the stage, onto a different bridesmaid and then down into the vomit.

The singer came back up in an instant, yanking Mike down at the legs and then leaping on top of him on the stage. They began to thrash and punch wildly. The crash of a knocked-over cymbal punctuated the beginning of what in a movie would've been a wackily choreographed barroom brawl, but was in real life pathetic and clumsy and just long enough to make things ugly for everyone.

Hotel security threw on the house lights and one of the guests—an off-duty county sheriff—took control. Thick-necked and crew-cutted, he forcefully pulled apart everyone who didn't have the sense to leave the dance floor on their own. But when he got to the stage, he seemed to employ added gusto to the lanky scuzzball in the blue jacket who was on the stage when the fight broke out.

He yanked Mike up from the floor by his lapels, but Mike came up swinging without sizing up the brawn of his adversary. Flailing with doped-up frenzy, he drove a decent punch into the sheriff's ear before the now-furious cop shoved Mike backward.

Taggert and some others held the cop back long enough for him to think better of kicking the shit out of Mike. Bleeding from his ear, he yanked himself away from the arms holding him back and produced his badge, pointing furiously at Mike.

"Sit down," he snarled. "Don't fucking *think* of leaving."

Beyond the cop, Mike could see the red and blue flicker of police lights dart across the ballroom's opaque curtains as a squad car rolled into the parking lot.

The vial that he stole from the bartender had shattered in his pocket during the fight. The broken glass cut his thigh; his pocket was sticky with nearly eight ounces of bloody cocaine.

When John bailed Mike out the next morning, he didn't recognize the torn, stained blue jacket his brother wore.

"What did they say?" John asked in the car, exasperated and mad. *"Exactly?"*

Mike was tired. His head hurt.

"Dunno," he sighed to the passing traffic. "The vial broke, the coke got mixed with the blood, so they can't measure it the usual way. If they can't prove there was enough to show intent to sell, they have to bust it down to possession. They might just give me community service."

"You punched a sheriff."

"He was off-duty," Mike complained. "They gotta cut me slack on that."

"With *your* record?" John asked skeptically.

"Yeah," Mike sagged dispiritedly. He turned to John for the first time.

"Don't tell Mom."

John tried to study his brother as he drove. Something new was at play here.

They drove in silence while Mike stared out the window. He unconsciously picked at one of the frayed rips in the blue suit coat and took a deep breath.

"For all those years, I wasn't around. Or I was, but I was fucked up," Mike began quietly. "Now, me and her are living in the same house, we got nothing but time. But even if I wanted to make things right with her, she can't make sense of it anymore."

John knew his brother never spent much time alone in his skull, contemplating. The morning he spent in that jail cell had obviously given him time to think.

"Intent to sell would get me a year. If I was *lucky*," Mike said hollowly.

"You've done the time before," John said.

"Yeah. But even if it was just six months . . ." Mike trailed off, staring dead ahead. "It doesn't look like she'll still be here when I get back.

"She'll *be* here, but . . ."

He tapped his head as the truth of what Mike was dealing with struck John hard. Because it was true. And because Mike had found his way to it.

The silence hung in the air. "She's going so fast," Mike said.

Another long silence. Neither knew how to be this way with each other.

"So then this is the time you have," John finally said decisively. "You just have to hold it together, *stay straight,* until one of you goes away. Until then, you've got time."

John saw his brother's eyes well up before he turned away. He watched his brother's shoulders heave as he tried to hide his crying.

This was the time Mike had, John thought to himself. Things could not wait any longer.

Forty

It began like this:

"Did you ever hear Dad talk like Donald Duck?"

John waited a couple days, until Mike's drug bust slid into a predictable state of legal limbo. With his fate forestalled by red tape and systematic indifference, it didn't take long for Mike to resume the grumpy pose John could now see through.

Mike reflexively shot back the baffled and barbed glare he leveled on his little brother whenever he spoke nonsense.

"What?"

They sat across a table at Rocky's, John mysteriously having invited Mike out for dinner. Mike ordered the prime rib sandwich and a series of beers; John looked sweaty and settled for a glass of water.

"I mean," John meandered unsteadily, "what do you really remember about him?"

"He was always in my shit," Mike recalled bitterly. "Twenty-four seven."

"That was at the end," John said quickly. "But you two didn't start going at it until you started getting high and pushing the bands, when you were thirteen or fourteen. All those years before that, when you got along, he was like . . . Dad. Right?"

Mike shrugged. John pressed on.

"Little League. Cub Scouts. Christmas morning. Before you started hating each other, you were a kid and he was your dad and, you know, things were *okay*."

"When he had time for us," Mike sniffed.

"Yeah," John agreed. "But, I'm just saying. Even with how it ended, he did all right by you for a long time. Longer than he *didn't*. Right?"

"You are so gay," Mike chuckled derisively.

Mike finished off the last of his sandwich, and instantly two huge sundaes were lowered onto the table. The brothers looked up.

"Do they have free sundaes in jail?" Sheila the waitress sternly inquired of Mike. She had been hovering throughout lunch, this being her first chance to nag Mike in years.

"No, ma'am," he said compliantly, without attitude.

"Are free sundaes important to you?"

"Yes, ma'am," Mike said.

"Any chance you can keep your skinny butt out of jail so that you and me can keep this good thing going?"

"I'm trying, ma'am."

"Try harder," she glowered good-naturedly before turning to John. "Why aren't you eating?"

"I'm not—"

"You take care of yourselves," the waitress decreed sagely to the pair of them, "you take care of each other, and you take care of your mom. I waited on your father long enough to know that's what he would've expected from the two of you."

"Got it," John smiled, grateful beyond measure for the bridge she provided to their past. She tallied up their bill and slapped it on the table.

"Tip generously," she said, then whispered: *"He's watching."* She pointed heavenward and winked.

John and Mike smiled as they watched her retreat to the kitchen. Mike shook his head with wry fondness as he dug into the sundae. John still had no appetite as he stared past his brother to the hospital.

The sun had fully set. It was time to cross the street.

Mike followed skeptically, sufficiently bonded with his brother from the nostalgia that enveloped them in the restaurant. But as John briskly led him around the back of the old hospital into the dense shadows, he began to get rattled.

"Dude," Mike laughed uneasily as his younger brother produced a key to the door behind the dumpster. "What the fuck are you doing?"

"I told you, you gotta check this out," John said in the rare position of being the bad influence on his older brother. "It's a trip."

He made sure to observe the illicit look of anticipation on Mike's face as the door creaked open. As intrigued as he was, Mike feared detection as he looked to confirm that no one was watching them.

"Man, I've got a sentence hanging over my head. I can't afford to get caught—"

"C'mon," John said cockily, holding the door open and gesturing him in. "Don't be so gay."

"Jesus, I remember all this," Mike whispered as their flashlights did their best to reignite his memories of the old patient wing. He looked to the dull, dusty tiles beneath his feet. "The floors were like ice after they got waxed. I'd take my shoes off, get a running start, and I could slide almost all the way down to that corner in my socks."

He smiled as he pointed.

"I'd run around, not giving a fuck that people were sick and dying inside these rooms. Dad finally took me into one of them; I must've been around six. This old lady was like a hundred, and she was crying. Crying, like a baby—just bawling—because she hurt so much.

"He told me to stop being such an obnoxious pain in the ass around people he was trying to help."

They explored every inch of the old building: the empty gift shop, the pharmacy, the chapel. Some of it was new to John and he enjoyed poking around the spooky new corners with his big brother.

They stood uneasily once they realized they stumbled

upon the old morgue; its cold, steel tables with drains and rotted hoses still on display. John hung back as Mike took it all in, his morbid curiosity undercut with something deeper as he studied one of the tables. His eyes followed the path from the operating surface to the trough to the drain that flushed everything away.

Maybe he was thinking of the dead girl he slept with in Rhode Island before his world caved in. Maybe he was thinking of their father.

John was imagining how best to tell Mike practically from the moment Walt Bolger told *him*. The slow buildup and the gradual reveal that the old man used with John had no doubt felt necessary, and it did its job in John's case. But accepting the full story, from Larry's stroke to room 116 and the decades in-between, required more cognitive dexterity than John knew his simple-minded brother could process. John would fill in the details after Mike's mind was blown by what he was brought to, but first he had to get him there.

"You need to get ready to get your head around something totally fucked up," John said forebodingly once they reached the room. Profanity from his straitlaced brother always struck Mike as amusing, but he stopped smiling when he saw John shaking.

Mike looked to the closed door, and then back to John. Something big loomed.

John let it come bluntly, to get it done.

"Dad's not dead. He's been alive, all this time," John said. "You're going to see him now." And he opened the door.

John stepped in. Mike did not. The words John just said, the macabre pristineness of the room inside, the form in the shadowy bed that was visible from the hallway—it all froze Mike in place as his mind began to churn.

John agonized as Mike's uncomprehending eyes met his. "Come on, Mike," he said gently, taking his brother at the elbow. "You need to do this."

John got him into the room, but Mike would go no farther. His chest began to heave from a shortness of breath as his eyes locked upon the man in the bed. John had earlier positioned Larry facing into the room, but with the dim light, the toll that time and disease took on Larry and the madness of the moment, Mike found it easy to push back the truth.

He looked to John, certain instead that his brother had lost his mind.

"What the fuck are you doing in here?" Mike whispered sharply, finally taking in the carefully staged comfort of the room.

"That's Dad, Mike," John whispered, gently but firmly. "It's him."

Mike wasn't having it. *"What the fuck are you doing in here?"*

"Look at him. Just look at him."

The plaintive urging of his little brother compelled Mike to take one step closer. The view was clearer now. Mike was old enough to remember his grandfather—Larry's dad—before the old man died at sixty-seven, eaten away by cancer.

The resemblance was there on the man in the bed. That family face was there.

Mike's legs failed him and he sank to his knees. His head filled with helium and white noise as wracking sobs overtook him.

If there were words for the moment, they came out only as choked, baffled gasps. John knelt beside his brother and held him as Mike quivered at the unexpected and relentless flood of emotion.

"I know," John whispered, rubbing Mike's shoulder beneath his long, dirty hair. "I know."

Mike finally made it to Larry's bedside, and John left the two of them alone. John stayed outside the room for as long as Mike needed, and then they sat in the hall as John walked him through the journey that brought them here.

As Mike sat beside his brother and John laid out the plot that Walt Bolger carried out, John saw the fury and disbelief pass across Mike's face. But it was tempered by a humbled calm that John had gambled would be there. It might not last, but the same momentousness that slammed John into accepting this as an opportunity to reclaim their father seemed to have struck Mike the same way.

Mike's eyes remained locked on the door to his father's room. "You end up hating somebody—really *hating* them," he said softly. "But the whole time, maybe you're thinking, 'On the other side of all this *shit*, maybe we could be cool with each other someday.' You know? When we were older, we'd work it all out.

"But then out of nowhere he up and dies, and we never . . ."

He gave into another bout of tears. John allowed him a moment, but then he resolved to get to the responsibility left to them.

"What are we going to do about Mom?" John asked.

Mike felt the shock as the full weight of what they needed to do hit him.

"Fuck!" Mike groaned hopelessly as he replayed what he just endured. "She can't . . . If we . . .

"Fuck!!!"

The answer wasn't going to come to them just then. They stood and sighed heavily in tandem. John turned to lead them out, but Mike wasn't ready to go. He stared at his father's door.

"Go on back in," John said, sitting back down. "I'll wait."

"You come, too," Mike said softly as he opened the door and gestured John in. "We'll hang out. The three of us."

Forty-one

Katie's school recognized her as one of the top artists in her class. While she invested predictable teenaged energy into deflecting praise and protested anything as humiliating as a party for her and her friends at her grandmother's house, John could tell at the gallery exhibit that she was shyly excited to be recognized for her talents.

Since the exhibit recognized the full range of her work, it went back a few years. The arc of her creative skills but also the swing in her persona were clearly charted, with mixed-media projects of simple beauty and whimsy gradually giving way to grim black-and-white photo studies and stark, disquieting charcoal landscapes.

Back at her grandmother's house, food sat uneaten as Katie's mopey crowd generally failed to attend. Friends from earlier years—freshly scrubbed and a bit dweeby—filtered through the house, grazing on snacks and making polite conversation with Katie's proud grandmother. They smiled nervously as Rose's disordered thinking tumbled out in tangles. After answering over and over again how they knew Katie and where they went to school, they graciously slipped away.

The handful of goths who stopped by gathered sullenly in the living room, sitting in the shadows and watching a 1982 episode of *Match Game* on the Game Show Network. They surrounded Mike, who had been ordered to the family gathering by his mother. Other than sleeping in the old family house at night, Mike stayed away since he found out about Larry. He barely said a word at the party.

"Hey," one kid mumbled to Mike when the game show went to a commercial. "Katie says you used to be somebody. In a band."

Mike stared back mutely.

"You still know how to score dope?"

Mike glowered and went for the sliding door into the backyard. John was on him before he lit his cigarette.

"Where have you been?" John asked.

"Around."

"You're supposed to be *here*."

Mike wouldn't meet his eye. John knew the signs.

"You're high," he said darkly.

"Whatever."

"We need to tell her!" John hissed. "You're supposed to help me."

Mike looked past him to their mother, standing in her backyard and chatting amiably with a longtime neighbor.

"This is gonna fuck her up," Mike said moodily but with concern. "If we tell her, this is gonna seriously fuck her up."

"We have to tell her. You agreed."

Mike took a long drag on his cigarette. "I brought up Don Huff the other day. She had no idea who the guy was," he laughed bitterly. "Asshole walked away with most of her money, made it so she's stuck living in this shitty old house, and she has no memory of ever knowing him. She doesn't even get to hate him anymore because as far as she knows they never met. How fucked up is that?"

"She remembers Dad," John protested.

"Who knows what's left of him in that head of hers? He could be all gone in there, until—boom!—there he fucking is again. Thanks to us.

"'Larry's back, Mom, deal with it.' You really want to lay that on her?"

They watched from across the yard as Robin sidled up to Rose and rested her hand on her back. She helped the neighbor understand what Rose tried to say.

"Dean Durning means it," John said to Mike. "I can't buy any more time with him."

"Dean Durning," Mike sneered. "I oughta go kick his ass."

"Yeah, that'll be good. An assault charge is all you need to keep you out of jail."

Mike sagged impotently.

"He's going to pull the plug," John said impatiently. "We may not even know about it until it's done. If we're wrong about giving her the chance to see him one last time, I don't want that hanging over my head for the rest of my life."

Mike drew on his cigarette icily. "You wanted my help figuring this out, I say we don't tell her. I think that's the thing to do, seeing where she's at.

"If we're wrong," he said with a shrug, "you get used to things hangin' over your head."

Later, Rose found her sons in lawn chairs on the back patio as the sun went down and Robin cleaned up in the kitchen. Their mother was in her nightgown as she sat down in the twilight.

"I'm tired," she yawned contentedly.

"You should go to bed," John said.

Rose looked across the yard. Some strands of a thought vexed her. "Wasn't that something, what she said? The whole thing?"

John had no idea what she was talking about but invested himself in wherever she wanted to go with it. "It was!" he said in agreement. "I couldn't believe it."

"Shouldn't someone know the way?"

"I think so. I told her I'd ask."

"Someone really should," Rose said. "Will you let me know? I really want to know. It's not right." It troubled her, whatever it was.

"I will. But I told her it would take two weeks. So just don't let it bother you until then. Okay?"

That seemed to bring Rose some peace.

Mike watched. He always got exasperated and cranky try-ing to talk to his mother, but he saw how John just rolled with whatever she talked about. It didn't seem to matter what you said back so long as you listened and returned words back to her.

"*You* should know," she said to Mike, who took a moment to realize he was drawn in. "For all the times it did it to you. Right?"

"I think so," Mike said awkwardly, sensing how it worked. "I think you figured it out."

"With the birds!" she smiled.

Mike clucked indignantly. "It's a joke without the birds," he said, like you'd have to be an asshole to not want it with the birds.

"See! *We* know," she grinned before giving into a fuzzy yawn. "I'm tired."

"You should go to bed," John said.

"I think I will," she said sleepily as she stood and then stooped down to kiss John's cheek. "Goodnight. Don't let the bed bugs bite."

"Okay."

She kissed Mike. "Don't be out too late."

"I'm in for the night," he said. "I'll be here."

"I like that," she said. "And then, three more! Can you believe it?"

"Three is really something," Mike agreed.

"Three!" Rose marveled as she turned to amble barefoot across the lawn. "I'll tell Robin."

She stepped unsteadily into the house and John and

Mike watched through the kitchen window as she spoke to Robin with fervor. Robin nodded earnestly as she dried a coffee cup.

Mike's cigarette ash dotted the dimming light as both men sighed and said nothing.

Forty-two

John had begun missing deadlines. Because of Next Step's reputation and relationships, many of the smaller foundations—donating a grand here, three grand there—would still accept a proposal a few days late and a bit fuzzy around the edges.

But Betty Stienke was not to be messed with. Dead since 1967, as a girl she married into a tannery empire that thrived in the Midwest for nearly one hundred years, and she died with millions. The Betty S. Stienke Foundation hovered over the philanthropic landscape as one of the richest sources of human services funding in southeast Wisconsin for decades, and Next Step earned tens of thousands of dollars every year from the foundation's long-serving and ruthlessly inflexible foundation manager.

Every year when it came time to reapply to Stienke, John felt the future of the agency—and the lives of those they tried to help—riding on his shoulders as he hunkered down and ground out the complicated grant proposal. He never failed to bring in the money.

But this year Stienke fell right in the thick of his Larry dilemma, and John cut corners. Five days past deadline, he finally cobbled together entire blocks of text from previous grants and knocked it out while sitting at Larry's bedside in the middle of the night. The budget he included with the funding request was a lazy approximation of predicted revenue and expenses.

It ate at John to turn in something so slipshod, but he gambled that almost two decades of a productive relationship between foundation and agency would earn him a pass for an off year. When Stienke came around again in twelve months, Larry would be gone and John's head would be back in the game.

He was asleep on his couch when Fred Kirby, Next Step's executive director, called and told him he needed to see him right away.

"What happened with Stienke?" Fred began gravely as soon as John sat down in his shambles of an office.

Past retirement age, Fred was a supremely decent man and as close to a father figure as John had ever allowed himself. It was Fred who trusted John to set his own hours and meet his deadlines without oversight, and John never let him down. So he despaired to hear the uneasy tone in his boss's voice.

"I told Kurt Stamper that I was going to be a few days

past deadline," John squirmed. "He was his usual grouchy self, but he was okay with it. Is he saying—?"

Fred held the proposal in his hand. Seeing a printed copy for the first time, half the thickness of a typical Stienke appeal, John's heart sank at what he tried to get away with.

"What is this?" Fred asked plaintively. "This is not what we turn in to them."

John went gray with regret. "There were things going on, at home. I had a lot of things on my plate, and . . ."

"I told Stamper you must have just emailed the wrong file," Fred continued hopefully. "This is a draft. Right?"

"Look," John protested weakly. "They know what we do here. They know we've never been anything other than one-hundred-percent responsible with their money. They expect us to jump through the same hoops for them every year, but just because—"

Fred flipped through the pages with alarm. "These are just pieces of past proposals. You didn't even take out the other funder's name on one page." Fred held it up; a crotchety circle was scrawled around the offending word. Kurt Stamper had caught John not even bothering to use search and replace to catch the mistake.

John winced and sagged.

"The foundation is spending down. They're cutting back on who they're supporting until the funds are gone. And now we've fallen off their automatic renewal list," Fred said gravely. "He's sending us to the board for review. They're going to be looking at us closely, asking a lot of questions.

"In this economy, if they decide there are other agencies who are doing what we do more efficiently . . . We could *lose* this."

John's face burned with regret. Fred studied him with personal concern that undercut this perilous threat to the agency.

"How did this happen?" the old man asked patiently. "What's going on?"

"It's just . . ." John sighed. More than once he longed to unburden himself to Fred about his father, knowing that he could trust Fred with a secret.

"I'm just going through a rough patch at home," he said.

"I knew your marriage was having some problems," Fred offered sympathetically.

"Well, you know," John said, sitting up defensively. "When you're married for a long time, things change, but that doesn't mean that . . ." He trailed off, realizing that the only cover he had was marital discord.

"We've been working through some things, but I think we're going to be fine. It's just been . . . hard."

"I understand," Fred said sincerely, before rattling the meager pages of the Stienke proposal. "But, John, this is serious." Fred had been dealing with health problems and John knew he had been trying to find a successor since before the economy went bad. If they lost one of their top funders, finding someone to take over for him would be impossible.

"We have nothing to fear going before their board," John said confidently. "We do good work here. It's about *time* they take a closer look at us, to see what all we're accomplishing with not a hell of a lot of money.

"Things are so tough out there, they might decide they want to give us—"

Ozzy Osbourne's "Crazy Train" rumbled out of John's pants. Mike almost never called; something had to be up. John squirmed awkwardly as he tried to fish his cell from his pocket.

"I'm sorry," he said to Fred. "I really need to . . ."

He answered the phone. "Hey, I need to call you back. I'm in the middle of—"

"You need to get down to the mall," Mike cut in sharply. "Right now."

John met his boss's eye with unease. "Can't you deal with it?"

"No. She went over to Macy's with Mrs. Ludlow and store security called and said I had to get over here and . . . I'm not dealing with this shit alone."

John grimaced. "I'll be right there."

He hung up and stood. "I'm sorry," he pleaded to Fred. "I'm on the tail end of resolving this. I won't let you down again. But . . ."

"Go," Fred said.

"Stienke's going to be fine."

"I hope so."

A store employee led John through housewares, intimate apparel, and travel accessories. The store on a Monday morning was sterile and half-empty. The piped in music played Céline Dion. Her heart was going on.

They moved from the customer side of the operation to the airless row of management offices. Passing a lounge area partitioned by a large window, John saw his mother sitting alone on a bank of vinyl chairs. Mrs. Ludlow, a neighbor since the day the family moved into the house decades ago, sat apart from her, looking ashen and unsure.

Rose sat compactly, staring at her hands.

Instead of being taken to her, John followed the assistant manager around a corner to find Mike, pacing agitatedly with an unlit cigarette in his mouth. His usual shabbiness clashed particularly harshly with the antiseptic corporate offices.

Mike came alive at seeing his brother. "What the fuck, man? What took you so long?"

"What happened?" John asked.

Mike was coiled to flee. He'd already heard the whole story. "Look, you're gonna have to—"

A door marked STORE SECURITY opened and a middle-aged man with a kind face emerged. He seemed relieved to see John but reticent to proceed following a tepid handshake. "You must be Rose's other son. I'm Ted Reichard, the manager here. Please, come in."

He gestured both brothers into the security room. Having missed his chance to escape, Mike warily followed John in.

The security room lacked any air of covert mystery whatsoever, just a cramped little nook off the employee lunchroom. Monitors over a video deck showed vulnerable corners of the store. Shoppers blandly went about their business as cameras spied on them.

John and Mike were directed to sit in the two chairs at the security console. The manager stood as he proceeded. He couldn't have known that Mike hadn't had time to tell John what happened.

"We are trying to be as sensitive to this as possible," he began. "We know your mother has her challenges, and I can't imagine how embarrassing this is for her.

"But when she became upset and started threatening lawsuits over how we have dealt with the situation, it became my job to protect the store's interests. I think you should watch what happened, and then we can talk about where we go from here."

John squirmed as Mike stared at the floor.

The manager pushed a button and one of the monitors played back silent, grainy images from a dressing room. The camera was trained on an empty stall as a store employee walked past.

On the tape, a customer emerged from behind a closed stall door, looking displeased with what she tried on. John leaned in as Rose and Mrs. Ludlow walked into view, each with prospective purchases draped over their arms. Rose loved to shop; even without the audio, John could see that she was in good spirits. She tried to chipperly follow Mrs. Ludlow into her dressing room before being redirected into a stall of her own. She closed the door behind her.

The voyeuristic queasiness grew as Rose's feet, a few

inches apart, showed through the gap below the stall door. She appeared to sit down. Her feet were still, apart from some unsteady shifting, then she slid down her clothes and they balled up at her ankles.

A deathly few moments passed, and then a customer walking past the fitting rooms slipped before catching herself.

She looked down, then registered disgust as she examined her shoes. She studied Rose's closed door with incomprehension, walked out of view for several moments, then returned with a young store employee. Both tried to avoid the puddle.

The angle and the quality of the image muted the full reality of it, but it was obvious what happened. John's heart constricted.

On the video playback, the store employee delicately knocked on the stall door. Rose's feet shuffled unsteadily before she opened the door, the camera for a moment catching her pulling up her skirt and realizing that everything was soaked in urine. The store worker was admirable for her discretion and kind handling, but Rose was obviously confused and mortified.

"My sister had Alzheimer's," Reichard said softly. "I can imagine what happened. Your Mom was overstimulated from being at the mall, she steps alone into a stall, she disrobes. She just forgot where she was, that's all."

Seeing Rose's stricken face on the video, cornered and ashamed in that tiny room, was too much for Mike as he bolted from the room.

On the monitor, Mrs. Ludlow stepped into view. Quickly

assessing the situation, she attempted to step into the stall with Rose and close the door behind them, but Rose quickly became obstinate.

Either to deflect her embarrassment or in a true inability to process what was happening, she began lashing out at everyone. Embarrassed shoppers moved past, trying to avoid the crazy lady, as Reichard himself appeared on the tape to try and gracefully defuse the situation. His concern and gentle touch was clear.

Mrs. Ludlow finally got Rose alone in the stall and closed the door. An employee quickly brought fresh clothes.

"We got her cleaned up as quick as we could," Reichard said. "We got her fresh clothes, which we are happy to let her keep. I believe that we handled a sensitive situation as delicately as we possibly could, but . . . She was *really* angry before we were able to calm her down."

John wasn't listening anymore.

He stepped from the security office. He was not surprised to not see Mike with their mother, looking tinier than ever.

Mrs. Ludlow smiled at John before leaving the two of them alone. John sat down beside Rose and put his arm around her.

"Hi, Mom."

"Hello," she said defeatedly. He kissed her temple. They sat in silence for a moment.

"I had to see a man about a horse," Rose finally said simply.

"Sounds like," he smiled as he pulled her closer.

She smiled, too, but then sagged. "I'm sorry."

"Nothing to be sorry about," he said. They fell silent again, neither anxious to leave. To have to walk back out through the mall, forever garish and carefree, felt cruel.

He finally rubbed her back. "It's past lunchtime, you must be starving. Let's go to Rocky's. My treat."

He stood, but she pulled away.

"Mom. Nobody is ever going to know."

"You don't know that."

"Nobody will know," he said firmly, offering his hand. "I promise."

Forty-three

John and Robin sat across their kitchen table. John cradled a cup of coffee as if its heat might cauterize what hurt him.

"She can't be on her own anymore," he said. "Mike is useless."

There were only two options left for the care of Rose. Robin would've been within her rights to lobby for the less intrusive one, but John wasn't surprised when she didn't.

"We'll fix up the spare room," she said without hesitation. "Your job will allow you to be here for her during the day—assuming you *keep* your job. We can all work with her at night."

John studied his wife, grateful for the compassion she had for his mother.

"This isn't a very big house," he pointed out.

"She isn't a very big woman."

"Things would really change around here," he continued, "for all of us. Christ, we're just heading into the worst of it with Katie. Can we really deal with her *and* Mom at the same time?"

"It would do our daughter good to be around someone with real problems, instead of the self-pitying drama she and her mopey little friends wallow in," Robin said, finishing her coffee and then standing to get more. "Maybe she'll start seeing them for what they are."

John smiled at her gruff wisdom and watched her at the coffeemaker. He waited until she returned with the pot and refilled his cup.

"You and me aren't a hundred percent," he said quietly, conceding the truth that had been living with them for too long. "Moving my mother in here isn't going to help with our . . . closeness issues."

"You think?" she drawled sarcastically. He smiled, but then she undercut the lightness with blunt reality.

"It won't be forever," she said. "She's changing fast, John. It's coming fast."

He knew this, but despaired at hearing it.

"I want to have her here, for as long as we can responsibly take care of her," Robin continued. "But there's going to come a time when she's going to have to go where she can be safe. We need to start looking into that now, because a decent place will be expensive and her long-term plan isn't going to cover all of it."

John's insides constricted at the problems yet to come. Robin saw this and took his hand.

"We'll deal with that when it comes. For now, I want you to be here for her."

Robin continued. "I've watched how you've thrown yourself into caring for your father, even when there was nothing you could do for him. You still have time with your mom. While she still can, I want her to know how lucky she is to have you looking out for her."

Tears teased their way into his eyes and he didn't bother to push back at them. "I love you," he told her.

"I know you do," she said. "I love you, too."

He swabbed at the emotion pooled in his eyes and tickling his nose, then sighed as he sized up their kitchen.

"This really *is* a small house," he said.

"It's fine."

"You know," he said tentatively. "That old house of hers has a lot of room."

"We are not moving into your mother's house."

"Okay," he said, surrendering quickly and wisely. She wasn't convinced.

"For a lot of reasons," she said firmly, "I am not moving into that house."

"Okay."

She bore down: "If we moved into that house, it would come with a fully installed *Mike*."

"Understood."

"I am only so wonderful."

Forty-four

John and Mike stood at the living room window, watching Rose in her garden with Mrs. Ludlow. A male cardinal sat on the bird feeder, and Mike guessed Rose was engaging Mrs. Ludlow in her search for the bird's mate as the two old ladies searched the trees. Paired-off cardinals never let themselves get too far from each other, Rose would always tell her sons when they were boys.

Neither took their eyes off her as Mike spoke with uncommon focus.

"If we tell her, about Dad," he began, having walked through this for himself ahead of time, "and it's a *good* thing, then we'll know we made the right call. Forever. No matter how bad things get as she gets worse, we'll have that—the three of us. The *four* of us," he recalculated, surprising both brothers. It would be kind of like getting the band back together, with all original members.

"No matter what fucked-up path it took to get us there," Mike reasoned, "if telling her turns out good, that's like a family thing we could all do together. It'd be all right."

"Yep," John agreed.

"But if we tell her, and it goes bad," Mike flinched darkly. "It could go really, *really* bad. Like, 'We had no idea how badly this was going to go' bad. Like, *'What the fuck were we thinking?'*"

"I know," John said.

"But," Mike continued hopefully. "Even if it went really bad, she might forget we told her. Eventually. Maybe."

"I don't know," John said doubtfully.

Mike conceded the point with a shrug before proceeding.

"But you and me, we wouldn't forget," he said bluntly. "If it's hell, if telling her turns out to be the most awful thing we ever have to go through, it's gonna stick with us until the day we fucking die. Letting her know could hit her as hard as the day Dad died, and *we* let it happen."

John had considered this. *A lot.*

"So," Mike began to sum up, "are we not telling her because of what we're afraid it will do to her? Or to *us*?"

The reality of his big brother's question stunned John, both for its implication and for the fact that Mike got to it first.

Mike had been spending most of his time at Larry's bedside, pulling from his father what he could, while he could. He had obviously been doing a lot of thinking. Maybe Larry, in his way, helped push his boys to take action.

"Because if we're saying there's a *chance* knowing about Dad will make her happy, then we gotta grow a pair and get this done," Mike continued. " 'Cause time's gonna come where she's not gonna get to be happy about anything. Forever."

The simple truth of this landed on John hard. It was right there.

"If we're not telling her because it's too hard," Mike summed up darkly. "Then fuck us."

They decided to practice on Katie first. Which meant convincing Robin.

"You two are crazy," she said, unfamiliar with the sight of John and his brother sitting as a team across from her at their kitchen table.

"Katie's going to have to be told eventually," John stressed.

"Why does she have to know? Ever?" Robin asked. "The only way this gets taken care of without turning it into a disaster is for as few people as possible to know. Just leave Katie out of it."

"I want her to know," John said flatly.

"And then what?" Robin asked. "She's a teenager. In a culture where every stray thought they have is broadcast to the world, the more outrageous and intimate the better. You really think this won't end up on Facebook and everywhere else?"

It killed John to hear how cynical Robin had become about their daughter.

"Sometimes you just have to trust people," he said simply.

"And what about your mother?" Robin pressed on. "Suppose telling her goes well? Suppose bringing her to her husband ends up being something beautiful? Which, my God, I would wish for that woman more than anything.

"But then what? You can't *trust* her to stay quiet about it. If she told one friend, which you know she might, the whole town will know, the way those women gossip."

John sighed. He learned a long time ago that *But then what?* is the phrase that separates people like him from people like his wife. *But then what?* is that irksome comeback that usually causes half-assed ideas to be smashed upon the rocks.

"Nobody will believe her," Mike said proudly, disarming his annoyingly logical sister-in-law. "Most of what she says anymore doesn't make any sense, people will just smile and nod their heads."

"So your whole plan is built on the fact that she's losing her mind?" Robin asked disapprovingly. "Nice."

"Sometimes life's a shit sandwich," Mike said. "But maybe the bread won't be moldy."

John and Robin stopped to jointly mark the moment at which Mike Husted uttered something approximating a genuine—if crude—profundity. He noted their looks of impressed surprise.

Robin looked at these two with an unexpected sense of bemused affection. For all her well-earned animosity toward Mike—and her suspicion that somewhere beyond all this he would earn gobs more—it was not displeasing to see the brothers coming together over something.

She could picture them as boys, working as a team to earnestly beg their parents for a dog, or to stay up late to watch something on TV. In the same way John found sustenance by getting back some version of his father, she was happy for her husband that he had found his brother. At least for now.

John grew earnest. "I don't want to believe that Katie would do anything to hurt the family," he said to Robin, quiet but firm. "And I don't want to believe you think she would."

Katie came home from school to find her parents and her uncle—who she barely knew, who was just a skeezy old loser to her—waiting. The heaviness in the living room and the funereal tone of the adults put her immediately on guard. But as they gingerly explained their way to the truth about Larry, John's heart sank at the glib sarcasm and ghoulish fascination that soured his daughter's reaction.

"This is *too* weird," she said with a mordant smirk, wishing she could escape to her room. "I mean, *seriously.*"

"We've all been having a hard time making sense of it," John said.

"Does he have really long fingernails? Like Wolverine?"

"No," John said patiently. "There have always been people, to take care of things like that."

"He has *people?*"

"He can't feed himself, honey," her father explained. "He can't do anything. Without them to help him, for years, he would have died."

"But wasn't that supposed to happen anyway?" she asked.

The adults sagged at the myriad ways this story strained reason. It didn't help that Katie's tone was both honestly curious and mocking.

"It was," John struggled, "but it became complicated. These people, who *loved* your grandfather, they thought they were doing the right thing. At least at first. So they worked really hard to take care of him. For a really long time."

"And now it's your father's job," Robin said, stepping in. "But it's not something we can keep doing. It's been very hard on him. On all of us."

Her father's behavior the past few months suddenly made sense. Her spine set as she pieced it together and recognized how to make this about her.

"*That's* where you go every night!" she protested haughtily to John. "You *lied* to me. It *wasn't* about Grandma. Really nice, when you're on me every day of my life about not telling the truth. *Perfect.*"

"He's been trying to help his father," Robin said with forced evenness. "And he didn't want to upset you."

"Whatever," Katie dismissed with airy superiority.

"Hey," Mike interjected sharply. "Don't be an asshole."

Everyone turned to Mike. Robin would later recall the unfamiliar desire to hug him.

"He's our *father*," he said, bearing down on his niece. "He fucking *died* on us, when we were *your* age.

"As much as you want to act like your dad is some fucking joke to you," Mike said, pointing to John, "you wanna talk about what that's like, havin' your father drop dead out of nowhere? You wanna try living through *that*?"

Katie blinked soberly, a little afraid. Her uncle probably hadn't spoken five hundred words to her since the day she was born.

"And now he's had to figure out *this*," Mike continued on John's behalf. "This has all been on *him*. This has all been out of *his* pocket. I can't do shit to help. Because I'm forty-five fucking years old, and back when I was your age—when I mighta started making something outta myself—I was the same hard-ass poser *joke* you're turning into."

Provoked, Katie made as if to shoot back. But she was way out of her league.

"You got it *made*," Mike continued caustically. "You got—holy shit!—you got more electronic, computer-cell-phone-miniature-TV *bullshit* than they had on space shuttles when I was your age—*that he pays for!!*—and now you're sitting here giving him shit when he's trying to tell you about something that's really hurting him? That we still have to figure out how to tell your grandmother—*our mother*—who might not think this is the *fucking cartoon* that you do? *Really?* You're proud of this?"

Katie's eyes began to water. "Mike . . ." Robin said protectively.

He eased off on his niece. "You're gonna be a grown-up someday, you know? And all *this*," he said, referring to her costume and her pose, "is just gonna be a bunch of obnoxious shit you did with some skanky dumbfucks you don't want to know anymore.

"If you're lucky, *they'll* still be around, the both of 'em," he said, pointing to her parents. "And you'll *like* it. Maybe

not like Walton's Mountain, let's hug it out over every stupid fucking thing. But it'll be something you'll be glad you
got, even if you don't show it all the time." He met John's
eye guiltily for just a moment.

"So, you know, you're a kid," Mike summed up gruffly.
"Have a party, see what you can get away with—whatever.
Just don't be such a dick about it."

Forty-five

By the time they slipped through the hidden door of the old hospital, the ironic detachment that Katie intended to drape herself in slipped away. The visiting party became four when Robin realized she had to be there for her daughter if this turned out to be an awful idea.

As the flashlight beams led the way and the dust and rot began to make her feel like she was suffocating, Katie wished she had stayed home. But that thing her uncle said—about how much her father was hurting because of everything that happened—made her take the ride.

She could tell he wanted her to come have a look at her grandfather. She could do that for him. But now here she was, whispering and creeping about in a deserted old hospital, feeling an impending sense of attack, like in one of the *Saw* movies.

They finally gathered at the door into room 116.

"It's just like he's asleep," John said to Katie soothingly. "You'll see."

He opened the door. But it wasn't like that at all.

Across the room, the shriveled, bone-thin old man writhed in anguish, his breath ragged and full of fluid. The familiar and calm lines on the vital signs monitor spiked wildly, the measures for heart rate, pulse, and oxygen all registering dire numbers as the unit blinked and beeped.

The familiar silence of the room broken alarmingly, John and Mike rushed to their father's side.

"Jesus, he's burning up," John said as he felt Larry's forehead. The old man's mouth snapped open and closed sharply, fighting for air. His lungs gurgled with phlegm.

"He's . . . drowning," Mike said with muted urgency. The involuntary contortions caused the old man's eyes to open for scant seconds before slamming shut again. Katie couldn't have known that parted eyelids—for even a moment—weren't normal.

Gloria came within fifteen minutes. The Husteds stayed out of her way as she intensely but unhurriedly took Larry's temperature and listened to his breathing. She had a log book that John wasn't sure he had ever noticed before. It was filled with pages and pages of meticulous notes. She entered her new records and shook her head.

John discussed her diagnosis in halting but sufficient Spanish that would have impressed his family any other time. They saw John's spirit sag.

"It's an infection of some kind. She thinks he caught something," he said. "His fever is nearly a hundred and three."

"Is this it?" Robin asked with stark sensitivity.

They all watched as Gloria injected something into Larry's IV line.

"She said she could flood him with antibiotics, see if he can fight it off. I said go ahead, but . . ." he trailed off. "Yeah, I think we're there."

"What about your mother?" asked Robin, impulsively but certain it needed to be asked.

John and Mike looked to each other for an answer, then turned to their father's bed. Gloria stood over him, gently brushing his matted hair with her fingers, holding his hand, and whispering something gentle in Spanish.

Forty-six

Alzheimer's patients struggle with dream states, as the agitation of their waking hours are set loose to jostle their minds insanely while they sleep. And then upon waking, the surrealism of their dreams dissolves seamlessly into the disorientation of their days. It was common for Mike to have Rose emerge from her room first thing in the morning, ashen and agitated and begging to know what was real and what had been a dream.

"Why would you boys do this?" she now asked her sons as she quivered, equal parts angry and scared when they sat her down a little past midnight. The shock of having them in her bedroom in the middle of the night, the craziness of what they told her—the funhouse mirrors of her mind were having their way with her.

"Mom, it's true," John said softly, sitting on one side of

her on the bed, holding her hand while Mike sat on the other. "Dad's alive. Larry, your husband, is alive. And we'll explain it all to you when we can, but right now we need you to come see him. He's waiting for you."

"Your father died. A long time ago," she said slowly and with grave solemnity. "You *know* this. *Why are you doing this to me?*"

She focused all her attention on John. For so long, he was all she had. He was the one to make things right. And now she was pleading with him to stop breaking her heart.

His eyes welled at her anguish. But before he could respond, Mike moved from beside her to kneel at her slippered feet. He took both her hands and looked in her eyes.

"Mom," he said softly, "we need you to trust us. Can you do that? Can you get dressed, and just come for a drive with us? We'll bring you right back, and we'll get you back into bed, and in the morning you'll forget all about this. Okay?"

Something long gone stirred inside her. This sensitivity, from her angry, unsettled son, was lovely. Even if this was only a dream, she was grateful to have him hold her hands and speak gently to her. She would follow him anywhere so long as he seemed to love her again.

Forty-seven

The work lights John had borrowed from his neighbor remained at the hospital, so before John and Mike left to get Rose he charged Robin and Katie with positioning them as best they could along the path to the room. Hampered by time and available electricity, the lights were stationed intermittently. They provided sufficient illumination, freeing John and Mike from having to guide their mother in by flashlight, but they cast jagged veins of shadows along the passageway. They had just finished when they heard them coming.

John and Mike walked on either side of Rose, their hands lightly on her back and guiding her forward. Rose became silent in the car, and now she seemed to have withdrawn completely into herself as she shuffled slowly.

"You okay, Mom?" John asked gently. "We could stop and sit for a moment, if you want."

She said nothing, just kept moving her feet in the direction she was pushed. John and Mike exchanged a look—there was no turning back.

They rounded a corner, and there stood Robin and Katie standing outside a door. Faces emerged from shadows—faces of loved ones, turning up in the oddest places. Rose felt comforted to see them, but confused that they should be here. She looked to them imploringly as Katie fought back a tearful sigh. She gave her grandmother a hug.

"Okay, Mom?" John said as Katie stepped back. "We're going to go in now. We're going to see Dad. Larry. He's right inside. Are you ready?"

She looked to her sons. What had gone wrong with them, that they would be part of this?

But she nodded. Because they were her sons. Because she trusted them.

Mike opened the door. John took her elbow and escorted her in. Robin and Katie stayed in the hallway as the door closed.

Forty-eight

John had asked Gloria to sedate Larry. In every scenario John spent the past several weeks imagining, all of them saw Rose reuniting with Larry as he lay peacefully, the moment soft and still. The agonized, disturbing struggle for breath that they unexpectedly found earlier that evening could not be the image that Rose would confront.

The lights in the room were muted and warm. John and Mike laid the softest support at their mother's back as they continued to ease her forward. The dry shuffling of her sensible shoes were the only sounds in the room as she drew toward the bed.

As they finally reached Larry's side, John drew in a deep breath.

"Mom. This is—"

"*Sssshhh!*" she said sharply, her gaze fixed on the man sleeping in the bed.

John and Mike met each other's eyes. There was anger in her silencing, as if their overly solicitous care irritated her. As if it offended her for them to think that introductions were necessary.

She took a step toward the bed, shaking off her sons. They stepped back to let her continue on her own.

Her eyes grew curious but skeptical as she slowly traversed the foot of the bed and came around the other side, her stare never once broken from the man lying there.

Returning to the head of the bed, she drew even closer. She stared at the drawn, depleted face looking back at her, the man's eyes closed as if caught in the deepest of sleeps.

She tilted her head to the right and then to the left, as if shifting her perspective might finally bring her husband into focus. But it didn't seem to come. It appeared that she might reject this whole insane premise and demand that John and Mike return her to her bed.

But then a clear shiver of clarity crossed her face as she looked closer. A very specific memory registered as she hesitated, and then slowly extended a finger to trace the scar beneath her husband's left eye.

As she made contact with his skin, a lifetime—both shared and denied them—infused her.

In an instant she was determined to climb into the bed to lie beside him.

"Whoa, hey. Mom," John said in an urgent whisper, both

he and Mike not at all prepared to react to this. Larry was as fragile as a china doll. The IV and feeding tube were at risk of being yanked out as John frantically came around the bed. "Hang on a minute."

Rose was tiny. The hospital bed was elevated, but she was not going to deny the driven, almost hungry need to restore herself to her husband's side. She silently started climbing her way up.

John tried to find a respectful spot on an arm or leg with which to ease her up, while Mike stood on the other side of the bed and pulled her forward with the same discretion. Rose did not utter a word as John and Mike did all they could to get her where she wanted to be.

"Okay," John sweated. "Just move this leg over here. . . . Watch your elbow. Good, now . . ."

As Rose found a comfortable space beside her husband, she appeared perilously close to tumbling off the bed. As beautiful as the moment was, John and Mike were afraid to step away for fear she'd fall.

"Mom . . ." Mike whispered with concern.

"Ssshhhhh," she said again, gently this time. Snuggling up next to Larry, she closed her eyes and gently laid her head on his chest.

Here was his heart, still beating for her.

She sighed and became completely still. As still as her husband. The image and the complete silence of the room riveted John and Mike as both blunted sobs that might break the spell.

They watched for as many moments as they could allow themselves, then they silently left the room.

John wept without restraint as he fell into the embrace of his wife and daughter waiting in the hall. Alone for just a moment, Mike gratefully stepped forward as the hug parted to accept him. The four of them held each other, their sobs and mutters of comfort echoing down the empty hallways.

They sat through the night. John and Robin tried numerous times to take Katie home—it was a school night—but she begged to stay. The hall at night was cold. The four sat close to each other to stay warm. They napped and talked and imagined ghost stories about the souls who once roamed these corridors.

Discreet glimpses into Larry's room confirmed that Rose had fallen asleep, but she would wake up soon. Between the confusion of remembering where she was and with whom, the chances of her falling from the bed as the realization hit her were great. They could not risk her waking up without them there.

A little after six, John and Mike finally crept into the room.

Rose woke up.

Larry did not. Finally, forever.

Forty-nine

The tapping skittered through the cemetery with a volume amplified by the dead-of-night still. This mission, he hoped, would be the last.

At Katie's instruction, John crept into Eastlawn a few nights earlier to apply the plaster to Larry's headstone, giving it time to set. Now, with sculpting tools borrowed from art class, Katie came back with him to chisel in 2015.

The year of Larry's death had been a lie. It was time to set things straight.

"It's vandalism," Robin had protested.

"It's *our* headstone," John replied. "We paid for it."

"Don't you think it's going to raise questions?"

"How much time do *you* spend fact-checking other people's graves?"

"It's going to look ridiculous!"

"Yeah, well," John shrugged. "Sometimes, so does my family."

It was not in Robin to back down. "What if you get caught?"

"I really think you're overthinking this."

There was plenty of careful monitoring of Rose after Larry died. When she woke up that morning next to her husband, she wasn't told that he was dead. And yet when she was led away from him she gave no indication that she expected to see him again. Disoriented and unable to focus, no one spoke as they returned her to her home. Mike stayed awake in the living room as she slept soundly until the next morning.

When she finally came to the breakfast table, John and Mike waited anxiously. John brought her favorite blueberry muffins and a big pot of coffee simmered. They watched her intently as she shuffled sleepily into the room, brightening as she found her two boys and a tray of goodies waiting for her.

"I could have slept the day away," she said sighed contentedly as she tucked into her first muffin.

"It's good to see you sleeping so well," John said warily, studying her closely.

"Shouldn't you be at work?" she asked John, and then appeared to confuse her two sons. "*You* have a job. Don't you?"

"Sure. And Mike, he's looking. Something will turn up," John said. "But, today, it just seemed like we should . . . You know. Hang out. If you wanted to talk."

John and Mike resolved to not bring up Larry unless Rose

did. It was cowardice, but it was also out of respect for the delicate state of her mind.

They did what they charged themselves with doing; they brought Rose the news of her husband. It seemed inconceivable that it hadn't stuck, but if she had to cope by folding the night before into the shifting sands of her everyday grip on reality, that's what they would allow her.

Hearing she had both sons to herself, Rose beamed as she laid her hands on their arms. "How did I get so lucky?"

They sat together all day, Rose intermittently slipping away to nap. Over lunch they watched *Days of Our Lives*. At some point in this ritual that Mike and Rose had come to share, Mike took on the job of making the soup and grilled cheese sandwiches. The bread was browned perfectly, the cheese melted just so.

"Is she the one trying to get Serena to leave town?" Rose asked as they settled in before the soap opera.

"No. That's Nicole. *This* one," Mike said, pointing to the TV, "is Paige. Remember? She's JJ's girlfriend, but JJ also slept with Eve, Paige's mom. Eve's trying to get Cole to set up JJ to get him arrested for drugs, but Dr. Jonas might rat out Eve first 'cause he just figured out that she slept with JJ. So . . . It's some crazy shit."

"*Language,*" Rose scolded Mike, as John smiled fondly at the two of them.

When by the next day Rose still hadn't mentioned Larry, John knew it could not be avoided. They had to make arrangements.

There could be no funeral. The empty casket planted in the ground in 1985 could not now be replaced by an occupied one without spilling the secret wide open. As instructed by Walt Bolger before he left town, John warily called on Todd Stanton at the funeral home. As he nervously ushered John into his office, Todd—a few years older than John and now the prosperous owner of his father's mortuary—was wary now that the mysterious burden his father bequeathed to him decades earlier was finally coming due.

Todd explained to John that his father gave him no details, just that if the day came that he received a call concerning Larry Husted he was to open the doors to the business to him and perform his duties with the utmost decorum and secrecy. Todd spent years wondering what the hell his father did.

John told Todd the whole story; here was one of the very few people who could be trusted with the secret. When John finished, Todd was pale.

"Holy shit," he said in awe.

"Tell me about it," John smiled.

"I mean . . ." Todd said, struggling to figure out what his obligation was here. "I'm *sorry,* about my father. If by going along with this he caused your family . . ." He trailed off, completely at a loss to make sense of it.

"It's okay," John said generously. "It turned out okay."

Todd chuckled with relief, shaking his head in wonder. "Those crazy fuckers."

Todd found a memory. "Your father treated me once, when I was eight. I broke my arm," he said fondly. "He was a really nice guy. I was scared and it hurt like hell, but he made me laugh."

John smiled gratefully.

"It will be an honor to see to this for your family," Todd said earnestly.

John called Dean Durning as soon as they got Rose settled back home. Durning had the good sense to receive the news respectfully and without betraying a whiff of the incredible relief he felt.

John wanted Larry tended to immediately; his body would not lie in that rotted building until the cover of night returned. Durning pointed out that sending the funeral home's van in the daylight, even around to the hidden back door, would be too big a risk. They agreed that Durning would drive his family's van and that he and Todd Stanton would remove the body.

Stanton firmly refused to allow John to be present. There was no way that the funeral home director, a respected man around town, would allow a family to endure such an indignity. Todd's father would expect no less of him.

Todd would cremate Larry's body after-hours. He offered to prepare Larry for viewing if the family desired, but John and Mike knew instinctively that they wanted their final memory of Larry to be the one in their mother's arms.

Rose, they decided, had seen enough. In time, they

would move Larry's urn into John and Robin's living room, where they would attempt to re-create a smaller version of the picture-filled family shrine Rose kept in the old house.

They knew that as her mind continued to fail and the disruption of moving her in with them caused her agitation, it would be healthy to provide her a quiet space where hopefully the photos and mementoes would comfort her where her memory couldn't. If she ever asked how that urn came to be among the family collection, and who was in it, they'd figure out an explanation then.

"Mom, it feels like we should do something. For Dad," John said in her living room, several days after Larry died. Mike was there, too. They still didn't know what she understood but felt forced to delicately try to address it. "Maybe go out to dinner, the whole family, and just raise a glass to him."

"That would be wonderful," she smiled, touched by the suggestion. She looked to Larry's portrait on the shelf. "He was a great man, your father. We were lucky to have him as long as we did."

This told them nothing.

"Mom," Mike said firmly. "Dad is dead. *Really* dead."

"I *know*," she said disapprovingly, offended by their need to tell her the obvious. "I was *there*."

"When?" John asked, tempering his exasperation.

"When he *died*."

In a perfect universe, this would be a delicious joke, Rose knowingly talking in oblique circles as she playfully drove her sons mad. As it was, John and Mike were beyond flummoxed.

John slid closer. "Are you talking about . . . a long time ago?"

She sighed and looked at one of the old photos of her with her husband. They were in a hammock somewhere, looking to be in their late twenties, before Mike came along.

Larry laid back contentedly, an arm cocked behind his head, while Rose lay beside him, her head on his chest. She smiled into the camera lens, while he drank her in.

"Everything was so long ago," she said.

She unexpectedly brightened, as if turning a page. "We could go to the Sunset. Your father loved that place!"

"Okay," John smiled.

"And Robin? And . . . ?"

"Katie," John said quickly. "Yeah, the whole family."

"And we'll tell stories. About your father," she said eagerly, before wilting sadly. "I don't know them anymore."

"You gave us the stories, Mom," Mike assured her. "We'll give them back to you."

She glowed at the idea.

Katie squinted in the dark and tapped on the chisel while John held the flashlight. As Robin predicted, the crudely etched new date on the headstone was turning out badly. Despite her talent and best intentions, this was an assignment that no artist could hope to pull off.

"It looks awful!" she sighed.

"It's great," John said appreciatively, pleased that she agreed to come do it with him at all. "Your grandfather would love it."

Katie etched out the final 5 in the year as she mumbled, mostly to herself. "Could my family *be* any more bizarre?"

John smiled. "Quiet, you. You'll bring your kids here someday, and you'll tell them the whole story. They'll think *you're* the freak for having played along with all this."

"Can I make up the parts that you're never going to explain to me?"

He studied his daughter in the dark. "I would expect no less."

Despite her dissatisfaction with her work, she applied careful attention to the job. As she finished, she blew away the remaining dust, then buffed the plaster with a fine abrasive sheet. John marveled at her determination.

After perfecting it as best she could, she sat back to assess the result. Grandpa now died at seventy-eight, not forty-eight. And he was back at the house, on the mantel.

She rested on an empty stretch of ground beside the grave.

"Is this where Grandma will go?" she asked.

"Uh-huh," John said, unprepared for the question but not thrown by the eventuality.

"Soon?"

"I don't know," he sighed. "Things are going to be hard for her. But maybe not for a while."

"Right," Katie said. "Not too soon. But not too long."

"Right," John agreed, loving her for the simple way she crystallized his hope.

She yawned and then shivered in the cold night air.

"Come on, let's get you home," he said as he stood stiffly.

Fifty

Dean Durning hovered anxiously as John, Mike, Robin, and Katie made quick work of clearing out room 116, hours after returning Rose home following their supper club send-off for Larry. The harried administrator knew he was unlikely to see the old building brought down during his tenure, but at least its final resident had taken his leave. By dawn, it would be left to the rats and raccoons.

The family divvied up the memorabilia on the shelves. Most of it went to John's living room, where new images and maybe new memories would surround Rose as she settled in with John and Robin.

Mike took the framed newspaper story about his band. John took the Lucite block commemorating the move into the new hospital. The brothers squabbled over the Donald Duck figurine, until Katie emitted a girlish giggle at holding it.

Soon there was nothing left but the hospital bed and the rotting boxes of medical records that John never returned to the gymnasium after he pieced together the Vicky Farragut story. Durning nudged a box with his foot and watched it crumble, the air filling with mold and dust.

"Jesus," Durning said, clearing his throat as it clouded menacingly around him. "This stuff could kill you."

John heard this with his ears, and then felt it punch him in the gut, and then staggered beneath its weight as the possibility announced itself:

It appeared that John might have killed his father.

The internal retelling of the tale would agitate and enthrall John's mind for the rest of his life. If, as it surely appeared, it had been his digging through the hospital's rotted files that ended his father's endless life, that would be okay. Poetic, really. And funny, kind of. If you were willing to go there.

These mad rationalizations would come in time; in the moment, what John might have done to his father ricocheted against the insides of his skull as the others left him behind.

The last to leave room 116, he forced himself to tamp down this new information just long enough to properly acknowledge the pure, uncomplicated silence he was leaving behind.

Then he closed the door, and thought it all over.

Acknowledgments

Thanks to Professor Ann Angel, the writing track faculty of Mount Mary University, and the talented and inspiring students who experienced this work in its earliest form. While merely scrambling to meet an assignment deadline as I pursued my graduate degree, they encouraged me to spin a thirty-year-old dream (literally) into a short story, then a thesis project, and finally the book you now hold in your hands. Only took an additional eleven years.

Thanks also to early eyeballs along the way, who read partial or "finished" drafts and never failed to send me back to work with new ideas and encouragement. A special shout-out to the well-read dames of the Wauwatosa Enablers, who made *Raising the Dad* a book club selection when it was only a fat stack of pages and gave me a spark when I really needed it.

Boundless gratitude to Marcia Markland, who responded to an honest-to-God cold query at the precise moment I came to think I had expended all publication options for a book of which I am so proud. Thanks, Marcia, and your able associates Quressa Robinson and Nettie Finn.

To family, friends, colleagues, and total strangers who have said kind things about any of my writing in any of the outlets that have been kind enough to give me a platform over the past thirty-five years: you have no idea how validating your approval has been.

And most of all to Pam, always my champion and my strength. The whole wide world opened up to me the day we met.